STELLAR INSTINCT

AN AGENT RENAULT SPY-FI ADVENTURE

JONATHAN NEVAIR

CANTINOOL BOOKS

First edition: December 01, 2022.

Cover art and design by Miblart

Editing: Jonathan Oliver

Published by Cantinool Books

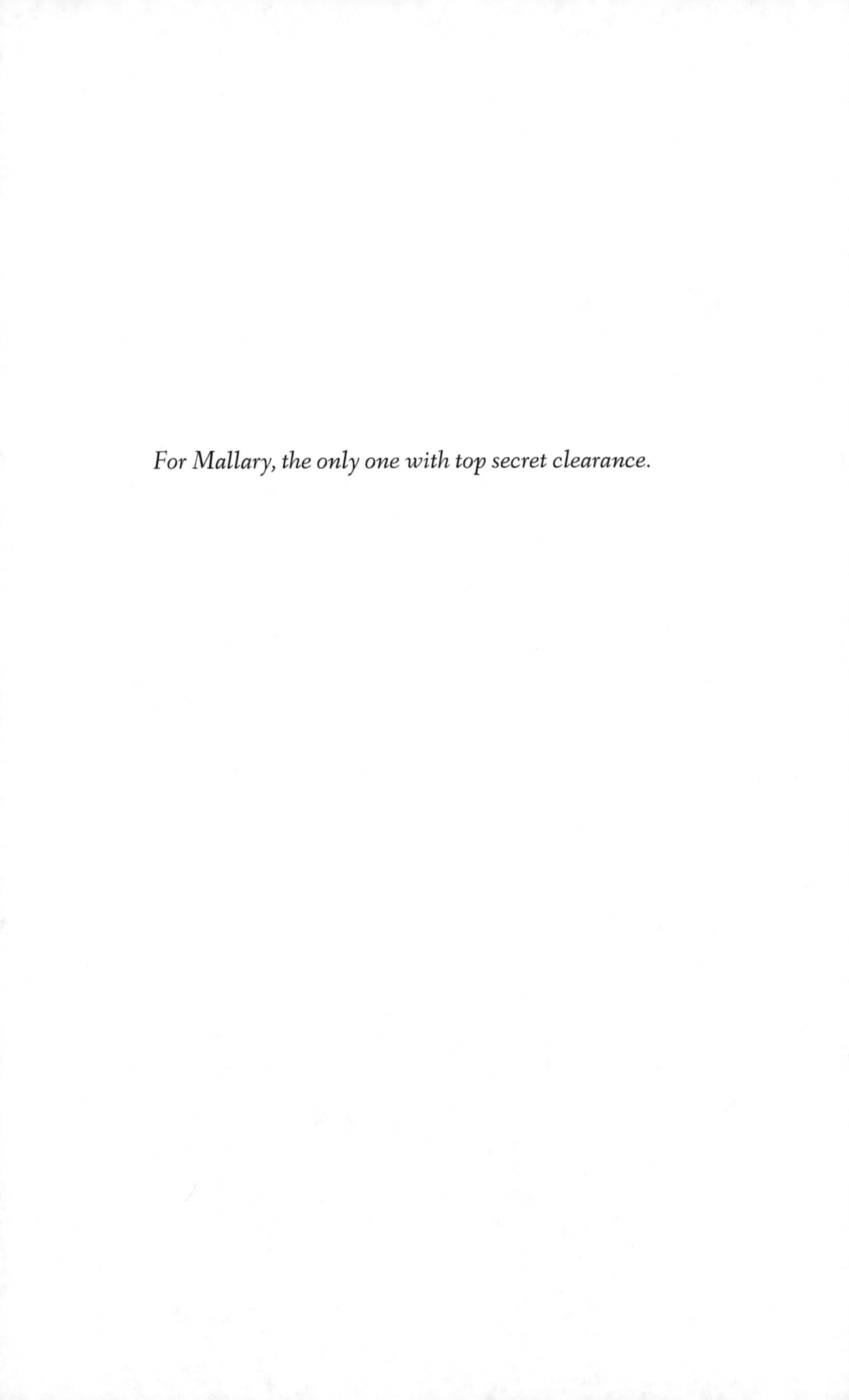

For Mallary, the only one with top secret clearance.

ONE

Agent Lilline Renault ignored the shadow slinking along the ice cave wall. She tore a strip off the dead guide's hyperchromium snow jacket and threw it onto the fledgling fire. Blood-stained fabric snapped and crackled, struggling to ignite.

"I know you're there," she said, huddling close to the orange flames. The blaster holster at her hip shifted as she knelt deeper to tend the kindling.

Hot fabric sizzled and popped. Jagged shafts flashed into existence in the fissure sheltering her from the storm. Lilline gazed at the fire's reflections. Narrow spindles danced in rhythmic patterns on the glacial ice. Whatever she'd seen a moment earlier had vanished.

"Yuk!" She coughed, the stench of volatile chemicals singing her nostrils. As if in riposte to the human intrusion, the cavern sent her voice bouncing back.

At least the smell of burning fabric wasn't as nauseating as the stink of the Dendari guide's entrails. Those lay a kilometer back on the treeless white expanse, spilled out in oozing yellow and crimson streaks from their face-down and soon-to-be frozen corpse. The hairy bipedal species native to Frebu thought her an easy mark, a foolish academic with no idea of the dangers that accompanied the illicit smuggling of rare gems and minerals. Her wrist-action blade had told the fanged and bulbous-eyed opportunist otherwise, penetrating all three layers of protective clothing to gut its furry hide in a single swipe.

Lilline had left the guide naked, sprawled out like a blemish on white skin. She'd stopped a short distance uphill in the snowy void to view the scene. Under the shadow of Frebu's towering glacier, staring at the mess of blood and organs, a line of verse had bubbled up. She'd tweaked and refined it on the march to the temporary shelter until it fit into a poetic box.

> *A chef in the kitchen,*
> *bowl of stew too heavy.*
> *Across a white-tiled floor,*
> *see them teeter, totter.*
> *Slip, slip, slip, splash and slide.*
> *Crash and bang!*
> *It spills under belly.*

"Total crap," she said and tossed another strip of the jacket into the flames. Shadows cast on the rippling ice grew as the fabric caught. Nothing besides the fire's reflection danced in a steady rhythm, yet she knew that the lurker remained in the cave, unseen. Call it occupational intuition or a human's sixth sense. Either way, another presence shared the haven of the icy refuge.

The poem didn't improve her mood. She'd done it again. A septet stanza with five lines of hexameter syllabic verse broken with one trimeter line. Derivative. Embarrassingly so. A classic parody of Den-shi. All her poems sounded like Den-shi. The editors who sent rejections said it. The friends she read them to said it.

"You need to find your voice," her peers in the poetry group repeated, ad nauseam. *"Let go. You're trying so hard it shows."*

Of course, she was trying. And how dare they?

So, her poetry sounded like Den-shi. Weren't you supposed to emulate the greats when learning the craft? None rivaled the degree of worship attained by the contemporary master of words. Den-shi, that anonymous poet whose populist verse tantalized the eyes and ears of billions going on forty cycles. A voice to emulate indeed.

"Yours will come in time, Lilli," Granny Kissy told her again and again. Lilline wasn't sure. She was starting to—

Movement on the cavern wall drew her eyes. The rogue shadow reappeared among the flickering reflections of firelight.

The poetic self-critique would have to wait.

With performed nonchalance, Lilline tore more strips off the jacket and added one to the flames. It ignited, the warm glow sending a wave of heat over her cold cheeks and lips. She lifted an arm and covered her nose as toxic smoke belched from the fire.

"I don't know who you are," she said, between hacking, "but I imagine you must be as screwed as me out here tonight."

Lilline lowered the hood on her jacket and kneeled closer to the flames. She blew to encourage the growing fire. Just enough additional oxygen to boost the starter sticks so they glowed long into the cold Frebu night. Too much and she'd collapse the fragile stack and smother them. If that happened, she was done for, like the Dendari guide lying dead out in the snow.

Too bad about that. She liked playing a professor of mineralogy obsessed with rare gems. It made for amusing personality quirks, and the diatribes about extraordinary geological occurrences and alluring, yet-to-be uncovered precious stones had made for challenging exercises in memorization. They'd also helped fill the uncomfortable silence on the trek across the tundra from where the two landed the Hyler Explorer Pod. Not that she sought anything related to gems or minerals at the coordinates programmed into her handheld comm-sat. On the contrary, she was after something more valuable: information.

It would have been entertaining to keep up the performance but with the guide out of the picture, Lilline could go back to being herself. Whoever that was.

Like a vampire gazing in a mirror, her identity cast no reflection. She could see it in her mind: the database ID bar blinking red in an error code. No wonder she couldn't find her poetic voice.

"Don't want to talk?" she asked, without turning.

No response.

Fine.

Lilline leaned in and blew to encourage the growing flames. With the starter sticks glowing hot, the smoke rose higher, trailing up and away along the ceiling into the glacier's deeper interior reaches. Across from her on the ripples of blue ice, the mystery shadow lingered still.

She glanced at the pile of clothes next to her to gain a wider peripheral view. Nothing appeared in her field of vision to that side. The unknown visitor had to be behind her. Her hands sifted through the red and white fabric on the icy floor. Most of the Dendari's jacket was left to burn, as well as their heavy snow pants and undergarments. If she were prudent with the portions, it should last through the night.

A strand of shoulder-length black hair dropped in front of her face and dangled close to the flames. She pulled off a glove and tucked it behind the wedge of brown skin over her right ear. The tress fell off. Lilline repeated the gesture in practiced response, pushing the hairs down into the seam over the canal's opening.

Five cycles since the Bukki tiger had taken that ear on Hesh-9 with a near-fatal bite to the head. She knew it would be easier to cut her hair short. Everyone back at HQ had been telling her so. That alone was enough to keep her from chopping it off.

Still no response or sound of movement behind her. Only the gusting winds slamming into the glacier's sheer face. The gales hit the ice wall like a giant's fisted blows against city buildings on far-off planets where less foolish citizens lived safe and routine lives.

That had never been Lilline's road. Her small taste of the mundane after graduating mandatory schooling was more rank than the smoky stink rising from the fire. Even the Dendari's entrails didn't come close to her disgust of ordinary life with a chipped identity, registered name, and twenty days of paid vacation meant to cover the burden of existence on an annual cycle.

She much preferred anonymity and license to deceive, bypass galactic law, and when the opportunity allowed, kill. Assassination wasn't murder when its purpose saved lives, not according to her employer's ethical philosophy. Her role was to be a piece on the board. She did what she needed, when she needed, to do the job. The greater good had no idea how hard she worked to keep them safe.

A gentle crunch behind her interrupted the tempest's pugilistic blows. Lilline drew her blaster and held it up by her side.

"We really going to do this? If you're here for the Starex crystals I hate to disappoint you, but you've followed a set of tracks to a dead end."

Another crunch. Judging by the shadow's height across the fire, she guessed whoever or whatever it was made its way prone. That would be smart. On a quick turn, a shooter would expect to confront a standing figure. Except that the reflection gave them away.

Amateur.

"I'm really tired, chump." She grabbed another strip of the jacket and tossed it into the flames.

"And frustrated," she whispered. If the Dendari guide hadn't smashed her portable comm-sat unit with a boot kick in their struggle, it wouldn't be an issue. Because of their lame attempt to subdue her and access bogus map coordinates leading to a non-existent horde of Starex crystals, it was.

Idiot.

All night in this cavern tending the fire and then she'd have to walk out far enough from the ice wall to send a location pulse before trekking back to the Hyler. That meant calculating the bounce trajectory to and from orbit which required math. *Difficult* math.

Applied mathematics was a nuisance in the field. Calculations slowed you down or got you killed. Worse, advice based on numbers wreaked of analysts who sat with their noses in statistics and so-called protocols. They had no idea of what it took to survive in the chaos of the galactic fray.

Pure mathematics was another story. A special kind of beauty and freedom of discovery lay in abstract numerics. That field of study shared a kinship with Lilline's weapon of choice: intuition. She kept it loaded with rounds of well-honed instinct.

Right now, her rational, equational mind was screaming out to turn around. Intuition told her not to... not yet.

For over ten cycles on the job, Lilline's abstract impulses hadn't failed her. Well, except for the time with the Bukki tiger but there were mitigating circumstances to that one. Namely, an opponent with *better* instincts.

Pop!

Compressed gas in the burning fabric sent a flash of light through the cave. The urge to turn and shoot lost out to discipline. She remained motionless; blaster raised at her side. Cold metal stung her trigger finger as she pressed down onto curved steel, readying to fire.

Crack!

The flames spit out another burst of light. A whoosh of air passed her missing ear. The shadow expanded, casting a blanket of darkness over the wall. Lilline rose to a knee and aimed the blaster. The mystery intruder landed on the cave floor. Its shadow diminished to a life-size replica.

"I almost shot you," she said and tossed the weapon onto the ice. Shivering fingers pulled off her other glove. She lifted both hands to the fire, rubbing them together to get the blood flowing. Her steamy breaths pulsed in waves inside the frigid cave. "I've read about you," she said. A rush of cold air from the storm shot through the cavern's narrow opening, fluttering the flames. "Don't blame you for coming in."

The owl paced back and forth, wings expanded, casting an angelic shadow. Lilline made out the distinct gray circle on its snowy white breast common to the species riding the glacier's edge, the Ice Ranger. It was thought that the owl's pattern mimicked Frebu's solitary moon, Eroton.

Another part of the job she enjoyed. Learning vital facts that might save your life undercover, rendered useless after the completion of a mission. Except for dinner parties and cocktail receptions where trivia and small talk led to charming party successes or one-night stands. Lilline didn't do social, not off the clock, but she was a master of conversation on the job. Sex was another matter and she had different tactics that avoided lengthy chatter and chase. Intuition, as it turned out, was much better than logic for that enigmatic social game.

"Well," she said, watching the owl fold its wings and strut back and forth. The familiar sound of crunching snow returned as it strode across the ice. "If you're willing to share a fire with a secret agent who can't find her poetic voice, be my guest." Lilline threw what was left of the Dendari's jacket into the flames.

Screw it.

She lay back on the cave floor. Plumes of smoke rose as the large swath caught fire, casting firelight onto blue ripples. Her brown eyes followed the spiraling streams as they bounced off the ice and snaked deeper into the cavern. Where the narrow interior passage led, she didn't intend to find out. There were creatures more dangerous and deadly than a Bukki tiger in Frebu's glacial labyrinths.

With no Dendari guide and the comm-sat crushed and broken, her chances of reaching the coordinates marking the source of the signals were near impossible. She'd have to ride out the night here in relative safety at the cavern's entrance and get back to the Hyler at dawn.

It wouldn't be easy after the night's storm blew the snowy tundra clean. It never was. In her twelve cycles as a field agent, she'd never completed a mission without at least one hiccup.

No matter. Her new priority was to send out a signal at first light. HQ didn't appreciate radio silence.

She shifted an arm onto her belly. Fingertips stung with cold as they came to rest on the silver belt buckle containing her emergency backup pulser. The crude piece of equipment afforded her no more than a general ping to a satellite connecting to *Yutu SS* orbiting along Frebu's equator. That hub networked to the Anu Het system mainframe and channeled back to a GAM-OPs sub-station four star systems away. The pulse wasn't a rescue call, only a "still alive" update and "track me please, if you can." Out here, with the planetary angle at the southern pole, even that possibility was doubtful.

She ran her fingertips over the buckle's edge and stared at the reflections of firelight on the cavern's ceiling. Lying on the hard floor, her soft and steady caress of steel sanded the edges of the howling gales pounding the glacier. It was the same rhythmic motion she used to calm Hiko. Light cycles away and part of what felt like another lifetime, the cunning feline she'd befriended outside her Domus-unit on Tavi-Prime had taken no time at all to warm to her. Lilline pictured the Nok-cat's yellow eyes glittering between flashes of red and blue air traffic lights on the wet pavement in the alley. Standing in her pajamas, plate in one hand and utensil in the other per usual dinner routine, she'd coaxed him closer with bits of her quick-meal. It had taken less than a week to have him on her lap and enjoying the same ebb and flow strokes she ran over the buckle at her waist.

As much as she preferred petting Hiko's silky coat to stroking cold steel, seeing the Nok-cat meant she was off the clock. Nothing was worse than being grounded. Out in the field, she had action and excitement, frustration, and obstacles to overcome, the allure of disguise, and the rush of danger. Most important of all, it offered poetic inspiration.

Life on Tavi-Prime entailed sedentary work at HQ. That

consisted of administrative tortures and nagging superiors. Her Domus-unit provided neither retreat nor refuge, only a mirror's empty reflection amplified to a silent scream. Unless she turned up with some intel worth sharing soon on Operation Snow Eclipse, she'd be back to quick-meals and snuggle time with Hiko. Four expeditions to out-of-the-way star systems seeking answers. So far, a mysterious rise in radio-wave frequencies on remote planets had yielded nothing solid.

She'd insisted on Frebu to her superiors as the last possibility. Her evidence was a thin pulse, a final thread in a trail of fraying links based more on conjecture than hard proof. Call it half desperation to succeed and half a desire to avoid being grounded, but she had a hunch. That wasn't something that Lauden, her boss back at HQ, liked to bet on.

And this time the kismet knife twisted deeper. Fate was going all-in to convince her this was a wild goose chase.

Lilline lifted her hand from the belt buckle and splayed her arm out next to her, fingers finding the handle of her blaster. She took the weapon in her grip, the cold metal of the trigger re-introducing itself to her index finger.

Maybe she was following a false lead. Lauden was itching for an excuse to sentence her to a boring, run-of-the-mill GAM-OPS post somewhere in the labyrinthine sub-levels of headquarters on Tavi-Prime. Ordinary wasn't an option. A desk job? Lilline would rather walk into a Frebu whiteout than return empty-handed on this one and face down that future. Despite what the chorus of naysayers at HQ declared, something was happening across the galactic commons. Lilline had been in the spy business long enough to know when something was worth the push and the pursuit.

If she was proud of one thing, it was her tenacity. She'd gotten that in her hereditary line from the most famous agent ever to grace the stage in the espionage game of galactic cat and mouse. For over ten cycles, Lilline had carried the familial torch well. Not anywhere near the legendary status of her Granny Kissy, but enough to become the go-to operative for top priority missions. Younger recruits might be quicker and stronger than her these days, but she was relentless. That made the wins, when they came, more substantial and satisfying.

Uncovering imminent danger to humanity and solving the puzzle of how to stop it was what built the reputation of GAM-OPS. For hundreds of cycles the covert organization had kept the commons running with civility, avoiding innumerable threats and disasters. GAM-OPS had lived up to its acronym: a galactic agency maintaining order, peace, and security for a diverse range of species across hundreds of star systems.

When and if this current mystery reared its ugly head, Lauden and the other bigwigs at HQ would thank themselves for her tenacity. She might even get a sculpture outside the Octagonal Club to pair with Granny Kissy's. Heck, maybe they'd put a Den-shi poem on her plaque. Or, one of her own compositions. Wouldn't that be something?

Tonight, however, Lilline would take what she could get: shelter, a fire, and as Frebu fate would have it, an owl as a companion. After today's turn of events, that suited her just fine.

She stretched her legs out on the ice and settled in for the long, cold night. The flames burned bright, chewing up the hyperchromium jacket. So, she'd be uncomfortable. It wouldn't be her first rough night in the field.

Through tired eyes, the trail of rising smoke blurred. The howling chorus dulled to a haunting, distant lull. She battled closing eyelids as flickering firelight played visual tricks on the fissure's ceiling. Despite her best effort, the world went dark.

The problem was, she hadn't yet closed her eyes.

Lilline flipped onto her belly and aimed the blaster in a two-handed grip. With practiced precision, her finger released the safety and switched on the infrared barrel light. Triangular green beams shot across the cavern. She scanned the weapon left and right, searching for a heat signature.

Squawk!

Out of the dark behind her came the familiar whoosh of flapping wings. The glitching form of the Ice Ranger passed through the IR's rays. The bird banked hard into the cavern's narrow exit and vanished. A second screech echoed as it rode the howling winds of Frebu's nightly storm.

"Who are you?" Lilline shouted, warm breath pulsing white static into the IR field. She shifted around, staying prone, and scanned the interior. Her grip tightened, trigger finger ready. The beam passed over the pile of hyperchromium clothes and across the cavern to—

"What the?"

She aimed the blaster back at the stack of starter sticks and what remained of the Dendari's jacket. No more than a faint outline indicated a clump of physical objects on the icy floor. Her breath continued to interrupt the IR beam with white light. No malfunction. The blaster's scope was working but the fire was out and left no traces of residual heat.

"Not good," she whispered.

Is it chemical? Or worse, radiation?

The slow creep of fear sent a chill up her spine.

Training took over. With disciplined cycles of inhalations and exhalations, she steadied her breathing. To wield her favorite weapon, she needed clarity and calm.

The pounding in her chest softened. Lilline narrowed her eyes and stared down the barrel of the blaster. *You're mine. And when I—*

A sound pricked up her ears. Underneath the gale's mighty blows pelting the glacier, a humming rose. Vibrations rattled her stomach, thighs, and toes inside her snowsuit and boots. Deep and low, a sonorous presence lurked.

Lilline lowered her head to the frosty surface. She ignored the burning cold of ice against her skin where the Bukki tiger had taken the earlobe and listened.

It's coming in waves.

The anomaly rose and fell, like a pulse. She wouldn't call it mechanical, but it didn't sound like anything natural, either. The odd thing was, she felt it as much as she heard it.

The signal wouldn't land. Like a pod circling in dense fog at a docking port, it sought the runway lights – or in this case, a linguistic destination. The problem was she didn't have one. More than that, Lilline's whole system – mind, body, even her "sixth sense" – told her this was beyond a deficiency in vocabulary.

It's a connection... and it's abstract.

She lifted her head from the floor and scanned the walls a second time. Something flashed into view to her right. She swung around, aiming the blaster across the extinguished pile of fabric and starter sticks.

"Who's there?"

Nothing shone in the beam's light.

"I know you're out there!"

A flicker of movement disturbed the IR field. She directed the weapon at it and caught sight of a long, thin shadow before it vanished.

The vibration in the ice grew intense, rattling her as if a mild electric shock ran through her body.

She searched the walls in vain.

"Sh-sh-ow yo-yourself," she said.

With a crunch, her ears popped. Her skin pulled against flesh and bone. Streams of vertical cracks appeared in the blue ice like a 360-degree mirror shattering. A symphony of buckling echoes bounced through the cavern.

Oh no...

Inward pressure squeezed her organs and muscles. She gasped for breath. Her heart thumped like a giant drum, sending an alarm pounding through her body.

The blaster dropped from her hands. Her skull screamed with pain.

The cave began to fade from view.

Boom!

A flash of light turned everything white.

In the momentary blindness, she felt the pressure release.

Lilline coughed and gulped in breaths, lying flat on her belly. Her ears picked up the crackling of the fire. She confirmed it burning steadily though blurry vision a few feet to her side. Nothing other than the howling gales outside competed with the sound of the flames.

Instinct, her primary weapon, made its long-anticipated entrance. That mysterious human awareness stepped up and tapped on her psychic shoulder.

Look up, it said.

Even prone, Lilline's stomach dropped.

Something was on the ceiling.

She weighed options in the time frame of a single heartbeat: Stay still or dash for the entrance? The latter would be the logical thing to do. The voices of analysts during basic training rang in her ears: *"When an unknown threat poses a risk, and they have the higher ground..."*

Lilline thought of the jacket she'd thrown onto the fire, ignoring prudence. And reason.

Screw it.

She grabbed the blaster, rolled over, and aimed it up at the fissure.

Her instinct had been right. And wrong. Something was there but it wasn't on the ceiling. It was in it.

TWO

Your finger shuts off the IR beam and you toss the blaster aside on the ice.

You didn't want to do that. You want to fire the weapon.

Why aren't you shooting?

It hits: you are not at the controls.

That fact screams through your bloodstream. It travels your neural highways.

You hate the feeling. Control is your friend, your shield against—

Deep down, the answer that you keep hidden from yourself rises. It breaks the surface of your psyche.

You try and ignore it.

But this thing above you is shifty and tenacious. It redirects its intrusion and asks a question.

"Who are you?"

You are no one.

That's not accurate. You are other people at the expense of yourself. You are whomever you need to be to do what is right for others.

But what about you? What about Lilline? Who is she?

You don't want to think about this and yet, you do. It is the work of that 'thing'. The violet, smoky specter above you inside the ice. It's probing you, learning about you. Feeding on you.

It wants my thoughts.

The cavern walls tremble. Your finger twitches with a glimpse of self-control.

It didn't like that.

You pushed back and broke the connection. You'd smile if you were able.

Your eyes watch the shadowy mass loom within the ice.

It wants me to think so it can learn, but it doesn't like when I think about it.

The walls tremble a second time.

You slide your arm across the floor.

You *can* move. If you push back, rather than let it inside you.

The specter flexes, stretching immaterial wings through blue ice.

You stare up, eyes burning and fight back.

The simple act of defiance enthuses you, but it takes everything you have. You're breaking again.

Your arm slides across the floor. It's back inside your mind, fighting you for control.

Of what you aren't sure. You struggle for the answer and strain to locate it, to push open a space for it.

You pry open a crack in its fierce psychic grip.

What is it seeking?

A flicker of conclusion rises.

You want something I have.

The specter snarls at your realization.

Your arm slides across the ice to the blaster. You feel the cold of the steel handle as you grab it.

The violet ghost retreats into the glacial blue. You see it diminish as if you sent it reeling back from a blow to its immaterial form.

If there's one thing you do well, it's fight for control.

The specter grows bold again, approaching the boundary

between the ice and air. Long, shadowy tentacles fan out like the fast-growing stems of a wraith plant.

It fooled you. You took the bait and told it your secret.

With smug delight, it bellows a sinister silence inside of you.

You rise to your feet.

You don't want to stand. You don't want to do anything it wants.

Your legs move, one boot in front of the other across the cavern. Your hand with the blaster comes up. It aims against the wall of cracked ice.

You halt. Firelight flickers off the cavern's ripples and undulations. Your arm bends at the elbow. The weapon makes a slow arc towards you. The barrel is approaching your face.

You are no one. You are always someone else, so there is no one to die.

Your eyes widen. Your heart races.

"I am no one," you say.

The cold steel of the barrel's tip touches your forehead.

You try and tell yourself 'no' but it comes out as 'yes'.

The specter probes deeper, taunting you.

You do everything you can to not tell it. You've never told anyone.

It pulls at the answer, drawing it up and out. You tug back, resisting.

Your grip against it slips. Your most intimate secret can't be kept from it.

"Because I want to be someone," you say.

The ghostly presence laughs. Your finger contacts the cold metal of the trigger. It starts to squeeze.

Fight it. Push back. Otherwise...

It asks you why, desiring to lap up every morsel with sinister arrogance.

Your hurt turns to anger. You forgot about that weapon.

Through your rage, you see a path. You know its course before you step onto it.

Your would-be smile is back.

You see the wall in front of you, but you sense the specter flexing, its smoky purple arms spanning out into the ice.

Satisfaction grows inside of you. Now you're pulling and its grip is slipping.

"I know your secret," you say out loud. Your words intrude on the chorus of faint, howling winds. Your hand with the blaster falls away from your forehead. You can't see the monstrosity above you. It doesn't matter, its presence is clear enough inside of you.

The internal battlefield grows quiet.

"Because you too need to be in control," you say.

A silent scream shatters the walls of ice.

THREE

Lilline covered her face seconds before hundreds of icy blue splinters showered her body. The floor shuddered. She stumbled and nearly lost her footing. The vibration returned, but its previous harmonious waves had transformed into an angry dissonance.

Her accusation during the internal struggle may have liberated her, but it caused her foe to rise in fury.

She shook off the shards clinging to her hair and bent her head back to get a view above. The violet shadow pulsed and glitched inside of the ice, its long wraith-like arms stretching and tearing away from the core. Flashes, like cloud-to-cloud lightning, streaked across the ceiling.

Boom!

A slab of the fissure overhead crashed down, opening a crevasse in the floor. Frozen splinters sprayed outward, echoing off the walls in an icy symphony.

Time to go.

Lilline bolted. The ground tilted this way and that, and she did her best to stay upright. In the flickering light, she made out the opening into the stormy Frebu night across the newly formed crevasse. Partially blocked by the fallen slab, getting through would be a tight squeeze. If she moved fast before more of the cave collapsed, she might make it.

Her eyes homed in on the exit like a bullseye at the shooting range. She ignored all other environmental obstacles, allowing her body to shift and counterbalance on instinct while her point of focus stayed fixed.

The walls buckled with streams of cracks. A thunderous boom rang through the cave. The glacier's bones were breaking.

Lilline gripped the blaster tight and flipped on a switch with her thumb. She leaped, soaring over the chasm, and pointed her arm with the weapon upward. Her trigger finger squeezed off round after round. No laser shots came out of the barrel. This wasn't for defense. She was on the clock, working. Call it intel gathering – of what, she didn't know. The image capture setting on the blaster would record digital renderings of the anomaly in the ceiling.

She landed across the crevasse and slipped. Her knee twisted and the hard crash of her hip and shoulder stung as she hit the unforgiving ice.

No scream of pain, only concentrated breathing and focus. And, of course, tenacity. She was, after all, a secret agent. Possibly the best in the galaxy. This was the job. It beat sitting at a desk crunching numbers.

Amidst the shuddering and collapsing cavern, Lilline caught sight of the violet mass pulsating and contracting overhead. That was all the intel she needed. You didn't have to be an expert in xenophysics or virtual mathematics, or whatever field it was this thing related to, to know what was about to happen. Good old common sense screamed out that this entity was going to collapse inward and then...

Lilline was on her feet and bolting through falling shards of ice towards the half-blocked exit. It was at times like these, amidst the chaos, when poetic inspiration rose:

> *From the ennui of night*
> *A new day ever dawns*
> *I will never give up*
> *How could I?*
> *If I did a world dies.*

That one wasn't half bad. The best ones always came under the worst conditions, at the most inconvenient times. Her mind was too busy to count the syllables, but the rhythm sounded like a 6/6/6/3/6. Maybe it was becoming more natural.

Lilline slid feet first through the narrow opening. She reached her blaster arm back and clicked at rapid-fire rates to capture whatever last images she could with the camera. Forget the pulse coordinates now. She'd found a stronger lead and evidence, of who knows what, in Frebu's polar zone. Operation Snow Eclipse's original mystery had been overshadowed by a whole new level of strange. Wait until she wrote this up for Lauden. He and the other T# agents weren't going to believe their eyes when they read her report and got a look at what she recorded.

She passed underneath the fallen slab and her prediction came true. The cavern lit up with bursts of yellow lightning. Electric currents streamed through the frozen tunnel. Her eardrums rattled as the roar of the collapsing cave shot out the small opening.

One final shove and she would clear the passage. Lilline pushed off the ice above her as something crashed with a thud. The collar of her jacket choked her neck and yanked her back. She felt the hard impact of ice against her head.

Frebu vanished.

Pain and nausea.

Flickering light.

Lilline struggled against obstinate eyelids, fighting the pull of unconsciousness.

Open your eyes.

Like a curtain rising, the visible world returned. She made out a blurry form inches from her face. On instinct, her hand with the blaster behind her head went into action. A finger switched on the IR ray. She withdrew the arm to her side and aimed the barrel upward. Misty steam from her breath crossed the beam and bounced off blue ice.

The cave. Frebu.

She blinked until she could focus. Pain pulsed in her left knee.

The thing in the ceiling.

A groan rang out, echoing for miles across the tundra. It bellowed with the gravitas of a foreboding creature lurking in mysterious ocean depths. The volume of the prodigious voice humiliated Frebu's howling gales. Lilline's prone body swayed as the glacier shifted.

A flash of memory returned: she'd cracked her head on something trying to escape through the narrow opening.

Doesn't matter. Just get out of here.

Lilline dug her heels in and drew herself forward with her calf muscles through the passage. The fabric on her jacket choked her throat and yanked her back. Now she understood. She'd hit her head on a fallen block of ice. Her hood was wedged behind her.

With a flick of her free hand, a wrist-action blade flashed out of the sheath over her palm. She slid it back and overhead. In one motion across the neckline, she freed herself and shimmied out.

Frebu's polar expanse was shrouded in swirling winds and snow. Squinting against a barrage of snowflakes, she made out nothing in the night.

The ledge rumbled. Lilline jumped back from the edge as an entire portion of the glacier wavered.

This isn't good.

The rocking of the ice meant one thing: imminent collapse. Forget about getting far enough away, she had to descend a thousand meters before running through the heavy snow. As terrifying as the moment was, Lilline lived for it. When you were a GAM-OPs agent, situations like this happened more often than most people knew. While billions of citizens around the galaxy rushed off to work, prepared meals, or slept, she and the other T# agents were in predicaments like this one. Lilline wouldn't switch places for anything. Well, maybe for a publishing deal of a book of her poems.

She holstered the blaster and reached back behind her head. Her hand slid inside the jacket below its severed hood and into the warm layer against her sweater. She ran it across the top of the jump chute unit. Her fingertips registered a tear along the edge of the pack where her blade sliced into it.

Lilline closed her eyes. Her fingers took on a vicarious touch-sight, following the GAM-OPs training that had taught her how to work in the dark. Taking apart and reassembling blasters, navigating her way out of a room with minimal contact with walls, or distinguishing objects through "touch-sight," as they called it. Her fingers functioned like eyes, probing the chute pack's opening. One tear to the fabric itself, judging by the slices to the folds. That would mean small incisions, but not enough to cause a significant loss of drag. The problem was the cords. She counted five cuts from her wrist-action blade.

The glacier groaned. A monstrous shudder echoed through the howling winds and blinding snow. The roar of collapsing ice resounded in the night. She was out of time.

Lilline ripped off her jacket and stuffed it into her belt strap. She'd need it if the jump didn't kill her. At this point, making it to the Hyler in the blizzard was a low priority. She had to get off this glacier or else nothing further mattered.

Boom!

A thunderous noise above told her everything she needed to know. Crumbling ice. Falling fast.

Time to jump.

If this was it, then so be it. Granny Kissy's critique on that piece of crap poem about the Dendari would have been nice, even if she knew her grandmother wouldn't tell her how much it sucked.

Lilline grabbed the chute cord on the side of the pack. Her head went left to right. *Which way to jump?* She knew from the climb up at dusk that there were rocks below, but with these winds, it didn't matter. Fate was in Frebu's hands.

Whoosh!

A familiar rush of air passed by her missing ear, against the gale's current.

A screech echoed in the Frebu night.

The owl!

The Ice Ranger danced around her, circling in the blowing snow. It let out another cry. The avalanche rumbled above, sending blocks and smaller shards down around her on the ledge.

"Get out of here!" she yelled at it.

Again, the owl circled in an arc to the left, dodging the falling ice with grace and ease.

It's guiding me.

Lilline leaped, following the Ice Ranger. Cold air rushed past. She let herself free fall, knowing that the longer she dropped without the chute open the less chance she had of the winds slamming her back into the glacier's wall.

Screech!

The owl soared past her, cutting a trail through the near blinding storm; danger and grace, fury and calm coming together in a strange balance.

"Best job in the galaxy!" Lilline screamed out.

She pulled the cord. The falling snow changed course, whizzing by in vertical lines as the chute deployed. Her left shoulder yanked upward as cords snapped and broke.

"No!" She reached up and grabbed hold of the few remaining cords. Her body spiraled, but it wasn't an uncontrollable spin. Wide and rhythmic, the descent flowed in a long, circular route. The owl flew past and around, mimicking the arc.

"Poetry of life!" Lilline called out to it.

The Ice Ranger crossed a few feet in front of her. A cold light shone on its white feathers. Lilline caught sight of a crescent moon inching into view below the storm cloud's break. Beams of white moonlight stretched over the frozen blanket of Frebu's tundra.

Eroton.

The owl cried out and arced away off into the night. In the growing moonlight, Lilline made out clear, deep snow below. She'd be able to make a soft landing. Better yet, glimmering in the distance to the southeast, the domed roof of the Hyler peeked out of the white void. Even with the injury to her knee, she could make that walk. Sunrise over the Frebu tundra from the warmth of the Hyler didn't sound so bad.

A smile broke through her frigid cheeks. It had been one hell of a day and night. She gazed at Eroton's rising as she descended. The poetic image of a small life form falling planetward while a majestic moon rose skyward in counteraction stirred her deep inside.

"Poetry of life, indeed," she whispered and peered up. The moonlit cloud line of the storm edge loomed overhead. Half the Frebu sky glittered with stars. The gales lessened and moved on, leaving her falling in a gentle breeze. Brilliant moonlight cast a cold, sublime radiance onto the snowy tundra.

"Eroton," she whispered.

The poem she'd write about this night had its title.

FOUR

GAM-OPs Headquarters | Planet: Tavi-Prime | Star System: Pesari-9, Galactic Core.

Lilline sat in the familiar wooden chair across Asher Lauden's desk, her finger tracing invisible lines on the polished surface. The GAM-OPs director stood, sipping tea by his office window, listening to her report through an audio translation feed in his earpiece.

Lingering traces of Queen Yaz Flake, Lauden's pipe tobacco of choice, hung in the air like morning mist. The tantalizing scent teased her nostrils, conjuring potent and nostalgic memories – her parents socializing with friends while she watched from a makeshift play area or listened from her second-floor bedroom. So many nights lulled to sleep by the rise and fall of laughter, like gentle waves on a shoreline. She could almost feel the comfy sheets, tinged with the scent of tobacco, as she gazed at Fentari's moons through the skylight. Yaz Flake was embedded in her DNA; the olfactory trigger pulled back a curtain onto the first act of her life. The leaf's thick and elegant smoke painted an image of good times before a crisis intervened and left her parentless and in the care of Granny Kissy, when she wasn't off saving the galaxy from the clutches of criminal masterminds.

Lilline stared at the sinuous trail of gray smoke rising from the discarded pipe on the desk. In its austere stand of Bartos marble, the wide bowl and curved stem offered a distraction from the tension Lauden thrived on in moments like these. Writing reports was bad enough but being present while her boss listened to them was pure torture. The poetry rose, as it always did when her emotions vied for dominance.

> *Both arrogant and stern,*
> *I think it gets you off.*
> *Because of your—*

"And then what happened?" Lauden knocked back the last of his tea and placed the cup and saucer down on a small circular table. He didn't rotate to face her, instead choosing to keep his back turned. That was never a good sign.

The GAM-OPs director's tall and gaunt figure cut into the rays of sunlight penetrating the dimly lit interior.

"It vanished," she said, "and the cavern collapsed. I was lucky to get out in time."

Lauden turned. All she made out in the strong backlight of the morning sun were his cravat and socks, both stark white and glittering. The rest of him, the prominent beak-like nose, austere and expertly tailored gray suit, and idiosyncratic translucent skin typical of all Gej-ti, were lost in shadow. That was Asher Lauden: CEO of the most powerful organization that didn't exist in the eyes of billions under its protection. His leadership cast an invisible, regulatory blanket over the known world, keeping it safe like a galactic watchdog.

"And you say it tried to feed on your thoughts?"

"As best as I can describe it." Lilline shifted in her seat, adjusting a leg. Her knee still ached.

"And did it?"

"Sir?" She looked at his silhouette. Lauden's face was nothing more than an oblong void. He was doing that on purpose.

"Did it communicate with you, speak to you?"

Lilline stared at the shadow. Faint traces of air traffic dotted the sky-lanes out the window. The endlessly repeating trails of morning commuters appeared like an army of insects on the move.

Did it communicate with me? The traumatic confrontation with the 'thing' on Frebu stirred her insides.

"T8?"

"I don't think so sir, no," she said, snapping back to the urban world of Tavi-Prime.

"You aren't sure?"

She knew where this was going. The scent of doubt and skepticism was usurping the Queen Yaz Flake.

"I'm reporting what happened, sir. As accurately as I can and in this case that means being unsure. GAM-OPs protocol requires—"

Lauden held up a hand, signaling for her to halt. "You know what I'm getting at." He strode back to his desk and sat. The shadowy silhouette metamorphosed into a visible, tangible humanoid now that he was out of the backlighting. One who, by the look Lilline recognized on his face, was about to say something insensitive.

"Let's play hypotheticals, shall we?" Lauden placed his elbows on the desk and clasped his fingertips together under his chin. The director's milky skin revealed faint traces of nerves and muscles, a reminder that the Gej-ti species once thrived on a planet in near darkness millions of cycles ago.

Lauden's eyes, pitch as night, cast their cold gaze across the desk. The pair of respiratory gills on either side of his neck, replacing the nasal passageway of humans, rose and fell in a steady rhythm.

"Scenario one," Lauden said, "this 'thing' is some sort of alien entity. Scenario two: you encountered a new weapon. Made by whomever it is who might be busy causing unknown radio signals on these far-off arctic planets. Scenario three: you had an episode of some—"

"With all due respect, I—"

"Be quiet." Lauden's calm austerity hit like a laser. "You had an episode of some kind," he said, continuing, "brought on by over-working yourself and stress. Or..."

Lauden was doing that thing he did, where he raised one of his black eyebrows. On his long narrow face, with its elderly statesman air, the gesture was effective. As much as she hated to admit it, it was a good look. It said, *I am now being reasonable.*

"Or," he repeated, "something out there triggered a neurological event or hallucination. The hyperchromium fumes, perhaps?"

Oh, crap.

It wasn't out of the realm of possibility. Her mind backtracked, running at high speed through the events on Frebu after she'd gutted the Dendari. She had inhaled a good bit of the noxious smoke.

And you tossed the entire jacket into the flames right before 'it' appeared.

"That doesn't explain the fire going out," she said.

Lauden did the other thing he liked to employ when he spoke with arrogance. Lilline and the other T# agents referred to it as "the thing with his hand." A gesture where he turned his palm up and over in the air.

Her boss made the action and waited for her response.

"It *did* happen, sir."

Did it? It had to have, there was no way it hadn't. The entire side of the glacier caved in.

"I'm sure of it," she said, pushing back. "There's no way that could be—"

A buzzer sounded, interrupting her defense.

"Yes," Lauden said.

"Sir, I've got the images downloaded and processed from T8's blaster-capture."

The voice was Carbrook's. He'd be in the lab. *Perfect timing.* The pictures from when she tore out of the collapsing ice cave would provide the visual evidence for her report.

"And?" Lauden said, the calm force of his gaze locked on her.

"Nothing there."

You've got to be kidding.

"I mean, there's the glacial cavern and patterned cracks and whatnot," Carbrook said. "But no sign of anything in the ice and IR scans on the data aren't bringing up anything either. Even my brand new multi-spectral resonator didn't provide anything."

"Thank you, Carbrook." Lauden cut the line and leaned back in his chair. "You didn't see signs of an installation or any kind of facility?"

He was doing the *"I'm being reasonable"* thing again.

"No, nothing else," Lilline said. "As my report stated, my effort to reach the pulse coordinates was compromised when the Dendari turned on me."

"Right. I'm putting you on psych leave for a week."

"What?"

Lauden's face didn't flinch. The cravat sparkled, but his face remained earnest. Even the visible nerves and cheek muscles were still. Only his temple arteries pulsed, as they always did, in a steady rhythm.

"You don't believe me?"

"I don't want you on active duty until we get you checked out with Dr. Zeglo."

The psych evaluator? In all her time at GAM-OPs, Lauden had never pulled her from a lead, even one as strange as this.

"Something is happening on Frebu, sir, and probably in the other systems that we're watching. We have to get back out there."

"Agreed. I'm sending T3 to give it the twice-over."

"Olana? She's a Pirtani thug. Searches and subtlety aren't her specialty. She's too thick-headed and brutish to know what to look for. This is my lead. With all due respect—"

"You're off Operation Snow Eclipse. I'll have my assistant set up an appointment with Dr. Zeglo. Day after tomorrow. Whether this was an episode of some kind or an anomaly like you say—"

"Episode?"

"End of conversation." Lauden swiped a hand over a sensor bar on his desk. A thin holo-field displaying a region of space Lilline didn't recognize, dense with star systems, rose between their faces. She peered through the glowing orbit lines. Her boss had moved his attention to the holo-field.

Arrogant bastard.

"And you need to rest that knee," he said, opening a file. "Don't think I didn't notice when you walked in."

Lauden didn't miss a thing. Four days getting back to Tavi-Prime and the pain and swelling lingered.

She'd been able to fool everyone on the return FTL journey. After landing the Hyler Pod at Frebu's orbit port, she'd ditched the professor ruse and boarded a luxury starliner under her favorite pseudonym – Keely Larkin. Lilline's database held almost twenty names, but Keely was her go-to preference.

An expedition scout for a company specializing in high-octane adventures, Keely Larkin was the perfect cover for someone who bounced around from one end of known space to the other. Lilline utilized the out-of-the-way locations on the job as fodder for Keely, describing daring solo excursions scouting potential destinations for the company she "worked" for – Galaxy Unlimited. When she returned from GAM-OPs missions banged up, no matter how severe, playing it off as a mishap in the backcountry for G.U. never raised suspicion.

GAM-OPs ran G.U. as a front, on the books, with real guides and actual tours for those seeking adventure. All legitimate down to a physical headquarters on the first floor of the building she was in now.

Lilline had become comfortable living as Keely Larkin. The cover identity was her break from work, a vacation from the job. And, if she were to admit it, a break from herself.

"You are no one."

She winced as the words from her encounter with the entity rang in her head. The haunting memory of the confrontation sent a chill through her psyche that wouldn't settle.

"We're done, by the way," Lauden said. He raised his eyes and locked them with hers through the holo-field. "I'll send this report to the analysts and have them look into it. If something is flagged and it fans out, then the galactic minister and her cabinet will be informed."

That will get nowhere.

The director was fooling himself if he expected number crunchers and data specialists to make any sense of what she'd encountered in the ice. At least when she got back from leave, they'd be no further along than they were now.

Lilline rose from the chair, using her arms to relieve the weight on her knee. She caught a hint of a smile on Lauden's face through the green star field.

"As I said," he muttered, "you need to rest that knee."

Lilline crossed to the office portal, doing her best to hide her injury. The morning light of Tavi-Prime faded as Lauden hit a switch lowering the shade. The watchdog was going back to his solitary work in atavistic comfort.

Her ears caught the sound of the pipe ignitor click.

"And T8?" Lauden's voice stopped her at the portal.

"Sir?"

"Have Carbrook repair that knee before you leave. He's been itching to try a new prototype on the Hyper-Healer. Should cut your recovery time in half."

But not my psych leave.

"My assistant can walk you down if you need a hand making it there."

"I'll be fine." She limped out the portal.

FIVE

Paragon Galactic, Inc. | District: Executive Estate | Star System: Sesstari, Galactic Core.

Mavron Nave focused on the small holo-screen hovering inches from his nose. An underwater section of the stream a few steps from where he stood appeared on the virtual grid.

"Good morning, Ke."

The words of greeting to his assistant were spoken with secondary attention, like a sidebar chat in the corner of a gaming system. His eyes tracked the yellow lure bobbing along the riverbed in the holo-display. Dexterous human fingertips flicked back and forth, working the radio wave thimbles controlling the underwater device. The bait danced in an experimental rhythm as if it were playing hopscotch, teasing the Cronkhead trout lurking in the shadows under a rocky ledge.

"I am sorry to—"

"I've told you about that phrase, Ke."

"Right." Ke's vibrato voice behind him was apologetic.

Nave knew without turning that the Rasp's fist-sized head, with its single eye and rusty-colored skin like dried clay, was bowed. He could see the signature squat frame and stocky muscular physique, with its snake-like neck rising to the small crown, in his mind. Ke was doing what they always did after foolish breaches of strict administrative etiquette, and an action typical of all Rasps, attempting to diminish their physical presence.

A shadow passed over the stream and surrounding meadows, blanketing the scene in temporary darkness. Seconds later, daylight resumed and Nave caught the distinct shape of a cargo ship's stern track across the field. He glanced up. The freighter crossed the transparent curvature of the orbital ring on its approach to dock at the station's central spoke.

"Report on Frebu." Nave returned his attention to the holoscreen and worked the thimbles. The Cronkhead showed little interest in the latest algorithm.

Damn this fish.

Nave liked data: quadron-code, meta-mathematics, binary sequences, and statistics. Rational logistics was music to his ears, the swirling numeric harmonies through which the world was meant to be understood. Even emotions, those distracting and annoying intrusions into calculative knowledge, could be nailed down and forced to confess to deductive origins by a mind advanced enough to locate the logistical wellspring unveiling its rational formula.

That one was still a work in progress. He'd conquer it soon enough.

Life for Mavron Nave was best lived in a world of ordered and formulaic design. So long as experience reflected a map of reason, he could remain focused on building things the right way, rather than inhabiting a world with faults. And hurt.

Fishing was his latest obsession, a pastime made of yet-to-be explained organic dynamics that didn't disgust him. Who knew that it would be so challenging. Despite his best efforts, the natural puzzle continued to elude him. Somewhere in the feeding decisions of aquatic species lay a pattern. Identify it, and a formula could be determined. From there, case studies and data collection would lead to deductions offering a rational solution. This was the way of the world. There was no mystery, only human ineptitude driven by lack of intelligence.

"There was an incident." Ke's deep voice passed out of the vertical neck flap with the distinct Rasp vibration.

Nave kept his eyes on the screen hovering before him.

"We were able to summon a thoughtform, a servitor, but—"

"But what?" His fingers increased their pace, dancing the lure in front of the Cronkhead. 'But' was one of his least favorite words.

"But we lost the facility."

"What?" Nave turned. The Rasp's crown, with its crackled red skin, hid a shameful eye aimed down at the blue and yellow wild-flowers in the meadow. The shadows of leaves from a lone apple tree dappled across their black company uniform with its gold logo.

"Something drew it from the lab area," Ke said.

"Through the shielding field?"

The Rasp raised their head and nodded. "The servitor crossed through that and the glacial ice. It moved through all physical matter."

Nave couldn't believe his ears. This was the best news he'd heard yet. *So, Dr. Hej was correct about the extra-dimensional frequencies.* "And?" He shut off the fishing system. The holo-screen with the view of the underwater stream bed vanished. With ease, his thimbled fingers navigated the lure out of the water and guided it forward until it hovered before him.

"Whatever or whoever it was that interfered caused a fatal error," Ke said.

Nave snatched the lure out of the air and gripped it tight. "What kind of fatal error?"

"The thoughtform imploded."

"Imploded?" He hadn't felt any psychic indication. It was supposed to be linked to him. "What did Dr. Hej say it was?"

"Well, you see... that's the thing, sir," Ke said.

His assistant's eye looked like glacial ice against the warmth of the meadow's colors.

"The entire facility is gone." Ke took a few steps back, their serpentine neck moving in a left-to-right rhythm.

The apple tree shaded their expression, but Nave knew it contained fear.

"The entity's implosion took out two kilometers of the glacier. All our equipment and architecture fell through the ice into the ocean." Ke lowered their eye. "Including Dr. Hej and the entire staff."

"Damn!" Nave spun around and threw the lure into the stream. He bolted to the water's edge and lifted a large rock overhead. With a raging scream, he turned and hurled it at the apple tree.

Ke dove away into the flowers.

The boulder tore a chunk of bark off the trunk and thudded to the ground. Nave strode to the tree, with its stupid and arrogant beauty. Rage and fury rose like a tidal swell in the blood coursing through his veins.

"Arrrrgh!" He yanked at a low limb, planting a boot on the trunk for leverage. "Damn!" The thick branch snapped and broke free, the release of force sending him onto his ass.

"Billions of credits!" he screamed, prone amidst the flowers.

He got to his feet and homed in on the tree. It stood quiet and stoic.

It's mocking me.

He raised the branch over his head and smashed it into the trunk. Once. Twice. Three times. So many times that he lost count. With each stroke, an end portion cracked and flew off and away into the flowers. After too many swings, a small stump the size of a knife blade remained in his hand. Nave spun back toward the stream and flung it at the rock on the far bank.

He bent over, hands on his knees, to catch his breath. The water flowed past as if nothing had happened. Unlike the apple tree, whose growth patterns remained undiscovered, the river's current ran at 3.4 volumes per second and did not taunt him. It was the perfect rate, according to his aesthetic formula. He'd designed the mechanics for the orbital, based on an innovative magnetic system that assisted the artificial gravity in sending the water downstream.

And it soothed his fury.

"The network," Nave said, gasping for air. "Was the network linked?" He turned around, still panting. Through his rage of blurry vision, he caught sight of Ke's snake-like neck and head rise out of the grass and flowers. The Rasp nodded.

"So, we have the data at least?"

"Yes," Ke said, their voice a whisper. The assistant stood and wiped off their uniform.

A small yellow bird, startled by the violent disruption a moment earlier, returned to the tree's branches and flitted about. It tried to land on the missing branch, circling in the air.

Nave's blood temperature lowered to a simmer. "What was it, Ke? You said something drew it from the lab. Do we know?"

The Rasp shook their ball-size head.

Something or someone? The other arctic locations where they had established preliminary stations reported prying eyes, but none had found their labs.

He walked to the stream, bent down, and splashed water onto his face. At the perfect temperature for his desired aquatic ecosystem, its nine-degrees Celsius water cooled his flushed skin.

Galactic security will be all over that site.

"Send someone to Frebu," he said, kneeling next to the bank. "Make sure they get the word out that this was a natural disaster. The sonic waves from the summoning can be cloaked as a seismic event.

Get a hacker to graft some additional data into the satellite network and override what is there."

He looked back at Ke. His assistant was already sending out the order on their wrist comm.

"Make sure you get 2112 to do it. Double the usual rate and tell them it's top priority."

The Rasp nodded and spoke into the comm.

2112 was the one hacker good enough for the job.

"Sir," Ke said.

Nave rose and wiped his hands on his shirt.

"According to the Frebu air traffic database, a Hyler was in the vicinity the same time as the glacial collapse. I've got someone checking the registration with the hopes of getting a trans-visa ID."

That was a start. If it was an individual or a group, they had been up against one heck of a situation. But they couldn't have survived. It would be near impossible.

"Working on the ID," Ke said. The meadow and stream turned to night as another cargo ship passed overhead, blocking out Sesstari, the star that gave light to the small independent empire that was Paragon Galactic, Inc.

Nave tracked the ship a kilometer above; the transparent ceiling revealed a backdrop of faint and distant stars. The ship's stern moved on and Sesstari's warm light dried the remaining dampness on his face. The star's rays entered his pores. Ultraviolet radiation – the calculation of its distance and intensity ran through his mind and soothed him more than the sun's glow.

"Dendari comm base lists a Hyler leaving atmosphere at dawn," Ke said. "I'll see about getting the data from its log."

"Yes, do that." Nave lowered his head. He opened his eyes and turned. His assistant stood next to the apple tree with its broken branch. The trunk looked like a sword dummy from where he'd damaged it.

Violence. It wasn't his area of expertise. Nor was killing, at least not in the physical world. He designed the means to do it in games better than anyone else in the galaxy. When something stood in his way that required it, others under his leadership did it for him. This time he would need to call on his best real-life player.

Whoever it was that interfered with his plans on Frebu was going to live a very short life.

"Get me The Preacher," he said.

SIX

"You have to get outside more, Carbrook." Lilline stood in the portal to the play space that was the personal fiefdom of creative human freelancer, Poz Carbrook. To her right, a floating platform tipped and swayed a meter off the floor. The eccentric inventor spun and ducked invisible enemies on the tilting surface like an action figure come to life.

"Be right with you, T8!" Carbrook's spiky red hair and yellow jumpsuit glowed like neon lights in the steel-gray sub-level hangar.

"I'll occupy myself," she said. "Plenty to fiddle around with in here."

"Don't touch anything!" Carbrook lost his balance and almost fell. "Just wait there a moment," he said and went back to swinging and shifting up and down while the disk tilted and pitched.

"Can't you pause that thing?"

The inventor waved a hand with a controller at her as if to say, *"not now."*

"What does that gesture even mean?"

"It means," he leaned hard against a sudden tilt of the hover-base, "it *means* that you're distracting me. Wait a moment!"

Lilline caught sight of the usual array of modified street vehicles, furniture with secret functions and deadly devices, and miscellaneous oddities designed to either kill you or save your life, scattered like discarded toys in the long, two-story hangar. At one end, in front of a weapons wall, a mannequin stood poised as if to spring into the air. Each hand was gloved with what looked like mini air burners like reversed thimbles on fingertips.

"What's that mannequin all about?"

"Not ready yet," he said, bending and twisting. "Don't even think about touching it."

She tracked further down the hall and recognized something that brought a smile to her face: the reconstructed *Velociter Bullet* shot to pieces on her last mission. It looked good as new. She turned to check on Carbrook. The techie was still absorbed in his virtual entertainment. Despite how much it pissed him off to have to do so much work to save the hybrid flyer from the junk heap, Lilline knew that underneath the veneer of frustration hid the pride at knowing it went to good use.

And it had. To call that thing unique was an understatement. The *Velociter* was the fastest two-person rocketed projectile ever built. If something was worthy of verse it was that gleaming beauty. Polished to a shine, its deep purple shell glimmered like a jewel in a display window. She'd written a poem in syllabic half-time, using 3/3/3/3/3/1/3, to celebrate its speed by accelerating the meter.

> *Bullet race,*
> *Bullet fly.*
> *Vapor trail,*

Streaks the sky,
Speed of sound.
Whoosh!
Silent strike.

The Velociter made impressive work of a near-impossible atmospheric blockade in the Myri-12 system. She had rocketed through the defense grid over the small inhabitable moon off Qo without so much as a glitching flash on the air traffic screens. The local government had no idea a GAM-OPs agent passed into the atmosphere, and they never suspected any foul play in the sudden and unexpected death of a political official with secret plans to initiate a coup within the week. If that had been allowed to happen, it would have set off a chain reaction of diplomatic crises leading to local economic and—

Blah blah blah.

Lilline didn't care about any of the details. What mattered was that she had stopped the line of consequential dominoes. Her actions prevented mass suffering for the potential victims of a small elite's greed and selfish lust for power, fame, or whatever other personal fetishes political criminals and deviants got off on. That kind of pain and death took away her parents and it wasn't going to happen to anyone else. Not if she could help it. No one deserved to live through the loss that she had. Not on GAM-OPs's watch.

Her mark on Qo fell in ignorance, with no idea of what had transpired. Lilline chose to do it old school, like the assassin guilds from the time of the First Collective. One server for the elegant private dinner at the embassy of similar size and build was given a brief dose of narcs and stuffed in a closet. A quick change into their outfit and she had served the Secretary of Galactic Resource Exchange an untraceable poison in a cocktail infusion. The Gej-ti hadn't even looked up at her when she poured the aperitif into her glass. The secretary was too busy bragging about a future that would never come. Lilline took it upon herself to allow for a small, personal satisfaction. After the cocktail shaker tipped to empty, she rolled the spy game dice.

"Anything else, Secretary?" she had asked, interrupting the woman.

It was against the rules. An unnecessary risk, but in the field, you always carried a wild card. That's what made an operation worthwhile – you played the odds for the moral jackpot. When no one else shared your cloak and dagger victories, this was how you got to walk away and gloat in private.

Lilline smiled as she stared at the *Velociter*, remembering the unbeatable hand she drew that night. She got the look she'd hoped for from the secretary. Their eyes locked for one brief instant, and it was priceless. The politician's gaze radiated arrogant annoyance at being interrupted. Lilline responded with an apologetic and meek subservience that veiled a silent smirk of anticipation at the inevitable victory. The Gej-ti dismissed her without so much as a word. She shooed her away with a wave of her hand, and an exaggerated exhalation through her neck gills, refusing to grace her with a verbal response. The woman was beautiful, that Lilline remembered. Stunningly so, with typical Gej-ti skin and hazel eyes pointing to crossbreeding with another human variant species, making for an aura both fierce and elegant. Most of her marks were like that – auratic, each in a unique fashion. You didn't rise to power or climb the rungs toward it in a galactic government system with intelligence and influence alone. Charisma, ugly or beautiful, could be wielded as a seductive and alluring social and political weapon.

That was a poem she might still write. Not only for the atmosphere of the encounter and anticipation of the poison's effect eight hours later, but because Lilline had re-routed the course of galactic civilization with one small interference at an elegant, private dinner on a moon off Qo. She, like her fellow T# GAM-OPs agents, served as stationary time travelers to yet-to-be-determined futures, making minuscule interventions in politics and culture like a boot crushing an insect in one millennium that sets off a chain of exponential consequences re-routing galactic civilization. Forever.

Most important for Lilline was that the course was for the better, at least according to her superiors and the intel driving her missions. No one outside of GAM-OPs knew that fate was more determined than—

"Too bad about the blaster pics."

Lilline turned away from the view of the *Velociter*. Carbrook stood, biting his nails.

"That's disgusting. You do know that, right?"

The inventor shrugged but didn't stop.

"It's not something that other people want to see, Carbrook. Including me."

"I don't ever see other people," he said, lowering the hand. "Except for you, Lauden, my new assistant, and the other T#s. And maybe the occasional sub-tech from maintenance or custodial when I need—"

Lilline held up a hand, halting the rant.

Carbrook's look made clear he wasn't offended. In all the time she'd known him, he'd never gotten upset. Except for when she banged up his stuff. Carbrook's inventions contained more emotional value than his pride or ego.

Lilline studied the inventor's face. Subtle crow's feet spread around his green eyes like newly sprouted seedlings. She'd always thought of Carbrook as young. A New-Gen, he was her junior by fifteen cycles. A typical New-Gen too, all punky when it came to fashion and attitude (but not politics) and more invested in virtual than physical reality. Odd to think that he too would grow old, and another set of galactic youngsters would make him look dated and uncool.

"What game was it this time?" she asked, nodding towards the hovering platform.

"Umm, obvious." The techie rolled his eyes.

Lilline held out her hand.

He pointed at it. "You're doing the Lauden thing! That's awesome."

"Carbrook, what game?" Lilline asked. "You know what? Why am I even asking? I don't care."

"Crak, you really don't know. That is *almost* cool."

"I'm almost ready to *lose* my cool."

"Alright, alright." He shoved his hands in the pockets of his yellow jumpsuit. "*Freestrike* 3. Brushing up my form." He tipped his spiky red head towards the hovering platform. "*Free 4* drops any day. The wait is all the rage. Like, everywhere." The glitter in his eyes was as bright as the stars on Frebu a few nights earlier. "The icon is going to change soon." Carbook gestured back to the platform. A meter-wide red holographic symbol spun above the circular disk.

"That thing?" Lilline pointed.

"Where have you been, T8? In a cave?"

Lilline kept the irony of the remark to herself.

"Everyone in all the networked star systems is waiting. *Freestrike* is the crak! It's overtaking the best games by Oui-tech and Gonzo. I'm probably the one other person in the galaxy with the tech capacity to do what they are doing. It's the biggest thing since—"

Lilline held up her hand to halt him. She knew the symbol. Everyone did. If you lived anywhere networked, which was ninety percent of known systems, Paragon's logo had been a ubiquitous phenomenon for over twenty cycles. Under the entrepreneurial leadership of the brilliant designer Mavron Nave, the company usurped its commercial rivals for market supremacy as the most popular entertainment technology corporation in the galaxy.

"You don't want to know what is going to happen?" Carbrook asked.

"Not really."

Lilline read genuine shock on his face. He looked almost disappointed. Out of kindness, she flipped her hand over in a gesture to proceed.

"Ha! You did the Lauden thing again," Carbrook said, withdrawing a hand from a pocket and pointing.

Maybe she did need some time off. It's like Lauden was getting inside her head, infiltrating her thoughts. A pang stirred her belly. The haunting memory of the shadowy specter in the ice cave flashed in her mind.

"T8, you cool? You look like you've seen a ghost," Carbrook said.

Enough with the weird coincidences. "Get on with it, and let's get my knee healed up," she said.

"So, the deal is," Carbrook said, "the icon is going to switch to a new one and when it does, the Avatar says..."

"The who?"

The inventor leaped back, his high-top sneakers smacking on the floor as he landed in an action pose straight out of a game. "You," he pointed, still in the stance, "are lame."

"Yes, you have told me that before."

Carbrook stood and straightened his jumpsuit. "I mean, poetry is lame." He shrugged as if to say, *"sorry, but it's true"* and walked back over. "But crak, T8, you don't even know about the Avatar? That's like granny-level lame."

"What is that supposed to imply?"

Carbrook's green eyes went wide, and he folded the fingers of both hands together on his head in exasperation. "Not that Kissy Renault is lame, I mean... she's awesome. Or *was* awesome, back in the day... from what I hear. Well, I'll bet she's still awesome even now that she's—"

Lilline held up her hand to stop him. "How about we fix up my knee and drop the whole *Freestruck* thing?"

"*Freestrike.*" Carbrook said in a low murmur, eyes down. He kicked a toe of his sneaker into the smooth gray paint on the floor.

"Whatever," she said.

The inventor gestured for her to follow him down the hangar.

"I see my *Velociter* is back together in one piece," she said, following behind him.

"Not your *Velociter*. My *Velociter*."

"Actually, it's GAM-OPs's *Velociter*," Lilline said, getting him back for the *Freestrike* razz.

"Whatever," he said. "The important thing is that you're going to like this new Hyper-Healer. I made some new mods to the earlier version. I'm guessing by the way you're walking this thing will get you to ninety percent in about fifteen minutes."

That was impressive. The previous Hyper-Healer she had used after mishaps on missions was good for getting past the worst of an injury, but you still dealt with the final stages of regeneration through the body's natural biological cycle.

"What did you change?" she asked as they approached the unit. The opaque green sphere, about the size of a small transport pod, rested on a pedestal with a series of cables running from its base. Lilline tracked them as they ran like a set of thick, multicolored snakes across the floor. The wires connected to a complicated wall unit that flashed and blinked like a carnival ride at night.

"Way over your intelligence scale," Carbrook said and crossed a palm a few inches over his red spikes.

"Depends on the kind of intelligence," she said, approaching the wall of lights and examining the machine. "Field survival intelligence or analyst statistical intelligence?" She turned to Carbrook. "The latter, I find to be quite useless in my line of work."

"The *science* kind," Carbrook said, switching on a set of buttons on the unit. "Abstract theory refined and confirmed by applied mathematics. None of your 'trust your gut' stuff that leaves my inventions looking like a target dummy on the blaster range."

"Fair enough." She might bicker with Carbrook and piss him off when she destroyed his toys, but she respected his brilliance. Plus, on the few occasions when she'd asked for explanations of new modifications to her equipment, it always ran a course ending with complex algebra. She and Carbrook learned that was a wall between them that could never be breached or climbed. She had grown to like the wall.

It kept things amicable even while being constructed of sarcastic mortar.

A green holo-board materialized in front of the computer. Carbrook punched in a set of codes and directed her to the sphere behind them. The opaque Hyper-Healer shell sparkled and turned translucent. The familiar med bay recliner she had come to know too well appeared through the flickering green magnetic shield.

"Check this out," Carbrook said. He waved a hand in front of them. A set of steps unfolded to ground level with a hiss.

"Impressive," she said.

"There's more," Carbrook said.

She caught a look of satisfaction on his face.

"I named it."

"I can't wait," she said. "The suspense is killing me."

"The Healer can help stay that damage." He smirked.

"Almost poetic."

"Why, thank you." He took a bow. "And now let me introduce you to..."

Lilline waited. He didn't continue.

Carbrook held his face frozen, eyebrows raised.

"What?" she asked.

"Aren't you going to do it?"

"Do what?"

"The Lauden thing?" he whispered as if her boss was listening in.

Lilline rolled her eyes and flipped her hand over.

"T8, meet Queen Yaz."

How could she not laugh? Somehow it did manage to relieve some of the seriousness that Lauden dropped onto everyone and everything at GAM-OPs.

"Not bad at all," she said.

Carbrook clapped his hands in satisfaction. "Queen Yaz, please allow T8 entry."

The translucent shell dematerialized above the stairs, leaving a human-sized archway open for passage.

"Get up and in and we'll get you on the mend," Carbrook said and extended an arm in a polite gesture.

Lilline took the steps gingerly, favoring her good knee.

"That is... if it doesn't malfunction," the inventor said. "You're the first run since my mods."

She didn't turn, but she did smile.

SEVEN

"Well? Can anyone offer Keely some feedback?"

Lilline read the usual expressions on the faces in her poetry critique group. Holographic heads hovered to her left and right, forming a circle from her seat on the couch in her Domus-unit. Scattered around Tavi-Prime's endless urban blanket, budding poets of a variety of species gathered virtually for the monthly meeting.

Writing poetry wasn't a big draw these days. Only a handful of enthusiasts pursued the literary art, despite its vast popularity across the galaxy. These were the die-hards, the ones whose minds were occupied with meter, rhyme, scansion, and an artistic drive to craft ideas and dress them in elegant words.

Was it a blessing or a curse? Looking around the room, Lilline wasn't sure. All eyes were lowered, per usual the signal that none wanted to contribute to her growing, near-perpetual, pile of poetic corpses stacked up from cycles of slash and burn criticism.

"It's a bit arrogant, Keely." Fehli, the group leader and poetry professor at T-Prime Academy, broke the silence. Lilline knew the tone well. The human instructor spoke as much to ease the awkward discomfort as she did for benefit of critique. Lilline couldn't blame her. Fehli was doing her job, juggling between managing the group dynamic and providing difficult commentary. When icy silences fell, the veteran poet shared what others were thinking but were too afraid to say for fear of hurting someone's feelings.

Lilline could take it. Her thick skin told a history of the unenthusiastic reception of her creative writing. A significant portion of her hardened exterior came from another source: her job. Not her fake job at Galaxy Unlimited. Her *real* job. The one that she couldn't talk about.

"Unless it's meant to be sarcastic?" Fehli ran a wrinkled hand, russet and worn with age, through her stark white hair. Lilline guessed the professor must be nearing eighty cycles. The benefits of her wisdom, appreciated by everyone in the group, were tempered for Lilline by the fact that she never failed to identify her poetic imitation of Den-shi. At some point in each session, it came up.

"It reminds me of Den-shi's work, but a bit too closely associated. If that's what you are going for then you need to think more about the origin of the parody and sarcasm."

And there it is.

Lilline kept her expression neutral and nodded. If she could do it while pouring poison into a glass for a diplomat, she could do it for a poetry instructor under her false identity.

"Let's read it again," Fehli said. "Keely, would you?"

Lilline re-posted the poem. The lines manifested in holo-form in front of her couch, hovering in an extra-dimensional sphere so that it faced every angle as flat text, allowing all present to read it.

From the ennui of night,

a new day ever dawns.
I will never give up.
How could I?
If I do, a world dies.

"I agree," Jejeni said. "It reads like Den-shi."
Not surprised to hear that.

The young Kreeli always supported Fehli in her wake. The band he wore across his oblong and hairless blue head shifted from periwinkle to magenta, indicating a vital internal adjustment to blood pressure. All Kreelis utilized the barometric regulator to survive outside their home world of Joranda.

"You're still ignoring scansion," Fehli said.

Lilline nodded. *Because I suck at it.*

"I mean, no offense Keely," Jejeni continued in what human ears perceived as a low-pitched and thick voice, "but 'a world dies'? It's not like one person's actions resonate across the galaxy."

Holo-heads nodded, supporting the remark.

Lilline's blood pressure rose. This was turning into a challenge worthy of a GAM-OPs operation.

You all have no idea who I am.

Her stomach twisted. Its source wasn't Jejeni's comment.

"You are no one."

The irony hit harder than anything the critique group mustered as criticism. Sure, telling them she was a GAM-OPs agent would be cathartic. It would release over ten-cycles of deception and secrecy. Arrogance had nothing to do with it. She wasn't after recognition for deeds unseen and unspoken. No thanks were required for keeping the galaxy safe. Pain and suffering were wrought too easily by those who abused power.

The irony lay deeper. She couldn't give them the answer, only reveal another layer of armor. Peel back Keely Larkin and you revealed Lilline Renault. But who was she?

I have no idea.

"Are you alright, Keely?"

Lilline caught sight of Fehli looking over with concern.

"I hope you didn't take that the wrong way. Remember," the professor's gaze went from holo to holo, "everything said here is about improvement. We're all already doing the work. That is what matters most."

Hovering heads nodded.

"I'm fine," Lilline said. "Thank you for the feedback. I'll look into the sarcasm angle." She smiled politely. "I've got no shortage of Denshi's volumes to go through." She lifted her leg onto a pillow resting on the table in front of the couch. Her knee felt one hundred percent after the short session in the Hyper-Healer but Dr. Zeglo insisted that she keep it up for a second day. Twenty-four hours since she'd been put on leave. It felt like an eternity.

"Knee injury, Keely?" It was Grego, the middle-aged human financier across from her. His round, cherubic face and smooth black skin carried the boy from his youth through to adulthood. Grego had that look gifted to some people where the traces of the child remained in the adult's features.

"Fine, thanks Grego. Minor work accident. Nothing serious," she said. Hiko jumped up onto her lap.

"Awww," a chorus of multi-species voices said in unison.

Lilline ran her hand over Hiko's black fur. He nudged against her with his nose each time she stroked him from head to tail.

"Say hello, Hiko," she directed his attention to the holo-group. As usual, Hiko ignored her instructions and purred. The feline homed in on the pleasure of her long, gentle strokes ending at the white tip of his tail.

"I think that's all the time we have," Fehli said. "Thanks to everyone who shared their latest and greatest."

Holo-heads nodded. Lilline did as well.

"I'll need to check my schedule before I send out the next group invitation. The end of term is approaching and that means extra admin work." Fehli rolled her eyes. "My favorite."

Several members chuckled and nodded.

"Bye all," Fehli said and waved a gaunt hand.

Lilline signaled goodbye and cut the feed. She let out a sigh and turned to Hiko. "You know my little secret, don't you?" She ran the fingers of a hand under his chin.

The Nok-cat's purring revved up like a motor. He pushed his nose into one of her wrists and dragged his head along her forearm.

"Alright. So, what now?" she asked.

Lilline eyed the mail stick next to her foot on the table.

"What do you say, Hiko? Get it over with?"

He purred on, oblivious to her question.

She lifted her leg off the table and reached for the device. "Ooof." She stood with a groan, sending Hiko jumping away with a disgruntled meowing. "Oh relax," she said and walked to her desk. Her side was still a bit sore where she smacked the ice in the cave. Recovering from injuries these days took more time than it had ten cycles ago.

Hip pain aside, Carbrook's new healer system didn't fail to impress. Her knee felt as good as new.

She inserted the stick into the slot on the desk and leaned forward, hands resting on the polished white surface, as the holo-field came to life.

"Two new missives," the computer announced. "One written. One audio/visual."

The text would be from her grandmother. Kissy was the only person who wrote to her. No one in networked galactic systems 'wrote' to anyone anymore. People sent correspondence as voice recorded audio or holo-vids.

Except Kissy.

Her grandmother wrote out her words the old-fashioned way, by hand. Her letters were then either scanned into the comm system as a single image or transcribed through typing with fingers. Or, more accurately, with *a* finger. Watching Kissy struggle on a holo-field keyboard was one of the few pleasures that gave Lilline a leg up on the former agent.

"You know you can use the voice transcription, right?" Lilline would say every time she witnessed her grandmother struggling to type.

"Yes, dear. I am very aware of that."

Lilline could hear her words now:

"If I wanted to speak with someone, I would call them or meet them for tea. If I am writing to them, then I will damn well write to them. And I expect them to read it when it's received. There's something to be said for the written language, Lilli. It has its own visual pace and rhythmic design. The eye-brain relationship is different than the ear-brain relationship. It's the same with poetry. You, as much as anyone, should know that."

She did know it. Mainstream communication may have moved on from the days of Agent Kissy, but the art of verse remained as proud and steadfast as the old woman. Poetry was an anachronism, a rare form of creative expression that relied on reading for consumption. Books, kinetic comics, and other textual media stayed popular, but most audiences consumed them through audio formats. Not poetry. That was done the old-fashioned way: reading. Many poets, Lilline included, penned their verses using voice recorders, but cultural tradition expected the final product to be transcribed into a textual layout. That reliance and focus on the written word was why so few practiced the art.

Lilline waved a hand and the holo-inbox materialized.

Sure enough, the first correspondence was from Granny. Or, as it read on the screen, "Imani Larkin." Kissy continued to use her pseudonym after retirement from the agency. She told Lilline it was because she'd gotten used to it, but that was a lie. Lilline knew it was out of concern for her safety. Now that she was continuing the family legacy, Kissy was being prudent. Her grandmother's decision ensured the baggage of a former agent and blood relative would not come back to haunt her granddaughter in the field.

As usual Kissy's missive was short and to the point:

. . .

Bored out of my mind.

Come visit before my brain shrivels so small that they put it in a museum of oddities.

Bring Dari cakes. MACHINE *SURE THEY ARE FROM MALARDI'S!*

-I.L.

Lilline snorted.

Typical Granny.

She had enough time for a visit to the retirement facility now. A few days at the guest chateau in the village of Villain might not be a bad idea. Its cobblestone streets and charming stone buildings under the snow-capped mountains of Tavi-Prime's moon were peaceful and inspiring. She wrote her best piece there when Kissy moved into the facility in the valley five cycles earlier: "A Lifetime in Villain." One of the few poems in her catalog where she strayed from a meter structure. She penned it with the modified Cinquain system. Popularized after its rediscovery by a scholar of language on the remote desert planet of Zeret, the poetry became all the rage across networked systems. Well, at least for those interested in esoteric literary form. Lost for millennia in a ruined temple, it had been kept safe by a reclusive spiritual sect. Poets and literati published a wave of poems using the style, imitating its unique linguistic mutation.

Exponential word growth, the same as in a Cinquain poem but with an equitable reduction, from one to five and back again. The form evolved out of the more traditional Cinquain verse, where the lines increase from one to four with a final line of a single word. The assigned grammar for each line in the traditional Cinquain is thrown out in the modified Zeret style. Syllabic design, per the older forms, is maintained with a 2/4/6/8/6/4/2 sequence. No scansion, which made Lilline smitten with the style. The lines of words crossing the page, and retreating again, contribute a visual component to the poetic aesthetics.

Lilline swiped her hand over the holo. "Pull up "A Lifetime in Villain"," she said. The words materialized in the cool magenta that was her favorite font color for poems that made her "best of" list.

Villain
Charming beauty
Speckled stones shimmering
Mountain air, resplendent vista
Table alone, tranquil
Glorious wine
Repose.

Yes, Villain will do.

Later this evening she would schedule a round-trip moon hop and book a room for three days at the Golden Pheasant starting tomorrow. If she left after her morning appointment with Dr. Zeglo she could be there by noon. Kissy would be thrilled. Instead of her usual stay of a few hours, the two would have some quality time together. Best of all, with the room in Villain she had an escape route and safe house.

"Always have an escape route," she winked at Hiko. Once she'd reached maximum daily Kissy level, she could retreat to the tranquility of Villain.

And write.

No interruptions. Only the sweet sound of the river running by at a quiet table on the Golden Pheasant's outdoor terrace. Glass of top-shelf Gondau and the best cheese this side of Res-94.

Hiko meowed. "Yes, I know sweetie. I'll be right there. Mama's hungry too."

She swiped her finger over the holo, closing the missive and opening the next one.

"Carbrook?" she said out loud. That was odd. She pushed start on the audio.

"My new assistant found something funky in your photo. Do you see it?"

Lilline opened the file. A shot from her blaster camera of the cave wall on Frebu filled the holo. Deep blue ice and long cracks ran through a portion of the frozen interior.

"No, I don't see it," she said. *Damn Carbrook.* He always did this.

Her eyes scanned the picture. Top to bottom. Side to side. Section by section. The way she was taught in training.

She recorded every detail in her memory and closed her eyes, bringing the visual data back to life as a mental image.

The cracks. The ice. The resonating and collapsing cavern. The cracks in the ice. The cracks in the—

"Oh, hello." Lilline opened her eyes. How did she miss that? "Way to go, Carbrook's new assistant," she said.

Hiko meowed.

The visit to Kissy would have to wait. Right now, she needed to do two things: feed Hiko and get back to HQ.

EIGHT

"Boss wants to see you."

Lilline hadn't taken more than a few steps inside Galaxy Unlimited when the familiar voice reached her ears.

Katar rose from a desk at her left and approached. The Kreeli nodded, his headband sparkling with a pressure adjustment, and joined her as she walked through the afternoon hustle-bustle of the expedition company's headquarters.

Katar was one of the G.U. employees in on the ruse. He'd served as a GAM-OPs field agent until a vicious revenge attack by an underworld syndicate left him without an arm and enough scars to play tick-tack-toe on his oblong forehead. Katar was a perfect liaison between the shell company and GAM-OPs. Nothing like putting a face with evidence of high adventure in front of customers interested in dangerous trips to hard-to-reach destinations across the galaxy.

Katar's story to potential clients about an encounter with a Ganghut lizard on the desert world of Elisia might be a twist on the truth but wasn't too far a stretch. He was barely alive when rescued from the hands of the syndicate. Lilline knew it because she had gone in, infiltrated and killed the ones holding her fellow agent, and brought him out safely.

"He's been smoking since noon," Katar said. The Kreeli, at almost four meters, leaned his bald crown down in her direction as they walked to share the confidential tidbit.

Lilline grunted a response as they strode through the central aisle in the three-story interior. Amidst its baroque architecture, holos of tourist packages ran in the open space above consulting stations. Adventure themes and expeditions of all types created an enticing collage of offerings. Lilline caught sight of a Bukki tiger bounding through dense foliage, at two times its usual scale, amidst the array of planetary destinations.

If Lauden had been at the Queen Yaz Flake since lunch that meant this was serious. So much for a private moment with Carbrook to go over the images from Frebu. If this had already crossed the director's desk, then more pieces to the puzzle were fitting together.

She followed Katar into the portal. The entryway crystallized into a glittering wall and blocked out the view of the G.U. offices. Lilline leaned forward and exhaled onto the control panel. The floor bounced as the hidden AI confirmed her breath-print and switched internal tracks.

"Anything floating through the office on this?" she asked.

Katar's elongated, hairless crown went back and forth, the scars on full display. "This is tight. No one is talking."

The crystals vanished and the hallway to the central rotunda of GAM-OPs appeared.

The Kreeli gestured out the portal with his remaining arm. "Good luck," he said.

"Don't trust it," Lilline walked out without looking over. "Prefer instinct."

Her ears caught the distinctive Kreeli huff that was the species equivalent of a human scoff.

So, this is big. Enough to keep Lauden puffing since noon and to have those sniffing for gossip coming up empty.

"Granny," she said in greeting and crossed the rotunda with its central fountain and statue of her grandmother. The clanking of dishes through an adjacent portal echoed off the domed ceiling as the staff reset tables in the Octagonal Club.

Two more turns and she was outside Lauden's office.

"Afternoon Cazshi, shall I go right in?"

Lauden's assistant kept his single eye down, focused on the task consuming him at his desk.

Lilline's nostrils picked up the sweet scent of Yaz Flake wafting through the reception area.

"Been smoking since noon," the Rasp said. His serpentine neck danced to and fro, but his gaze remained steady on the holo-documents.

"Yes, I heard."

The Rasp raised its head. Rust-colored skin and scales shimmered in the cold office light. Cazshi hit the button to open the portal.

"Good luck, T8," he said.

Something told her she might need it on this one.

"T8, join us."

Lauden didn't turn. His silhouette stood in its usual position, backlit at the office window. The Gej-ti gestured with an arm to take a seat by his desk.

Carbrook's spiky red head turned from the adjacent chair. The techie's entire appearance, from the hairstyle to the bright yellow jumpsuit, felt grossly out of place amidst the elegant restraint of the director's office.

"Finally," Carbrook whispered as she sat. "Been dying of tension in here."

Lilline inhaled deeply, a lingering cloud of Queen Yaz flake soothing her nostrils with nostalgic memory. She hated being here, but she loved the scent. A fitting irony for her entire relationship with GAM-OPs. The job was a dream. The downtime and necessary social and administrative portions at HQ were a form of professional torture. And then there was the anonymity – a beautiful thing. In the field, she could be anyone she wanted, go anywhere, and do almost anything, all on the company's bill. The cost? A life of accomplishments unrecognized and unacknowledged by billions. No ability to talk about work off the clock. Captured in poetry, inspired by some of the most extraordinary experiences and locales in the galaxy, others consumed her words with the pretense of hyperbole. But the scent of Yaz Flake took her back to a time before it all began. A time when her motivation for doing the job hadn't yet even sparked the smallest kindling of her life story.

"You've seen the images?" Lauden's voice broke her olfactory reverie.

"Yes, Carbrook sent them over the secure line."

"Odd isn't it, considering you were so far out on Frebu?" Smoke plumes exited the director's gills, clouding the afternoon light streaming through the window.

"Frebu?" Carbrook said.

"Yes," Lauden turned. "And that is what troubles me." The Gej-ti strode to the desk and sat.

"I didn't realize you were on Frebu," Carbook whispered.

"Need to know, Carbrook. And you didn't." She smiled at him.

Lauden waved a hand over a sensor, pulling up the images in holo-format. Her blaster capture from the ice cave hovered next to an image familiar to everyone in networked systems across the galaxy.

"The similarity is undeniable to the eye," Lauden said. "What do the computers say, Carbrook?"

"The algorithmic software confirms the probability of chance association to be too small, sir," the techie said, shifting in his seat. Lilline was enjoying the discomfort he displayed with being in Lauden's office. She was used to it, as much as she didn't like it.

"So T8 observes an unknown entity on Frebu that is linked to a company logo," Lauden said. The director repacked his pipe.

So, this is going to be a long meeting.

"To be clear, sir," Carbrook said. "It's not the company logo, but the icon of Paragon's most popular and successful game: *Freestrike.*"

"It's the current version, to be precise," Lilline added the clarification both to contribute to the discussion and to let Lauden know she wasn't ignorant of the details, even if she'd learned it a day before in Carbrook's lab.

The techie eyed her, aware of the dialogical tactic.

Tough. She was being a good agent. Quick on the uptake with intel and knowing when and how to use it. Carbrook was outside the lab now. He had to get used to how the social dynamic worked in GAM-OPs if he wanted to be part of their game.

"Sir."

Lilline smiled as Carbrook's head went up and around at the omniscient voice.

She winked when he looked at her for an explanation.

"Go ahead," Lauden said.

"T3's report from Frebu pinged in," Cazshi's voice from the outer office spoke through the audio system.

"And?" Lauden leaned back in his chair, smoking.

Carbrook's legs jittered up and down. Poor techie was dying in here. She loved it.

"Report: network data shows no activity at the polar region related to T8's report. The logs indicate a seismic event. Not uncommon, but larger than usual."

What? That can't be.

"Physical examination of the site: zero evidence of any facilities or traces of intrusion into the natural landscape. Glacial collapse is consistent with a polar quake."

"That's not possible," Lilline said.

Lauden put his hand up, stopping her. "And the signal hasn't re-started since T8 was there?"

"No, sir."

"Right, send T3 back to HQ."

"Sir," Lilline said. "You know as well as I do that doesn't mean —"

"Quite agree, T8," the director said, interrupting. "And you can relax. There's more to this than you know. Now that the link is established on Frebu, I have no doubt something is afoot."

Lilline eased back in the chair. She was in, and this was bigger than she thought. *Now, what is he on about?*

"What do you know about Mavron Nave, T8?" Lauden asked.

"The entrepreneur?"

The Gej-ti nodded.

"A billionaire. Owns and runs Paragon, Inc. Fancies himself as the latest and greatest entertainment producer in the galaxy and has the financial record and sales to prove it. Even Carbrook here is smitten with his systems."

Carbrook rose. "I should get back down to—"

"Stay," Lauden said, swiping a hand and pulling up another holo. A star chart appeared, replacing the parallel images of the entity and the gaming icon.

"If this is related to Mavron Nave's entertainment endeavors, you might be able to contribute."

"Sir," Carbrook sat back down.

Lilline gave him a smirk that said, *"Welcome to my world."*

"He's also recovered well from the hit Paragon took after some egregious labor practices a cycle back," she added. "Was quite contested in the courts if I'm not mistaken."

"Indeed," Lauden remarked. "The company has a long history of issues. What has our attention is Nave's recent activities. He's been buying up property in out-of-the-way systems for a few cycles now." The Gej-ti took a milky finger and touched various stars on the holo. The selected highlights expanded, opening to display planets and their moons. "We hadn't noticed a pattern between his purchases and the signals from polar regions until Frebu. That made five, which as you know, is my clinch number."

It was true. Five was Lauden's number that crossed the threshold from chance to certainty. *So that was why I was approved to go to Frebu.* The bastard could have told her rather than have made her beg for it.

"But Nave buys property all the time, all over the galaxy," the director said. "He's a billionaire and an entrepreneur, so establishing the links wasn't obvious."

"But now it is?" Lilline said.

"Now it is," the Gej-ti pointed the stem of his pipe at her.

These were the moments she did like in Lauden's office. The game *was* afoot.

"We have five planets, all of which were purchased by Nave, emitting signals like this for brief periods in the last two cycles. And we have evidence of activity witnessed firsthand by a field agent that has vanished. That's as much motivation as the images."

"Do we know anything about the signals, sir?" Carbrook said.

Good. He was learning and mustering up some courage to speak and contribute.

"As of yet, they don't appear to have a translation or a consistency that we can decipher," Lauden said. "That is what I'd like you to work on."

Carbrook nodded.

"This isn't the first time, either." The director's eyes homed in on her.

The intensity of his gaze pierced like a laser. She stayed firm and held it, but underneath the surface of her agent armor she was rattling. *Is he testing me?*

Lauden broke eye contact and swiped his hand, pulling up a new holo of star systems.

"We had reports of similar frequencies a few ten-cycles back. Just chatter, mind you." Lauden pointed the stem of his pipe at the holo.

"Radio department was unable to identify or track the source, but it was consistent enough to catch the attention of the team leader, who flagged it." He picked up the heat ignitor on his desk and relit his pipe. "We took the necessary precautions."

"Precautions, sir?" Lilline knew that phrase meant anything from adding the signals to a benign list to authorizing an active surveillance/investigation.

Lauden nodded and 'humphed', pipe clenched between his teeth.

She knew that one, too. It translated to *"not your need to know."*

A few ten-cycles ago? That was during Kissy's days as an active agent.

"Was Kissy involved?" she asked. It was a bold question, but within bounds, if the evidence was linked.

Lauden took a series of puffs of Queen Yaz Flake. The surface-level veins and nerves visible above his collar fluctuated in hue as his system absorbed the nicotine. Gej-ti had a leg-up in lung capacity over other human variants. A larger respiratory tract allowed more of the smoke's chemicals to enter their bloodstream. Their metabolic rate was unique as well. Even though the average lifespan of a Gej-ti was over two-hundred cycles, the unhealthy effects of smoking ran apace with their unique biological aging. A non-Gej-ti human in their fifties, in bad health from a lifetime of smoking, shared the same effect as Lauden's species when they passed one hundred and fifty cycles.

"Yes, she was... briefly. Nave's parents were mixed up in things related to the case as well."

"His parents?"

Lauden nodded.

She wasn't going to get more than that.

"The visual connections on Frebu are quite convincing, despite the lack of on-site evidence," the GAM-OPs director said, "well done, by the way." He nodded at Carbrook.

"Thank you, sir." The techie gave Lilline a clandestine wink, taking credit for what she knew originated with his assistant.

Idiot. He had no idea how perceptive Lauden was – the Gej-ti had spent a ten-cycle as a field agent before the director's post. She had to admit, it was easy to forget how long Lauden had been doing this job. He'd been in this office, shades drawn and smoking before Granny Kissy earned her T-rank.

Lauden stood and crossed the room to the window. He waved an arm and the translucent filter vanished, revealing the endless urban skyline of Tavi-Prime. The Gej-ti gazed out, puffing on his pipe. From her seat, Lilline caught signs of the afternoon commute picking up. Ships and smaller personal carriers drew implied lines across the open spaces above the buildings.

Thick smoke plumed around the director. This was the make-or-break moment; a decision was coming.

"I think—"

A chime interrupted him mid-sentence.

"What is it, Cazshi?" Lauden didn't flinch. He remained fixed like a statue, his back to her and Carbrook, gazing out the office window.

"Sir," the Rasp's voice came from everywhere and nowhere as if speaking from on high. "Carbrook's assistant is here. She says she has something that you should see."

NINE

"I'm sorry to interrupt."

Lilline turned. Carbrook's new assistant stood at the portal. Her four arms, two extending from the shoulders with double elbow joints and two smaller ones with single elbows mid-waist, were shoved into her white lab coat. Her wide and circular frame, typical of most Oltari, was punctuated by two small and stout legs without a knee joint that made her walking stilted. The species wasn't at home in a pedal-designed world. On her back, there rested a set of double wings that gave Oltaris their preferred mode of locomotion. They never flew more than a few meters off the ground, and never more than a kilometer at a time. On their home planets, where most Oltaris lived in preferred isolation, forests were their main ecosystem and habitat. Low-lying branches offered a mazed world where flocks congregated in self-governed communities. Oltari were gifted with broader sensory capacities than all other sentient species and those that integrated tended to gravitate to positions that challenged those limits.

"Pin, this is highly irregular." The voice was Carbrook's. The techie swung back around to face Lauden across the desk. "Sir, I apologize."

Pin lumbered forward. That was the other thing about Oltari. Their social skills in a mixed-species civilization lacked empathy, at least from the position of those who interacted with them. Communication occurred at an intense rate and Pin and others like her were responding in ways inaccessible by human variants, Kreelis, or Rasps. Lilline never was able to connect with an Oltari. None were in her poetry circle, and they tended to shy away from written media. They did, however, love music. Oltari made beautiful sounds when aroused, excited, or angry. Uncontrollable utterances emitted from their small mouths. Lilline delighted in the sonorous quality of the phrases, while others found them baffling.

"Do you know what cymatics is, sir?" Pin asked, in a thin yet determined voice.

Lauden shook his head.

"It's resonance visualized," Lilline said. "A way of transcribing the frequencies of sound with a moveable, malleable material."

"Yes," Pin said. "That's the general idea."

Lilline caught a look of satisfaction on Lauden's face. He kept puffing at his pipe, but she knew he was impressed. This was what was expected as a top agent – to function and perform with a vast array of knowledge under various conditions. T# operatives were chameleons, comfortable across a range of esoteric information while carrying expertise in the specific disciplines related to espionage.

In this case, cymatics was something Lilline had reached through poetry. Her interest in linguistic cadence and rhythm, written and spoken, led her to a long history of experimentation and studies on synesthesia. The idea that sensory stimulation and experience crossed, mixed, or re-routed via the avenues available to a species intrigued her. She'd ended up in cymatics, an adjunct area of study, which explored similar phenomena.

"If it's complicated, perhaps it would be better if you wrote up a report." The director's eyes were on Carbrook.

"Quite right, sir," Carbrook said.

Lilline read the embarrassment on the techie's face. His cheeks were almost as red as his hair.

"It's very simple, sir," Pin interjected.

Good for you, Pin. That was bold. Lilline couldn't wait to see how this played out.

"Pin, a report is what the director requested," Carbrook said. "If you go down and get started I will—"

"I can demonstrate it, right here." Pin said.

Carbrook's eyes went wide at being cut off. Lilline caught a small break in Lauden's otherwise stoic face. *Is he amused?*

Pin pointed at an elegant bonsai on a stand adjacent to Lauden's desk. "Sir, may I have a handful of the sand from that pot?"

Lauden gestured with his pipe to proceed.

Lilline smiled. This was the most entertainment she'd had at HQ in a long time.

Pin snatched up a seven-fingered handful of sand and looked around the office. "I need something thin... a surface of some kind like a plate."

"A plaque?" Lilline pointed over at an award leaning against the wall on a small end table.

"It won't damage it, sir," Pin said.

Lauden acquiesced with a silent gesture.

Pin took the plaque and walked back over to the bonsai. She lifted the pot off the stand with her two smaller arms and placed it on the table. With her fourth arm, she flipped over the base so that its four legs were sticking up in the air. The Oltari balanced the plaque on top. "I think this will work," she said.

Pin withdrew a small cube speaker from a pocket of her lab coat and fiddled with some buttons on it while another hand sprinkled sand over the surface of the plaque.

"Ready?" she asked.

Lauden gestured to proceed.

"If you wouldn't mind coming over, sir."

The director rose and approached. He was being a surprisingly good sport.

Pin held the device under the plate and turned it on. A high-pitched whine bounced off the walls of the room. From her seat, Lilline watched as the sand on the surface formed into a series of symmetrical patterns.

"And again," Pin said and hit a button on the cube under the plaque. Lilline's ears picked up the change to a lower frequency. The pattern shifted and formed a new design.

Pin shut off the cube. "Cymatics," she said. "Thank you for allowing me to use your belongings, sir." The Oltari cleaned up and re-arranged the items in Lauden's office.

The director walked back to his desk and sat. "Alright, then. We have the basics. Now, what have you got?"

"Well sir," Pin said and took out a portable holo-projector. "When I ran the frequencies from some of the other planetary sites through the standard computer analysis, I didn't get much. However, I couldn't help but notice how some of the signals irritated me."

"Irritated you?" Lauden asked.

"Well, I have some sensory ranges that are unique, unlike any of the other sentient species. It got me thinking and, on a whim, I decided to run some cymatics."

Now she had their attention. Lilline edged up in her chair. Lauden put down his pipe and focused on Carbrook's assistant.

Pin activated the holo-projector. "Here's the first one, from Xeni-5."

A square field of glitching static, blue and white, filled the air in the office next to the window. Pin played the signal. The digital noise coalesced into a geometric design, simple and octagonal.

"And here's Keth." This time the static shaped into a formation of four dots.

"Gelaris." Three wavy lines in a concentric pattern.

"And the fourth: Binto." One triangle formed.

"And now I'll play them all together."

Lilline couldn't hold back a smile.

Pin played all the frequencies in chorus.

"I don't believe it," Carbook whispered.

Neither could she. It was right there for all to see.

"The current version of *Freestrike*," Pin said and turned to face them, leaving the holo of the icon hovering in the smoky office.

"Well done," Lauden said.

"Thank you, sir."

"And Frebu?" the director asked. "Does that one fit?"

Pin hooed, making the involuntary sound when something exciting hit an Oltari's system. "Get ready," she said and switched to a new frequency.

An odd visual formed. Lilline felt a shiver run down her spine, Frebu's chilling psychological pain and mystery returned to haunt her.

"What is that?" Lauden asked.

"No idea," Pin said.

"Carbrook?" the Gej-ti turned to the lead tech.

He shook his head.

"And the most disturbing part is..." Pin switched the button on the speaker cube. The Frebu frequency cymatic was added to the others.

The new shape fit snugly in the middle in an area of negative space, forming a new and sinister-looking icon.

Lilline shivered.

***

"Why polar regions?" Lauden asked.

"They're remote. Away from prying eyes," Lilline said. "That's the obvious answer, at least."

The Gej-ti shook his head. "No, it's got to be something more than that."

"You think it's related to the signals?" she asked.

"It might be."

"Would the temperatures have any effect?" Lilline addressed the question to Carbrook and Pin.

"Not that I can think of, no." Carbrook looked to be deep in thought.

Lilline caught Pin nodding agreement.

"Pull up the planets, if you would please," Pin said. "The ones in systems where we know there have been signals emanating into space."

Lauden brought them up on the holo.

"Would you mind displaying the stats on one, sir? Any of them is fine," the Oltari said.

Lauden selected an example. A series of basic and more esoteric scientific data appeared over his desk.

Pin edged closer. "Another if you would, please."

Lauden drew up another planet from the group of five.

"Core similarity," Pin said. "The mantles."

Carbrook nodded. "It works as an enhanced conductor."

Lilline understood. "So, the planet piggybacks to amplify the range and power of the signal?"

"Exactly," Pin said, eyes fixed on the data in the holo.

"But why?" Lilline asked.

"To transmit as far and as wide as possible," Carbrook said.

"One thing is certain," Pin added. "There are more than gaming technicians working on these sites. Whatever they are toying with is exploiting high-end science."

"And we have how long until this new version drops?" Lauden asked.

"Less than a week," Pin said.

An eerie silence pervaded the office. Nothing moved except the wafting clouds of Queen Yaz Flake.

Lilline knew they weren't going to get anywhere sitting in HQ. It was time to get out in the field. "Can you think of any way to get me a meeting with Nave? Or with someone in the organization that gets me close enough to investigate?"

Carbrook's red spikes went right and left like a metronome, unsure.

"There is the release event," Pin said.

"What's this?" Lauden asked, gills fluttering.

Pin covered her mouth with a hand and coughed.

The assistant was struggling with the lingering smoke. Lilline had too as a rookie.

Pin nodded at Carbrook, passing the opportunity to share the information.

"Oh, that," Carbrook said. "I guess that could work."

"What is it, then?" Lauden said, pulling the pipe from his mouth. "Out with it already."

"Yes, sir." Carbrook straightened in his seat.

It was nice to be witness to someone else getting the treatment from the director.

"Well, sir, Nave's hosting a big event. A gala of sorts to celebrate the upcoming release."

This was it. Her ticket back into the field. She cut in: "Sir, this could be—"

Lauden held up a hand. "When and where, Carbrook?"

"I'm not entirely—"

"On Nave's ring orbital," Pin said, a meek look on her face as all heads turned to look in her direction. "At the company headquarters in the Sesstari system. It's all over the gaming feeds. Very VIP."

"That place is like an independent nation," Lauden muttered. "Isolated in space in a planetless system."

Lilline followed the plumes of smoke exiting his gills, a familiar sign that he was thinking at a rapid rate.

"Do you have any influence with this crowd?" Lauden eyed Carbrook.

"Influence, sir?"

"Can you get T8 in?"

Lauden's veins above his collar shifted color. Carbrook needed to get with the program and pick up on signals. Working alone in a lab might make you king of a personal fiefdom, and able to work without disturbance, but it failed to provide social and conversational exercise when strategizing for a potential mission.

"Hack the invitation list, sir?"

Lauden nodded.

"Piece of cake," Carbrook said.

"How long until the Gala?" Lilline asked.

"Four days," Pin said.

The assistant was growing bolder. *Good.* This was the first time Lilline had spoken with her beyond a *"hello"* in the lab. The Oltari wasn't afraid to contribute if she had an answer that furthered the conversation and made time management more efficient.

A glance at Lauden confirmed an expression Lilline knew well, too. The director shared the sentiment.

"Sir, Sesstari isn't a big hop," Lilline said, seizing an opportunity in the dead air. "It's about two days if I take the Celix Racer." She'd wanted to get in the seat of the high-end ship GAM-OPs purchased for half a cycle. That bird was a beauty. And fast. If you were a thrill junkie like her, it beat even the highest-class ticket experience on a public cruiser. Forget exquisite wine and cuisine, gambling, and other first-class amenities. She'd take speed. Not to mention, that thing had lines more beautiful than a Razor-tori fish. She'd heard talk of its weapon and cloaking capabilities, too. Special installs by those working under Carbrook.

"And," she added, "it would fit the outward-facing image for a VIP attending the Gala."

Lauden's lips pursed.

He doesn't miss a thing.

"How is your gaming knowledge?" The director's eyes fixed on her, calling her ruse.

"Not good," Carbrook muttered.

Damn it, Carbrook. Lilline couldn't deny it, as their conversation the previous day attested. The one tidbit she'd spouted out earlier wasn't going to keep her afloat.

"You could take a cruiser if you left tonight," Lauden said, tapping out his pipe on its stand. "Have plenty of downtime to go over things and get up to speed. Carbrook and his assistant can put together a file in a few short hours, I'm sure."

"Certainly, sir," Carbrook said.

Lauden was having fun at her expense. This implicit bartering went on every time he sent her out in the field.

She wanted that ship. Not just for the privacy and thrills, but because she needed a free day tomorrow to look into something.

"If I might..."

It was Pin, who coughed again.

Lauden did the gesture with his hand. Lilline caught Carbrook giving her a quick rise of an eyebrow in amusement.

"Perhaps a companion might be less suspicious, while also solving another problem."

Companion? Lilline didn't like where this was going.

The Oltari gestured ever-so-subtly at her.

What's she getting at?

Lauden nodded. "Grand idea. Well done. Pin, is it?"

"Yes, sir," the assistant said and stifled a cough.

"You'll need to get used to that," Lauden said, indicating the smoke with a wave of his pipe. "Good strategic thinking."

"Thank you, sir."

Pin looked as if she would faint. Lilline wasn't sure if it was from the smoke or the fact that the director of GAM-OPs was complimenting her.

It didn't ease Lilline's concern that the word 'companion' had been included in Pin's suggestion. Did the Oltari mean to come with her? Or... *Oh, hell no.* Not for all the Celix Racers in the galaxy.

"Sir," Lilline broke in, "are you recommending Carbrook attend the Gala along with me?"

"Not a recommendation, T8."

"With all due respect, he's not a field agent."

"But this is my field... technically speaking," Carbrook said. He gave her a look to emphasize the wordsmithing.

She rolled her eyes.

"I'd be in my element," Carbrook said. "Plus, you aren't versed in gaming. I can make it appear that we belong."

"Together? As in a couple?" Lilline snarked.

"Hoo."

The strange Oltari vocalization was like a bird calling out in the forest. "Excuse me," Pin said, two of her four hands covering a smile.

"I mean," Carbrook said, "belong *there*. As in, at a Gala for an upcoming game release."

The idea of working undercover with Carbrook was not the kind of field experience she was after to inspire her poetry.

"Yes," Lauden said. "This will do. And show more initiative next time, Carbrook. Pin is making you look bad." The director nodded at the Oltari.

What was Lauden thinking? Putting Carbrook in a sensitive undercover situation? Lauden's expression made clear there was no point in pushing back. Thankfully, some strategy remained on the table.

"Well, sir, if Carbrook is coming then I won't need as much time for intel prep. Perhaps taking the Racer is a better option? Not to mention, we might bump into some other attendees traveling on a cruiser. The less socializing beforehand the safer to maintain our covers. I can go as Keely Larkin, usual job. It's alluring enough for the Gala. Excellent for small talk, and unconnected to the professor I used for Frebu. And we can make him," she gestured at Carbrook, "new money. Avid gamer or some such. Green enough to lack too much... intelligence."

Carbrook shot her a look.

Lauden leaned back in his chair, the milky fingers from both hands forming a triangle under his chin.

Come on, you old fish. Give me the Racer.

The Gej-ti leaned forward and nodded. "Done. Pin, you and Carbrook go down to Intel and help them work up a good cover for the gala. We don't need to worry about your appearance in any data-bases." Lauden spoke to Carbrook. "Go as you are and you'll fit right in with that crowd, I assume?"

Carbrook and Pin both nodded.

Lilline smiled inside. The Racer. Even if she had to share it with Carbrook, she would get to fly that bird and arrive at the company station in style. Its defense and evasion weapons weren't bad insur-ance, either.

The gala, on the other hand, didn't sit so well. Carbrook could barely get through a difficult conversation in the director's office. His social limitations might blow their cover.

"Operation Freestrike," Lauden said, waving a hand to open a new holo-file. "I'll have Cazshi establish first-phase mission objectives."

"Thank you, sir," Lilline said and rose from her seat. She nodded at Carbrook and Pin, who were frozen in place and unsure of etiquette, to follow her out.

"You take tomorrow and rest that knee, T8," Lauden said. The office dimmed as the director activated the shade.

"Yes, sir." Sure, she'd do that. There'd be plenty of time to relax where she was heading.

TEN

Location: Virtual | Network: Encrypted.

You connect to the server. The pain and anguish fall away in the pristine space of Infinity. This is your world, the dominion where you reign supreme.

The filth, the social bacteria of mundane 'reality' is wiped clean like an operating room sterilized before a procedure. This is where your nimble hands and brilliant mind perform surgery on the world.

An under-respected entrepreneur, you will not sit idle on your mountain of newly accrued wealth and fame. That measure, that scale of judgment, will not suffice. Nor should it. You are, after all, a gracious benefactor. A philanthropist. Your due respect will arrive in the gesture of kindness to come. Those who cannot grasp what they need nor muster the courage to live as richly as they do vicariously will thank you. They will hail you. Bow to you.

Soon.

With concentration, you open the portal to your dominion. The neurosensors communicate with seamless grace. Let those who are your criminal collaborators continue to navigate with crude physical gestures through surrogate appendages. None deserve to share in all your secrets. You are, after all, their soon-to-be king.

You enter the hallway. The one you designed for this purpose. The others can't use it. They arrive in the board room through the main menu options. You grin as you walk, confident strides taking you past portraits of predecessors of various species from when galactic civilization was less closed-minded about rules of progress and morality. Each one you pass nods, just as you programmed it to as if this were your coronation. The throne they crafted and shaped but never finished awaits you.

The icon that will change the world glows blood-red on the mahogany double doors. In its pattern and meaning lies the last stage of an esoteric evolution leading to your ascent to the throne.

You pantomime its design with a virtual hand and the doors retract to the left and right.

"Welcome. Let us get started," you announce.

Your words surprise the ten figures gathered in the board room. Their virtual heads turn, some from the view of your perfect world out the floor-to-ceiling windows and others from conversations as they mingle, waiting for your arrival.

All your minions of the lower Tiers express shock. You hide your pleasure at the reminder of your superiority and gesture for all the members to take their seats.

You proceed to the chair at the head of the table, the one unique in design and larger than the rest. The seat of the Ultimate Leader. Everything in the room is to your liking. Of course, it is. You created it.

Those gathered around you might have autonomy over fiefdoms in the 'other' world, but here they submit to your grand design. They are at your mercy. This is your reality, shaped and crafted by genius, and they select options provided by your creative vocabulary. How ironic that you will grace the rest of the galaxy with the same path to freedom. That thought is too complicated and brilliant to share with those present, despite their criminal intelligence and knowledge of the ancient texts. They have one purpose for you: they are your thought-pawns. There may be cleverness among them, but it is the holistic force of wicked immorality you seek by inviting them to the table.

When the world flips on its head, the game will turn to life. Will that which you summon be unstoppable? Win or lose, the course of civilization will be forever changed. History will mark the prodigious moment as an evolutionary turn that re-directs a cowardly society onto a path of bravery and moral transcendence. Your name and that of your Order will forever be engraved into the galactic annals by cosmic hands that wait in the shadows. You desire unending fame as much as the next genius, but more important for you will be the lived experience of being its curator.

You gaze out the window from your throne at your virtual creation. From this great height over a city in your name, nature and technology run in sleek kinship to the horizon. The perfect harmony and beauty soothe your anger and resentment. Disgust at the ugliness of the 'other' world with its imperfections, its faults... its false values is quelled by your architectural and natural utopia. Why is it so difficult for the rest of the world to know what perfection looks like?

You let the members wait in silent tension. They dare not speak before you do. The one who did last time was made an example. Not here, but on their return to the mundane. Your executioner never fails at her task.

Sitting before you as avatars, their physical identities brought to a clandestine, virtual ideal through the beauty of your craft, they are ignorant fools. Let them have their false empowerment and security. They do not know and understand the deep secrets as you do.

You fix your gaze on the empty seat on the right side of the table. Eleven are present where there were twelve. Absence speaks volumes. None will challenge you again.

You relish the silent power. It screams from their subservient faces.

Once their thoughts are fused with your superior intelligence, there will be no stopping your ultimate creation. Already in its early form, the entity has proven extraordinary. Frebu was not a failure. Only a misstep.

None can stop the power you wield. It will pass through all security networks, all galactic fleets, and orbital defenses at will. The ones who ruined your family name and legacy will rue the day. They will be humiliated and made to suffer.

Your avatar smiles. Hesitant faces around the table, unsure of the source, remain stoic.

The angled light through the wall of windows casts an efficient beauty.

Restraint is power made cunning. Everything here reeks of it. From the shape of the room to the furniture in it, down to the trickling echo on the interior water wall, all is as you desire it. Isn't that the way it should be for those with the supremacy of mind?

A shadow rises and slashes a psychic blade across your soul. A burning wound sparks like fire inside of you, casting shadowy silhouettes onto your utopian walls.

Painful memories kept hidden for decades dance in flickering rhythms as the flames feed on your doubt.

There is one cure, and it drives everything: revenge.

"The Mind is the ultimate eye," you declare with the rhythm taught by those who came before you.

The lower Tier members respond as one, with like tone and cadence.

"Let us begin."

Taut expressions on the faces of those gathered around you release their tension.

Your voice resonates with perfect pitch and timbre. "Our ascendancy starts in five days."

ELEVEN

Moon: Beisho | Planetary orbit: Tavi-Prime | Star System: Pesari-9, Galactic Core.

"I'm here to see Imani Larkin." Lilline spoke into the entrance monitor at the gate to the Rolling Gables Retirement Facility. Her hover bike purred, the twin blue-stream air burners cycling down after she'd pushed them to the limit.

She loved Beisho's topography. Tavi-Prime's small moon, with its alpine mountain passes and gorges sporting frigid streams and water-falls, made for some of the most challenging high-speed hover biking in the galaxy.

"Are you a relation?" the AI responded, per usual visitor protocol.

"Her granddaughter," she said through the flipped-up helmet visor.

Beyond the well-groomed grounds of the facility, Lilline caught sight of the village of Villain up on the mountainside. From the valley, the Golden Pheasant's outdoor seating area was a speck, dotted with its signature red umbrellas. Dark green fir trees rose in strict spires on the steep slopes, surrounding the chateau's old stone exterior like sentinels guarding an ancient ruin. She wouldn't have time to stay over and write on this trip. Yesterday's meeting at HQ changed that plan. A few hours with Kissy and then it was back to Tavi-Prime on the moon hopper. If Carbrook hacked the system and got them on the invitation list for the gala, she would be off to Nave's orbital tomorrow morning.

"Retinal scan in ten seconds," the AI said.

Lilline removed her helmet and tucked a loose strand of hair in the wedge over her missing ear. She leaned forward, aligning her face with the scanner.

"Thank you, Ms. Larkin. You may proceed."

She hooked the helmet to the side of the cycle and twisted the throttle, firing the burners. A roar echoed through the valley in the crisp, morning air. She fought the urge to tear ass on the straight-away to the facility. That would put a shock on the faces of the retirees strolling the grounds. Then again, Kissy made enough of a ruckus daily that they'd do no more than shake their heads. At almost ninety cycles, her grandmother was still firing on all cylinders.

Lilline kept her speed within the limit on the long straight-away and parked the cycle in the lot. She grabbed a small box out of the bike's side compartment and made her way up and into the front entrance of the grand estate. The building, made of local stone, had once been a manor house of a wealthy citizen of Tavi-Prime. After their death, it had been donated to the government for civil use.

Holo-letters manifested in the air when she stepped inside the first portal:

Attention: low gravity environment through the lock. Please select the appropriate weighted ankle straps before proceeding.

Lilline pulled a set matching her body weight off the rack and attached them around her black riding suit. The bands would keep her grounded and able to move about like standard gee, while residents enjoyed a lighter gravity environment to soothe their ailing bodies and make mobility easier. It was a simple workaround – all the items in the common rooms, from decorations to furniture – were either secured in place or constructed with special metals that gave them additional weight. To access the dining areas and sleeping quarters, residents passed through a lock taking them back to standard gee. Floating forks and knives, and hovering soup and juice, invited disaster.

"Good morning, Ms. Larkin." A Rasp dressed in a blue uniform, their neck dancing to and fro, greeted her on entering the lobby. Lilline's mood softened, as it did whenever she entered the Rolling Gables. The interior decoration was tasteful, reflecting the previous owner's penchant for comfort and homeliness. It looked old in the right way for those in their later cycles, like a well-worn pair of shoes.

"Good morning. I'm here to see Imani," she said and gestured with the box in her hand. Why she wasn't sure. The employee didn't care if she'd brought her grandmother a gift.

"If you keep trying to stick that thing in me—"

"Ow!"

Lilline peered around the Rasp. Down the hallway through an opening to the living area, an elderly woman employed a finger lock on a human orderly.

"I think I found her," Lilline said and gestured with a nod.

The Rasp twisted their head around on their serpentine neck. "Good luck," they said, turning back and raising their single eyebrow.

Lilline hustled down the corridor, trying to keep the box level in her hand.

"You need to let me take some blood for your monthly check-up!" the orderly winced in pain, crumpled on the floor.

And that would be my grandmother.

Kissy twisted his digit, grasping the hand into a full wrist lock. The orderly's body responded involuntarily, splaying flat.

"Granny, stop it. The poor man is just trying to do his job."

"Keely, darling. What a pleasant surprise." Kissy didn't release the man from her grip. "Oh, you brought me Dari cakes. You are a dear."

"I'm sorry," Lilline said to the orderly at her feet.

He winced as Granny twisted a bit further.

"I won't have them sticking me with those needles. My body's fine how it is without them probing and prodding. Leaves a bruise, dear... every time."

"You want these?" Lilline held out the box. "They're from Malardi's." She raised an eyebrow, making clear if Granny wanted the cakes, she better release him. "Or should I give them to the staff?"

Kissy let go of the orderly's wrist and snatched the box out of her hand.

Damn, she's still fast.

"Come, let's sit in the sunroom." Her grandmother swished off towards the open portal to an enclosed transparent sitting area like she was lord of the manor. With her light and frail frame and the low gee, she bounced with the grace of a weightless fairy.

A secretly deadly and cunning fairy.

"My granddaughter, Marcy," Granny said to an elderly Kreeli sitting on a couch. The band on Marcy's oblong forehead showed little signs of pressure adjustment. "She brought me Dari cakes from Malardi's," Kissy waved the box in front of Marcy, who looked up with confusion.

"What did you say?"

"Oh, never mind." Kissy turned back to Lilline. "You see what I mean? I'm the one who is dying here." She sauntered off towards the portal to the sunroom, humming with a spring in her low gee step.

"I'm very sorry," Lilline said and helped the orderly up.

He wiped off his uniform. "She needs to get her lab work done. It's been five months since the last time we were able to pull blood."

"Someone got a sample? I'm impressed," Lilline said.

The orderly shook his head. "She's all yours." He walked away.

"Darling, aren't you coming?" Granny gestured with the box of cakes at the portal.

Lilline smiled at Marcy as she made her way to the sunroom but the Kreeli's oblong head was down, back to watching a broadcast on a tablet in her lap. Lilline entered and Kissy shut the portal. Her grandmother fiddled with the template on the wall.

"Granny, what are you doing?"

"Nothing, dear." Kissy hastened through a sequence of numbers with her wrinkled fingers. The light on the portal control went out. "Giving us a bit of privacy, that's all."

"Did you just break that?"

"What? Me?" Granny pointed at her chest. "I'm a little old lady. I'm not capable of such things." She shot her chin up in the air and walked to a set of chairs near the transparent wall overlooking the grounds.

I pity the staff in this place.

"Come, dear. Sit." Kissy patted the seat next to her.

Lilline approached and sat. Her grandmother held up a cake, a look of concern on her face.

"What's the matter? You said Malardi's."

"I didn't say damaged and jostled Dari cakes from Malardi's." She pursed her lips. "Your driving always left something to be desired."

Maybe a few hours this afternoon is better than three nights at the chateau.

"You rented a cycle when you should have come in a pod."

This now?

"It's safer, you know. For you as well as the Dari cakes," Kissy said and bit into the pastry.

"Well?" Lilline asked. "Still as good as they used to be when the world was perfect, and everything was better than it is now?" She crossed her legs, getting comfortable.

Granny huffed.

That was a 'yes' in Kissy's vocabulary. As close to an admission of pleasing her as you'd get.

"So," her grandmother said between bites, "what brings a busy secret agent out to the sticks of Beisho?"

"Granny!" Lilline whispered.

"Oh relax, darling. No one can hear us. I took out all the audio sensors in here myself."

"You what? Granny you aren't supposed to be—"

"I have important things to discuss sometimes too, you know." She took another bite. "So?"

"First of all, I came here to see you. I even travelled under another identity for extra safety." It was true. She'd taken the moon hopper as the professor of minerology. Her wig and prosthetic ear were sitting in the side bag of the cycle parked outside.

"All of that fuss just to see me?" Granny batted her eyelashes.

"You practically cried in your letter."

"It is nice to see you, dear." Kissy patted her thigh like she was twelve.

"And..." Lilline hesitated. *Should I bring it up?* Her eyes went around the sunroom. She'd come all this way to ask about the Nave situation, but now it felt like it made the trip inauthentic.

The heck with it. Kissy was in her shoes once, too. She knew the score.

"And I need to ask you something confidential."

"Oooo!" Her grandmother's eyes came alive with excitement. Around their vibrant glow, Kissy's face told a different story. Aged skin and withering features spoke of the unavoidable cycle of life taking its toll. She wasn't immortal, though it felt that way with her statue in the rotunda at HQ.

"It's about Mavron Nave."

"The billionaire?

Lilline nodded.

"I don't keep up with that kind of news, dear. All those entertainment gadgets and alternate realities." Granny shook her head and selected another Dari cake from the box. She pointed the pink pastry at Lilline. "This younger generation is going to reap what they sow with these games."

Here we go.

"We needed our wits more than anything when I was in the field."

"Every time," Lilline muttered and smiled the same smile she made every time the soliloquy started. This trip the jab entered the script sooner than usual.

"Don't get too reliant on that stuff from those lab rats at HQ, either. You never know when you'll be somewhere with nothing but your mind as your weapon."

"I know, Granny," Lilline said.

Kissy gave her a look that said, *"you say you know, but..."* with a raised eyebrow.

"About Nave, Granny. It's not the news I am after. It's history. Lauden said you were active when some unknown frequencies came in from random planets."

She mumbled a "yes" with her mouth full.

"He said something about Nave's parents and that you were involved."

"Mmmm, this pink one is very good," Granny emphasized her chewing.

"You're dodging my question."

"Am I?" Kissy gave her an innocent face. She took another bite and gazed out over the grounds. "It is a lovely view, isn't it dear?"

Lilline rolled her eyes.

"How's your poetry coming?" Kissy asked, licking her fingers.

"Don't change the topic."

"That bad?"

She didn't need that on top of this.

"I thought your latest one was better. It still rings too much like Den-shi. You ought to focus on finding your own voice."

"You too, now? Can we get back to my question?"

Granny huffed. "I don't know anything important about that. It was a long time ago, and anyway—"

Lilline's comm buzzer went off. The vibration in her thigh pocket sent a subtle signal up her leg. She held up a hand to halt the conversation.

"HQ calling?" Kissy gazed out the window as if enjoying the view.

Lilline shot her a look. *How did she notice?* It was impossible to see it inside her riding suit.

"I have to take this," she said. "I'll only be a minute." Lilline rose and walked to the opposite corner of the sunroom. She removed the communicator from her thigh pocket. The director's code number scrolled across the thin screen. "Lauden?" she said in a whisper. He never called direct. It was always someone else in Communications as an intermediary.

"Did you say that was Lauden?" Granny threw the box on Lilline's chair and approached. "Let me answer it! He'll be so surprised."

"Absolutely not." Lilline turned with the communicator in her hand like a child not wanting to share candy.

"I still have clearance at the highest level, Lilli."

The use of her proper name, and her nickname specifically, felt strange coming from Granny in a public place. Even if they were isolated in a 'soundproofed' room.

"Go sit down over there, Granny, and be—"

"Hey!"

Kissy had the communicator in her hand and was already frolicking across the sunroom in low gee glee.

Damn, she's fast.

"Asher? Is that you?"

Lilline winced.

"Kissy, darling. How is my favorite agent?"

Lilline rolled her eyes.

"Oh, stop it." Kissy giggled like she was five. "Favorite retired agent, Asher."

What is with the 'Asher'? Since when are they on a first-name basis?

"Retired but never replaced," Lauden said.

Gimme a break.

"I assume T8 is with you?" he asked.

Lilline cringed.

The audible click of the director's lighter, followed by the faint sound of fluttering gills, came over the line. He had her right where he wanted her.

"Oh yes, Asher. She's right here."

"Damn it, Granny," she muttered.

"Of course, you know that by now since it's her communicator." Kissy turned and winked at her.

"I thought you were resting that knee today, T8?" Lauden said, his tone growing stern.

Kissy walked over. Lilline snatched the comm back.

"Yes, sir. I wanted to see Imani," she used the public name with emphasis, "before I left Tavi-Prime. It was my original intention when you first gave me medical leave to come and spend a few days here."

Kissy fake clapped her hands.

"But unfortunately, something came up, as you know, so I made a quick hop today." Close enough to the full truth of it.

"Right," Lauden grumbled. "Well, visiting Kissy is always a top priority."

Granny gave her a smug look.

"Sir, is there a problem?" Lilline asked. "Do you need me to find a secure location to speak?"

Granny's eyes screamed with insult. Lilline wanted to extend a finger and point for her to go sit down but considering the scene when she'd arrived at the facility, she thought twice about placing a digit within reach.

"Nothing I can't say in front of your grandmother," Lauden said. "You've still got your clearance, Kissy, even though we retired your T number."

"Always the flatterer, Asher," Granny said, leaning up and into the communicator.

This is getting unbearable.

"T8, Carbrook hacked into Paragon and secured two invitations to Nave's gala."

"Gala?" Granny whispered. "Are you going to wear a dress?"

Lilline shooed her away.

"I want answers to what is going on with these frequencies and what Nave is planning."

Lilline caught Kissy raising an eyebrow, her face turning more earnest.

She does know something.

"We need this wrapped up quickly before it gets any larger... whatever it is," Lauden said. "Get back down planetside and make sure you're ready to go tomorrow morning at star rise. The Racer is being prepared for you."

"Yes, sir. Thank you."

"A pleasure, as always, Kissy," the director said. "I hope you'll come down for lunch in the Octagonal?"

"That would be delightful, Asher. If I can get my granddaughter to let me out of prison." Granny eyed her, the cunning and wit fully honed and working at full tilt.

"As soon as we wrap this up, I'll make sure to send T8 up to get you for a lovely luncheon."

"You are a darling, Asher," Granny said, head bobbing in delight.

"Get ready for work, T8." Lauden cut the line.

Lilline tore through the mountain pass, throttling the hover-bike to its limit. She banked left and right, cutting tight corners on the virtual lanes illuminated inside her visor.

So, Granny wasn't talking. She knew something about Nave's parents and the frequencies. As did Lauden, or 'Asher' as Kissy now referred to him. *What was that about?* This was either personal between the two of them or something so hush-hush at GAM-OPs that even another T# agent couldn't be in the circle of 'need to know'.

She revved the cycle and broke through the virtual boundary, making straight for a cliff wall ahead.

An alert tone cut through the space metal blasting into her ears.

"Warning, outside designated travel lane. Collision imminent."

"No kidding." She yanked the steering column back mere meters from the rock face. The turbo booster fired and shot the cycle up the steep cliff. Beisho's gravity battled the bike. She leaned in for aerodynamic advantage, rising skyward, fighting back. It wasn't enough, not today.

"Recorder," she said, activating the helmet's database. "Voice capture." The space metal halted.

> *"Put a wall up for me.*
> *I will scale it with ease.*
> *Block my way with your thugs.*
> *Watch as my clenched fists fly.*
> *Try and stump me with clues.*
> *Not this time.*
> *Not next time, not ever."*

But this wasn't a challenge. It was frustration. She wanted information and got denied. That pissed her off.

And where did it leave her poetry? Too much anger in the words. The verse was all showmanship and bragging, no theme and not worth the milibytes it took up in her helmet's drive.

Total crap.

"Recorder... delete."

The cycle broke over the lip of the mountain's face. Lilline gripped the handles tight and pushed on the steering column, leveling off. The bike crossed the snow-capped peak and a second vista opened below her. She leaned forward. Her stomach dropped as she plunged over the forests and pastures into the valley.

A few kilometers ahead, the Wenassi River snaked its way through a seam in the mountains. Mist tinged with spectral colors from afternoon sunlight dotted its course where waterfalls and deep pools interrupted tracks of steady and level flow. At top legal speed, it would take her thirty minutes to run the river before the turn at the farming grids to the spaceport town of Hikari.

The trip wasn't a total loss. Besides seeing Kissy, who never failed to entertain, there was a takeaway: she learned enough to conclude that Nave wasn't up to no good because he was unhappy being a billionaire and wanted to play around with his toys. There was history involved in this mystery. She'd be sure to read through his file in earnest on the hop to the Sesstari system. Anything to keep her from having to kill time with Carbrook on the Racer.

She reached the lower hills of the valley and straightened out the cycle. At least the ride over the river offered her time to let go.

"Screw it," she said and cranked up the space metal. She dove the bike down to a meter over the river's surface. The alert tone returned.

"Warning, outside—"

A finger flicked off the nav software on the handle grip. If a hidden camera tagged her it didn't matter. The staff at HQ made those violations disappear as easily as—

Pang!

The cycle wobbled and fishtailed. She struggled to keep it under control. Sparks reflected off the river's surface on her right.

Pat! Pat! Pat!

Blaster fire ripped the water alongside the bike. Lilline veered hard left and glanced back. Two hover cycles were tearing ass in pursuit. One of the riders raised an arm. A burst of red flashed from their hand.

Lilline hit the throttle and swerved right to avoid the shots. They struck close enough that water splashed up and speckled her visor.

She checked the damage gauge. The starboard burner read as compromised. She wasn't going to outrun them without full power. A hand went into her riding suit and pulled out the mini-blaster from under her armpit. She reached back and fired off a three-round burst at the one who took the shots.

The driver dodged the fire and revved up their cycle, closing the distance. The second rider split off to the other side of the river.

"Activate!" She turned the cycle's AI back on. "Report on engine 2."

"*Overheating. Minor damage. Please proceed to repair facility #479 at location—*"

"Deactivate!"

She didn't need that idiot rambling in her ear. She looked ahead. A half kilometer of straight run and then a drop with a large plume of mist. That meant a waterfall.

Pat! Pat! Pat!

More blaster fire.

Pang!

The cycle took another hit near her calf. Smoke trailed out along its side.

Lilline's eye went to the temperature gauge on engine 2. It was off the charts. That pointed to a coolant leak. She needed to get it down into a safe range for one final burst of speed before it blew out. She swerved the cycle in an ostensibly random pattern. In fact, it was a pre-determined formula taught to all GAM-OPs agents. Its rhythm and course were said to be the most difficult for the human mind to process and make determined predictions. No such patterns existed, yet, for the other species in the galaxy. Judging by the anatomy, size, and shape of these two pursuing her, they were human variants.

Engine 2 sputtered. The riders would be on her in under a minute.

Now or never.

She tucked the blaster into her suit and revved up the cycle. It shot across the river on a run for the waterfall. She leaned the bike right while shifting her body left, attempting to glide it horizontal over the water's surface.

One... two... three.

She released a hand from the steering column, grabbed the blaster, and poured out rounds across the river to hold off both riders. The cycle dropped lower and the burner tube on engine 2 broke the surface. Steam hissed as the hot metal hit the icy water. The temp readout on engine 2 changed from red to yellow.

Come on, give me green.

The drop to the falls approached. She had about twenty meters and ten seconds, at most.

Pang!

A shot grazed her hand, sending the blaster spinning away into the river. Pain surged through her forearm as the laser's trace burned through the glove.

The bike wobbled and dipped. Lilline grabbed the steering column and worked to right the cycle. No good, it was going under, and she was going in the air over the falls. One of the riders shot up parallel to her. She caught a twinkle in their eye as they aimed the blaster.

She waved.

Their expression changed to confusion.

Took you long enough.

Lilline bent the wrist of her injured hand and twitched her forearm muscles. The blade shot up and into her palm.

She threw it five meters ahead of them. It bowed in the air and plunged into their chest, sending them off the bike. She let go of her cycle, pushing it down into the water for leverage and launched off the machine with both legs, her angle following the knife's course.

The river gave way to a hundred meters of clear air and mist as the water plunged into a deep pool.

Her hands caught the other bike's grips as it went over the falls. The engine whirred in neutral as she and the machine plummeted towards the crashing water. She yanked back, legs dangling in the air, and the seat planted into her crotch. Her wrist pulled the throttle back. Mist and water raced by, followed by rocks, and then the view of the valley ahead as she arced upward. It was too good an opportunity to pass up, so she kept the steering column back. The extra speed from the plunge fueled her momentum. She swirled overhead, mist spraying her visor. The second cycle tore past while she was inverted. She completed the loop and hit the turbo booster.

Her hand went to the side compartment. Like back on Frebu, the eyes of her fingers searched inside.

She smiled at what she found.

The cycle broke through the mist, and she pulled up next to the other rider. They gave her a thumb's up, indicating success to who they thought was their partner.

She winked.

They did a double take. The rider reached for their blaster. Lilline fired, sending him over the side with a perfectly aimed shot. Their cycle skidded into the water, skimming like a thin rock over the surface before crashing into the far bank and exploding.

"Activate," she said. "Recorder on."

The title for this one came easy.

TWELVE

"Where did you get this?" Carbrook reached for the chip in her hand.

"Off a dead guy."

"What?" His eyes went wide. "Where?"

"Need to know, Carbrook. And you," Lilline twirled the chip between her fingers. "Don't need to know."

Celebrity Crush was a beauty. The ship's open plan gave Lilline visual access to the bridge in one direction and the lounge and office sections aft. Top-of-the-line interior design spoke of casual refinement with plush breakout areas for in-between work sessions. It defined space travel at its most up-to-date and expensive. GAM-OPs had spared no expense.

She handed Carbrook the chip.

He scrutinized it. "Cutting-edge." The techie swung around to his portable computer terminal and inserted it into a slot. He rubbed his hands together.

"What's up, Carbrook?"

"Need to know, Agent Renault." He started typing. "And you—"

"*Do* need to know. Get it straight. You are working for me on this op."

"Yeah, yeah." He sighed. "Take it easy, will you? I was honing my wordplay."

"Yes, I couldn't not notice," Lilline said, "Very subtle."

"Really?"

"No."

"Well, I need to sound refined at the gala so—"

"Keep the talking at a minimum on the orbital. Now, what's up?"

Carbrook opened a set of holos from the chip's data. "Usual smokescreen." He shook his head. "Gimme a break." The techie worked the board doing who knew what.

Lilline didn't care so long as he got her an ID on who had tried to kill her on Beisho. Other than the chip, nothing of value was on the dead rider she'd pulled out of the Wenassi River. He was a Gej-ti. Both were, Lilline guessed, even though the other's body never reappeared after going over the falls with her knife in their chest.

The truth was it could be anyone. After so many cycles working in the field you tallied up a lot of enemies, even under aliases. As sadistic as it sounded, she preferred death whenever it presented itself as an option. Declarations of retribution are hard to make from the grave.

"Damn, this is no joke," Carbook said, biting his nails.

"What do you mean? And stop that. It's disgusting."

"I've never seen this configuration before." He spat a nail out into the air. "It's like they've taken the data and put it somewhere on the chip that isn't part of the 'space' in the chip."

"That makes no sense. You know that, right?" Lilline examined the data. She had no idea why she bothered. It was a foreign language.

"Yeah." Carbrook wasn't listening. His hands and fingers worked the information labyrinth.

Lilline smiled at his determination. This was his version of 'in the field.'

The techie leaned back. "Oh, you crafty..." He rose and walked past her to the lounge area.

"What's the matter?"

"You're lucky I'm obsessed with gaming." He pulled something out of his bag and came back over. His hand held up a small eye-unit and gloves for her to see.

"I don't get it."

He slipped the visor on, fitted the gloves, and sat down. "You will if I'm right." He waved his hands, pantomiming an unrecognizable sequence. "Whoa!" Carbrook's head went back and forth as if sight-seeing the various rides at an amusement park.

"You cracked it?"

"This is rad."

"What is?"

"It's a virtual drive. *Inside* a hard drive." He giggled. "Brilliant." The techie gestured with both hands from the sides of his head as if it was exploding. "I've never seen anything like this. I wonder how whoever did this managed to—"

"Is anything in there?"

"Hold on." He gestured a few times as if swiping through pages. "Yep. There's something here alright."

"What is it?"

"You."

"Me?"

"Yes, Professor."

Professor?

"Pulling it out now," Carbrook said. "I'll bring it up on the board."

Lilline turned to the view of the FTL tunnel streaming by out of *Celebrity Crush's* bridge window. *Did someone mark me?*

Her gut rattled. She'd been targeted one other time as an undercover agent. It made for a harrowing few months until they found the source and eliminated it. But it came with costs. Another T# agent's life and her ear lost to a Bukki tiger.

"See it?"

Carbrook's voice pulled her back. A holo field blipped up next to the terminal.

There she was, in high resolution as her undercover persona for Operation Snow Eclipse, floating in holographic form. Full stats: Professor of Minerology, detailed visual description of her disguised identity, and even her fabricated academic work address on Tavi-Prime. Worse, there was a tracking record of her movements from the time she left the planet to visit Granny right up to when she killed the thugs on Beisho.

"You should be flattered," Carbrook said and waved a hand. Another holo appeared with a price: five million credits.

"That's not funny," she whispered. *Five million?* "No line back to the source of the request for the hit?"

"I'm trying, but this thing is like nothing I have ever seen. There's no way into the vault, not the way it's set up. Whoever requested it wanted to be sure no one traced them as the client." Carbrook shook his head. "Amazing."

"Who else could do this? I mean, the tech side of this?"

Carbrook pulled off the visor. "This?" He swung his chair to face her. "Maybe two or three hackers in the whole galaxy."

"Like?"

"You mean who are the best?"

She nodded.

"2112 for sure."

"Who is 2112?"

"Anonymous hacker. Works freelance. Takes pretty much any commission worthy of their abilities that pays enough. At least, that is what we think. Whoever they are, they're kind of a myth."

"A myth?" Lilline's gaze shifted to the FTL streaming through the bridge window. She didn't like all these veils, physical or virtual.

"Some don't think there is a 2112."

Carbrook's voice was like a narrator for a broadcast dubbed over the faster-than-light display.

"'Some' being those of us in the highest reaches of the tech world. Most think it's a moniker used by a collective, a kind of hive hacker mind that takes on commissions. A pseudonym as a cover for a bunch of individuals who like a challenge and who pick up jobs when they come up."

"What do you think?" she asked.

"I think it's one person. And they're damn good."

"What's with the name?" She turned back to find him biting his nails.

"Dunno, but it's clever." When he noticed her gaze burning into him, he stopped tearing a nail with his teeth. "Sorry. 2112 is a weird sequence in coding. It's a palindromic number."

Interesting.

She knew that from poetry. Certain modes used syllabic versions of it. It wasn't unlike the modified Zeret style of Cinquain.

"Send all this off to HQ," she said. "Including the bit about 2112."

"Will do, Boss." He raised an eyebrow and smiled.

She rolled her eyes but appreciated the effort – both the clever language and the deference to her leadership.

Something about this wouldn't settle. Her mind went back through all the ops that had been left with loose ends. There were more than she liked to admit.

"Man, this is wild," Carbrook said, fixated on the chip's information. "This is breaking open possibilities that were unthinkable just a ten-cycle ago."

"Approaching Sesstari system. FTL exit in three minutes." The ship's AI voice was as smooth as the Gondau they poured at the Golden Pheasant.

Lilline walked up and sat in the captain's chair, taking the ready position on the controls. She checked the navigation display. The entry point was close to the orbital. It would be quite a sight.

The empty seat next to her stared back. She swung around. Carbrook remained at the computer terminal, finishing the transmission to HQ that would shoot off after they dropped out of FTL. He was biting his nails. Again.

A tinge of guilt ran through her system. *I'm going to regret this.*

"Carbrook," she said, eyes back on the streams of faster-than-light speed travel passing the ship. "Get up here. That's an order."

A moment later the techie plopped down next to her.

"Straps," she said, indicating the safety sleeves on the sides of the seat.

He pulled them over his yellow jumper and clicked them together.

"Ten seconds," the AI announced.

The streams of light stopped. Instantly. It was like going from 160 km an hour to zero on a hovercycle in a centimeter. Out the window, a prodigious gold orbital spun in the emptiness of space. Its surface glimmered with reflected starlight. Around its edges, small shining specks were caught in Sesstari's rays. Lilline guessed them to be massive freighters coming and going from portions of the immense circular station.

"Whoa."

She smiled at the techie's response to the sublime view.

"I knew it was big," he said, "but even in 3-d it doesn't have the same effect."

"The real world, Carbrook. It has its own pleasures."

"And dangers," he whispered.

She nodded and flipped a set of buttons on the control panel. He was right about that. No replays out here. Once your power bar is wasted, you're toast.

"Nervous?" she asked.

"Admittedly, yes."

"Pre-op jitters. That's good," she said and hit the throttle. They shot off towards the orbital.

"Now what?" Carbrook asked.

"We go to the ball."

THIRTEEN

Paragon Galactic, Inc. | District: Grand Promenade | Star System: Sesstari, Galactic Core.

"Stop looking around."

"I can't help it," Carbrook said. "It's amazing."

"It's a space station." Lilline strolled down the corridor. "They're all over. You should get out more."

She had to admit that the orbital was extraordinary. In all her travels, she'd never seen a space-based habitation quite like this one.

A hundred or so meters to the right, over the walkway's sleek railing, the station's curving transparent shell offered a dramatic view of the cosmos. Vibrant red, blue, and green lights danced overhead on structural supports running in a complex geometric pattern, casting a kaleidoscope effect.

"Here we go," Lilline said as they neared a line of well-dressed guests. "Remember, mark anything you can to memory that appears unusual. If you see or hear something that relates to why we're here or otherwise urgent, let me know."

The techie nodded, staring up at the light display.

"Subtly, Carbrook. Don't blurt anything out. Take your time approaching me, as if you don't have anything important to say. Wait for me to start the conversation."

"Do I need a signal?"

She stopped and grabbed the sleeve of his tailored jacket. "I told you to be subtle."

"So, no signal?" He looked disappointed.

"This isn't one of your games or a broadcast drama. It's the real deal. Act like you would when you are out and about on Tavi-Prime."

"I don't get out and about."

And that was the problem. *Damn Lauden. I should be here alone.*

"Try and blend. Take no initiative at all. That shouldn't be too hard."

They strolled up to the waiting guests. Rasps, Kreelis, human variants, and a few Oltari formed a crowd at the official entrance.

"Remember what I told you when we docked." She had taken five minutes to go over undercover conduct before they stepped off *Celebrity Crush*. Five minutes. She'd trained for two cycles before going out into the field. Now she was walking into an op with a lab rat who'd had a five-minute pep talk.

They joined the queue. Lilline marked two exits and three security personnel, all Gej-ti, posing as guests next to the reception table.

"No way," Carbrook said. "It's in AR."

"Augmented Reality?"

He nodded and pointed. Lilline caught sight of a Kreeli couple at reception being handed sets of glasses shaped for their oblong heads. Three well-dressed Rasps donned mono-goggles over their large single eyes as they headed down the walkway.

"How is the back necklace working?" he asked.

"Perfectly." In the corner of the contact lens in her left eye, a small window displayed the view behind her, networked to a camera in the pendant dangling down her open-back dress. When she'd unpacked the outfit prepared by the Intel Department and Carbrook's team, she couldn't help but laugh. Granny got her wish. She was, indeed, wearing a dress. The accessories that accompanied it were more her cup of tea. She'd even put her hair up for the occasion.

Lilline had to give the Oltari credit, the new gadget was simple and straightforward yet extremely effective and useful. Now, she had eyes in the back of her head. She intended to put them to good use if she could get close enough to the entrepreneur. Who Nave interacted with, and how, would tell her as much as what she might gather from the spectacle of dazzling technology around the release of *Freestrike*.

She and Carbrook gave their names and accepted the glasses made for human viewers. Carbook put his pair on straight away, giggling with excitement. Lilline waited. She wanted a clear take on the physical layout inside before experiencing the augmented perceptions.

"Are you seeing this?" Carbrook said, head titled back as they continued walking over what looked like a natural preserve. Lilline's eyes were down, peering over the side of the railing. A transparent ceiling made, she guessed, from a molecular field divided them from a lower level two hundred meters below. It had to be for temperature regulation and sound reduction. Amidst an arid and rocky environment, two Ganghut lizards lounged by a pool of stagnant water. Those things were best not disturbed or roused to anger by unnecessary noise. She knew the fury of a Ganghut firsthand. The extraction op to rescue Katar included a near disaster with an ornery Ganghut as they made their way off the planet. She'd never seen another beast so destructive and malicious when harassed in its territory.

"You have to see this," Carbrook said.

Lilline put on the AR glasses. Her body swayed before catching its equilibrium. Bold red letters, at least three times the size of an average human, flew by and through them on the skyway. The sequence spelled one word over and over in caps: *FREESTRIKE.*

A flaming arrow as large as a passenger pod erupted from thin air, indicating they should turn left.

Carbrook laughed like a giddy child. "Crak, that is rad!"

Lilline shifted toward the indicated direction. She couldn't help but be impressed.

The arrow raised her interest, but the next view flooded her senses. A grand spectacle of lights and billboards five stories high exploded into life. It looked like the shopping district on Tavi-Prime at night ramped up to a bonus level. Various slogans and advertisements related to *Freestrike* shot across the open air above them. Sleek ships whizzed around in dramatic dogfights. An elegant human dancer moved with grace through a sparkling and misty void at five times scale. Lilline had been to a carnival once as a child, and this brought back memories of that experience. The difference was this was less real but more vivid.

"Now that's what I hoped for," Carbook said. She followed his gaze to the side wall. All manner of gaming displays related to *Freestrike,* as well as some additional offerings she recognized from the intel file, presented a playground for attendees. Down the center of the gala space ran an elegant run of food and drink. That was more to her liking.

"Well Carbrook, I imagine this is something like the afterlife in your version of whatever destination lies at the end of the road for people like you."

"Yeah," he said, half listening.

Lilline lowered her glasses. The five-story room remained but the spectacle in the sky and visual gaming systems vanished. A cool, minimal interior packed with attendees chatting and laughing competed with the loud music pumping in through speakers in the walls. At the far end of the space, the skyway resumed with an adjunct promenade overlooking the nature preserve.

"This is like the chip," Carbrook said.

"What do you mean?"

"Somehow it's blending augmentation and virtual tech, especially along the gaming walls."

Lilline marked four exits without the augmentation, three visible with the glasses and one without them. She now had at least five security personnel on her radar, all of them Gej-ti and disguised with nondescript costumes through the AR. *Clever.*

"Keely, look."

Lilline followed Carbrook's indicated direction, happy to hear him using the appropriate cover name.

"It's Nave."

She donned her glasses. Amidst the throngs of attendees, a floating head hovered, crowned with a dazzling display of astronomical phenomena dancing around it as if in a cosmic whirlpool.

"Crak, but that is great," Carbrook said. "The mind of the universe! A perfect avatar for the occasion."

Lilline wasn't sure what she thought of it. Certainly not humble, but what did you expect from a billionaire entrepreneur. She tipped the glasses down to the bridge of her nose. Nave stood, body and all, speaking with a Rasp wearing a black uniform with the gold company icon on the chest. She put the glasses back over her eyes. The Rasp vanished.

Interesting.

She'd heard of seeing through objects with AR. This was another use and a sneaky one at that.

Back down on the bridge of her nose with the glasses and she watched Nave hand the Rasp something. The stout employee spoke through its throat flap and put the item in a pocket. Lilline wasn't well versed in Rasp behavior but knew enough to read the nervousness in their movements.

"Who's the Kreeli?" she asked, putting the AR glasses back on and spotting a large figure on a platform in front of a crowd.

"Which one?"

"The one in the religious garb. On that pedestal." A Kreeli, decked out in an elaborate priestess outfit, held a group of guests transfixed with their animated gestures supporting what appeared to be powerful words. The orator's oblong blue head reeled back and forth as she shouted, arms pointing here and there.

"That's The Preacher."

Lilline kept her gaze on the Kreeli. "The Preacher?"

"She's a customer evangelist for Paragon. Preaches the consumer gospel."

Lilline had heard of the phenomenon. A persuader and influencer, whose fanaticism drove customer conversion from other companies' products. They boosted sales and increased followers' devotion to their products so they fell in line with a corporate piety that bordered on blind obsession.

"What's she saying?" Lilline asked.

"It sounds like cryptic nonsense unless you play the game. If you do, it's filled with esoteric meaning."

"Meaning if you buy the game and play through it?"

"Well, obviously."

Obviously. The integration of a secular devotion via pseudo-religious code and worship added a disturbing layer to her idea of Nave and his empire.

"Welcome."

Lilline lowered her eyes to find an Oltari hovering a half meter off the floor in front of them, wings flapping. The uniformed host glittered like a four-armed fairy from a childhood story.

"Oh, that is so cool!" Carbrook said. "Your appearance is crak."

"Thank you, and welcome to the gala." They gestured with four arms at the spectacle around them. "You are about to experience the most innovative and advanced entertainment technology in the galaxy."

The Oltari looked to Lilline.

"I can't wait," she said. "Although, I admit to being out of my element. It's my partner who is the invitee." She gestured at Carbrook. This was it. Go time.

"Are you in tech?" the Oltari asked, hovering and glittering. "Mr. Carbrook?"

"How did you know my name?"

The Oltari fluttered a half-meter off the floor. "It's accessed on my AR screen." One of its lower, two-elbowed arms bent around and pointed at the glasses.

So, everyone was ID'd here by the company. Another clever move.

"I'm a start-up," Carbrook said. "But I've been in the gaming industry for a while now. Nothing like this, though."

Not bad.

"Well, you'll find things are a bit different tonight, Mr. Carbrook. This is a teaser of what's to come when the next version of *Freestrike* drops."

"And when will that be?" Lilline asked, acting like she knew almost nothing. Not far from the truth.

"Oh, that's something only Mr. Nave knows."

Lilline nodded. She tipped the glasses down to keep track of the Rasp.

"So how does that integration work?" Carbrook pointed over at a game system running along the wall. "Is it like a virtual safe within a physical drive?"

"You know about that?" The Oltari stopped flapping its wings and dropped to the ground on its small, stumpy legs.

Lilline kept her gaze calm but inside she was roaring. The idiot was referencing the tech they found on the chip!

Carbrook looked at her for help.

"What would that be, dear? One of your crazy theories?" She looked at the Oltari. "He comes up with these impossible technological concepts. I always tell him he's living before his time." She did something revolting. Leaning in, her lips pecked him on the cheek. Talk about wanting to barf. It was worse than Granny calling Lauden "Asher."

She couldn't tell if Carbrook was more stunned from realizing his slip-up or from being kissed by her.

Lilline peeked over the edge of her glasses. The Oltari's AR lenses hid their expression. Not that it mattered all that much anyway with their species' idiosyncratic social skills.

"Well, darling," Lilline said, "go on then, it's why we're here. Give it all a try. I'll go and enjoy the view." She gestured to the railing overlooking the animal preserve.

Carbrook nodded, looking like he'd seen a ghost.

Never again. When I get back Lauden is going to get an earful. I don't care if he puts me on leave for it.

"Enjoy," the Oltari said and moved on to greet more guests.

"Have to go, Carbrook." Lilline's attention was on the employee making their way towards the exit not visible on the augmented system. "Don't do or say anything else stupid."

She kept her glasses below the line of her sight and tracked the Rasp, heading on an intercept.

FOURTEEN

Lilline swooped a drink from a passing server's tray and snaked her way across the plaza. She hustled through the crowds parallel to her mark until she gained the lead. Ten meters ahead of the Rasp, she turned on intercept.

"Oh, I am sorry. Excuse me," she said, grazing their side as she went by.

The Rasp didn't react. It stumbled once and kept going, long neck swaying.

No matter. Whatever Nave passed it was no longer in their pocket. She had it clasped in her hand. Lilline made her way through the gaming area amidst flashing lights and pounding music to the far side of the room where the promenade overlooked the preserve.

A quick check in the screen of her left eye showed no one following her after the lift job.

She knocked back the drink and placed it on a cocktail table before walking up to the railing. A few hundred meters below, a snowy landscape ran for a quarter kilometer in each direction. Dangling her hands over the edge, she opened her fingers far enough to inspect the item. As she suspected it was a drive.

How ironic.

For all the high-tech equipment Nave and his company had on display, they still passed things by hand using simple drives. *Good.* She could copy drives with simple things, too. She reached into her dress at its break on her chest and slipped out the small copy slice. The rectangular device needed to be within ten centimeters of a drive to take its contents, if the level of encryption fit its capabilities.

That was Carbrook's department. He was the best, or so he said. Lilline hung both hands over the edge of the railing, close enough to activate the drive. It lit up, initiating a data exchange. Her eyes focused on the blinking light peeking through clasped fingers, waiting for it to go full green.

She caught sight of the desert environment off to the right bordering the snowy region, cut by a strict boundary. Why did Nave have all these artificial ecosystems? Was he a naturalist? A philanthropist preserving threatened and endangered species? Or was he playing God?

She gazed out over the arctic landscape. It looked a lot like—

"Frebu."

Lilline's left eye focused on the small window of her contact lens streaming from the pendant cam. Nave was behind her.

The drive went green.

"Excuse, me?" She turned, slipping her device into the crease at her breast. She clasped the lifted drive in a closed hand.

"The inspiration for that ecosystem, Ms....?

"Larkin." She held out a hand. "Keely Larkin."

"Mavron Nave."

"Yes, I know."

He smiled. "I get that a lot."

"I'm sure."

Dancing with words. That's all this was other than the initial entrance, which was either a random coincidence or meant to put her off-balance.

A Rasp server approached with two glasses of wine. She imagined they appeared dazzling in the AR, but with her naked eyes, they wore the standard company uniform.

"May I offer you a glass of Gondau, Ms. Larkin?" he asked, taking the drinks from the tray held out by the Rasp.

"That depends," she said. "Is it pre-Roncheau?"

"Of course." Nave lowered his head in appreciation of her oenophilia. "You know your wines, Ms. Larkin."

"I know many things." She accepted the glass and gestured to him. Her eyes locked on his, sniffing the wine's aroma. As she expected of someone with billions to spend, he'd spared no expense. "The '52. You have good taste, Mr. Nave."

"I'm impressed. And please, Mavron is fine."

Lilline chose not to reciprocate.

"I don't often come across others with an appreciation of Gondau, least of all pre-Roncheau," he said. "There's a little village on Beisho, famous for its cellar. I'm sure you know it?"

She felt his gaze scrutinizing her own.

"Oh, yes. I've been there many times." Was it the wine or was he taunting her? She shifted back to the view over the railing. "You're not wearing glasses, Mavron. Odd, at your company gala celebrating your upcoming release."

"I prefer to have important conversations with discretion." She caught him glance towards the crowds at the gala in her contact lens. "And you, Ms. Larkin. I see that you are abstaining from the augmented reverie."

"That's my world, down there." Lilline gestured with her glass of wine. As she moved the hand, she slipped the lifted drive into the side of her dress with the other.

"Well, that makes sense now." Nave shifted next to her. He placed his forearms on the railing, dangling the wine glass over the edge and swirling its contents. Out of the corner of her eye, she observed him gazing out over the reserve. In the view through the pendant's camera, she noted at least three Gej-ti bodyguards nearby, eyes fixed on the billionaire.

Coincidence? Or was Nave's private security force an all Gej-ti company?

She faced him and brushed a strand of hair back behind her missing ear. "Did you figure something out about me that you can't access through your other reality?"

She decided to go on the offensive.

Let's see how you take it.

He grinned. "You've just confirmed it, Ms. Larkin."

"What's that?" She took a sip of the Gondau. Strange signals crossed with its robust flavor: Villain. Her private and safe space at the Golden Pheasant. And now, the cunning rhetorical sparring of a mission. She regretted taking the wine, as if the exchange had tainted its taste.

"Quite simple. As an expedition guide, you prefer the tangible world over its augmented and virtual improvement."

"Improvement? I beg to differ."

"I'm sure you do." He sipped the wine. "The world is full of faults, Ms. Larkin. It's a complex design, but no more than a foundation. A prototype for a galaxy that can be crafted to perfection."

"And whose ideal forms the guiding hand?"

He laughed. "I'm enjoying this conversation."

"Look at that," she said and smiled. "Having fun in the real world."

He raised his glass at the remark. "But it does present dangers. Especially in your line of work."

Now we are getting somewhere.

Nave's eyes went to her missing ear. "Bukki tiger, wasn't it?"

"On Hesh-9," she said. It was public knowledge. What she wanted to know was what the explicit reference veiled. If anything. "And how did you learn that piece of biographical information, Mavron? Through a pair of those fancy glasses of yours?"

"Oh no, Ms. Larkin," Nave turned back to the view. "I make sure I'm briefed on all guests, especially those added at the last minute."

So, he couldn't resist punching back.

Movement below inside the snowy landscape caught her eye. She tracked the flight of a bird across the tundra.

"Ice Ranger," Nave said. "Remarkable creature. Quite rare. I was lucky to secure one."

The flash of memory from the encounter in the cavern cut into her social game.

"Makes sense," she said, "if Frebu is the inspiration. But you are missing something."

"Oh?"

"Eroton. Without it, the Ranger's symbolism is lost. Perhaps you can build a moon out there for your perfect little world." She gestured to the cosmos through the transparent shell of the orbital.

"You are something of a birder, Ms. Larkin?"

"It comes with the job."

"You've been to Frebu, then?"

There it was.

"I've been to many places. It's a big galaxy. Like you said, full of danger. But then again, that's my business." She turned to him. "We live in separate worlds."

"Don't be so sure," he said. "The two are closer together than you know."

The Rasp she'd lifted the drive from approached and whispered in Nave's ear.

"I'm neglecting my other guests," he said, swigging down the rest of the Gondau.

In her camera, one of the bodyguards moved position.

"It was a pleasure meeting you, Ms. Larkin." He held out his hand.

She shook it, choosing only to smile.

"I hope the real world proves as exciting for you as the other is for me," he said. "While it lasts." He proceeded back into the crowds, donning a pair of AR glasses.

The bodyguard returned to their position. That wasn't the concern. The problem was the one called The Preacher. The evangelist passed a departing Nave, who stopped her and spoke into her ear.

Time to go.

Lilline put her back to the crowds and held her left eye shut for two seconds. The contact zoomed to a full lens view of the camera's field of vision. Carbrook's red spikes bounced up and down near one of the gaming stations. She turned with the casualness of someone without a care in the world and strode in that direction.

Her hand made as if to rub her eye, giving her time to close it and return the cam to a mini-window. The Preacher spoke with two Gej-ti security guards. One made for the exit and the other accompanied The Preacher on a direct course for her.

Lilline did her best to draw Carbrook's attention, but the techie was consumed in an augmented spectacle, head darting back and forth as a gamer ran through an ancient stone maze, battling monstrous creatures with a skilled set of hands.

Damn it, Carbrook.

The Preacher and the Gej-ti were closing.

"Come on," she said passing the techie. "Now."

It took him a moment to snap out of the game, but through the pendant she caught sight of him hustling to catch up.

Not subtle.

"Time to go," she said as they made their way to the exit. "And don't look back."

He looked.

Damn it!

Sure enough, it triggered the two in pursuit. They increased their pace, still trying to maintain a level of social behavior that didn't draw attention.

Lilline caught sight of the Rasp who spoke with Nave. She

grabbed Carbrook's shoulder and steered them towards the employee.

"The exit's over there," he said, pointing in the opposite direction.

"Get ready," she said.

"For what?"

The Rasp stood speaking with another guest by the railing across from the exit.

"To take a tumble." She shoved him into Nave's employee. The two collided and crashed to the ground. The Rasp's drink spilled, like she'd hoped.

"Oh, I am sorry!" She was down, grabbing the thick body to help them up. One hand went to the scaly skin at their neck and the other into their jacket pocket, replacing the drive she'd taken. She caught the name 'Ke' written under the company logo on their uniform. Her hand slipped out and she patted them once on the shoulder in apology. It wasn't as graceful as pouring a poisoned cocktail, but it worked.

"Excuse us," she said and pulled Carbrook to his feet, making for the exit. "When I tell you..." she dragged him along, "make for Level Five, cargo bay."

"But the Racer is in the guest port on Level Two."

"Just do it," she said through gritted teeth. Carbrook lost his collaborative privileges after ignoring her last instruction.

The Preacher and other Gej-ti were ten meters behind them and closing. The other guard was at the entrance fifteen meters ahead.

Another five steps.

"Three," she said, "two... one. Now."

She shoved him to the left, away from the direction of the guard and a crowd of guests. Carbrook stumbled through the opening to the hallway they'd come in and dashed down the corridor.

Lilline reached a hand around to the back of her head. The hairpin came out of her bun in one fluid movement. Black hair cascaded down her back as gracefully as the motion of her arm that hurled the thin dart into the neck of the Gej-ti at the entrance. Lilline kept walking at the same steady pace, passing through the reception area.

It was time for Pin's second surprise.

Two fingers undid the clasp on her chest holding the elegant back-drop necklace in place. It fell to the floor, the impact sending up a cloud of fumes that blocked out all vision.

Three... two... one.

She didn't need the cam to know that everyone inhaling the gas was out cold. She was starting to like Pin and made a mental note to thank her for the pendant.

With the gas cloud and havoc rising behind her, Lilline glided down the skyway with full-on secret agent grace. Once far enough from the mayhem, she bolted. A portal that she'd marked when they arrived approached. She ducked inside and peered back in the direction of her escape. Someone made their way through the cloud of fumes, hightailing it in pursuit.

The Preacher.

FIFTEEN

Lilline hit the descent button for Level Five. If her plan had worked, the ship would be there.

Her one weapon was a wrist knife. GAM-OPs had yet to figure out a workaround for electromagnetically charged weapons and security scanners. Nave's orbital ran on the latest technology and she had been forced to leave everything behind.

Nine... Eight... Seven... The portal opened and a side thrust kick shot toward her chest. She ducked and came up with both hands on the underside of the attacker's thigh, using a favorite technique: *mountain rises through silent mist.* Her shoulders shot the leg up and forward, sending her opponent out of the tube and onto the floor.

A Gej-ti security guard.

He rolled right as her heel came down at his groin, dodging her counterstrike. The brute was up in a flash laying into her with a flurry of punches. She blocked the first three, dress fluttering, and spun in and around as he drove forward with more swings. Her arm rotated in a wide arc, the fist crashing into the back of his neck. He collapsed in a heap on the floor. *Typhoon fury arms*: the first advanced technique she'd learned at the monastery.

She checked the portal's display screen. Level Seven. That didn't make sense unless someone overrode the system.

Her hands searched through the Gej-ti's suit for a weapon. She felt the handgrip of a G-type proton blaster under their shoulder.

Score.

She withdrew it from the holster and, with a deft set of fingers, checked its charge and took off the safety.

Level Seven? That meant she had two more levels to—

Blaster fire whizzed past her in the corridor. A Gej-ti ducked in and out of view at a corner, firing off shots. Lilline responded with a three-round burst and took off down the passageway.

A hallway leading right with a hazard symbol neared. She veered around the corner, ducking as blaster fire sent sparks off the wall over her head. So much for the smooth secret agent exit.

Suites of cages behind glass walls passed as she bolted down the corridor. In one, a Rasp in a lab coat fed a small furry creature what looked like a handful of vegetables.

The comm on her thigh buzzed.

You've got to be kidding.

Lilline took the next corner as shots whizzed close to her ear. Her free hand slapped the comm's thigh band under her dress. *If this is Lauden...*

"Dear Ms. Larkin, thank you for submitting your poem, 'A Night with Hiko' to the Inner Core Poetry Society's special issue on pets. We regret to inform you—"

She spun around and released a burst of rounds to buy herself time.

"... we received many wonderful poems..."

The Gej-ti peeked around the corner. She squeezed off a shot that would have made a bullseye on his forehead if he hadn't hastily retreated.

"Poetry is subjective and..."

She slapped off the comm and rounded the next turn. *Great confidence boost.* Well-timed. Rejection was just what she needed right now.

From the delay between the Gej-ti's laser fire, Lilline guessed her pursuer was alone. She halted and leaned up against the wall to wait for them, blaster at the ready.

"This way," someone shouted. Judging by the distance of the voice it had to be the one she'd engaged.

At least two other voices responded not far behind.

So much for that plan. She took off down the hall. On her right, the arid and rocky landscape of the nature preserve stood behind a transparent floor-to-ceiling magneto-shield. She spotted an airlock ahead.

"Time to visit the desert," she said and made for it.

Her free arm rotated the airlock's wheel. A hiss unsealed the entrance to the intermediary chamber. Lilline heaved the circular door open and made for the other end to enter—

Crack!

An impact to her back shot her forward. She crashed into the interior airlock. The handle's bars slammed into her gut. The blaster flew out of her hand and clanked to the floor.

She spun around, gasping to recover the wind that the steel bars knocked out of her.

The Preacher stood, hands in the air as if receiving a message from on high. Her oblong head shook as she roared with laughter. The Kreeli sent both arms down in a double punch. Lilline rolled forward between her legs. With a flex of her forearm, the wrist-action blade shot out. She came out of the somersault and slashed The Preacher's thigh with a perfectly aimed cut – right through the Kreeli's artery that lay lower than in humans and nearer to the underside of their thick muscles.

The blade twanged as it hit something hard underneath their clothing.

"Ha!" The Preacher bellowed and, with a step back, sent a back-fist across her chin. "Divinity is my protector!"

Pain seared the side of Lilline's jaw as she crashed into the wall.

Damn, but this is one big, crazy Kreeli.

"The power of gospel guides my hand!" The Preacher rocked their oblong head back and forth, cackling. The killer picked up the blaster and broke it in two in its massive hands.

Lilline wiped the blood from her mouth and released the blade from the wrist strap, gripping the handle. In the corner of her eye, two Gej-ti peered in through the open airlock. She held up the weapon for The Preacher to see and smiled.

The Kreeli snarled and taunted her to throw it.

Lilline sent it spinning through the air, wide of the Kreeli. It hit the piping on the wall. A perfect shot. Steam erupted in the chamber as the pressurized system went into a wild decompression. She dove for the closed lock and spun the wheel open, dashing into the preserve.

Brutal heat slammed into her as she ran. A rocky outcropping ahead looked familiar from the view on the skyway. She dashed off and over the boulders out of sight.

A sinister laugh bounced off the butte. The Preacher was inside.

Two Gej-ti appeared a hundred meters to her right, entering through another airlock. Red flashes erupted, mismatched with the clay palette of the landscape. Lilline ducked as the shots ricocheted off the craggy outcropping, spewing pebbles and dust in the air. She slid down a twenty-meter cliff into a basin with a pool and yelped in pain when her feet impacted the dusty ground. Hopefully it carried far enough to be heard. Around the stagnant water a boulder offered the protection she needed. She made for it and ducked behind the rock, panting.

The two Gej-ti came over the butte's rise. They proceeded forward with their blasters at the ready.

"I'm over here. I give up," she yelled and held up a hand, waving. No blaster fire.

The analysts would have a heart attack, but her instinct told her it was the right move.

She dragged herself into view struggling across the sand and dirt as if one leg was useless, trying to flee. She held up a hand as if to say, *"don't shoot."*

The two Gej-ti called back, most likely to The Preacher.

It didn't matter. This performance wasn't for them.

The two slid down the side of the rock and approached with slow and suspicious steps.

A little more. Come on.

"Sorry, but not this time," one said when they were across the pool, gills fluttering from the chase.

The other smiled and raised their blaster.

"Our orders are—"

Both Gej-ti flew off their feet and into the mouth of the Ganghut lizard that burst from the cave behind them. Screams echoed off the rocks as the creature's massive jaws closed on their flesh. The distinct Gej-ti green blood splattered the surface of the stagnant, murky pool.

"Pays to know your beasts," she said and rose. Atop the outcropping beyond the pond, The Preacher appeared. The Kreeli spread her arms wide as if to part the waters.

Lilline picked up a rock and displayed it as if she would throw it.

The killer's expression, as expected, was one of hilarity at her pathetic last-ditch attempt. The Preacher bellowed a laugh that echoed over the landscape.

Not too smart, are you? Lilline threw the stone far too low to hit her.

A massive roar erupted as a second Ganghut burst from the cave.

"There's always two," Lilline said.

The evangelist reeled back as the lizard rose to its full height. The creature swung around and sent the Kreeli diving away to avoid its hideous claw that swiped the top of the butte.

Lilline bolted for the exit on the opposite side of the preserve.

The cargo deck on Level Five appeared as Lilline hoped it would: calm.

She caught sight of *Celebrity Crush* tucked behind a medium-sized freighter. Carbrook's red spiky head leaned out the ramp door.

She dashed across the tarmac. The dock master emerged out of the office on her left.

"Hey, are you taking that Racer out?" The Rasp's neck snaked back and forth.

"Yep." Lilline withdrew a credit chip from inside her dress and tossed it to him without stopping.

"Wow, thanks."

It was double what she had negotiated with their colleague.

"Just open the bay doors," she yelled back. "Gotta run."

"Can do." The dock master's voice trailed off as she rounded the mini-freighter's bow. You could always count on traffic workers to keep their word. They weren't Paragon employees. All transportation ports in networked systems were managed by independent contractors. Give them enough credits and they always hooked you up. Lilline had never met one yet that hadn't delivered.

"I can't believe the ship was here," Carbrook said, leaning out the ramp. "It's so weird that—"

"Here." She slapped the copy slice into his hand and shoved past him, bolting for the cockpit.

"Shut that door and strap in," she yelled back.

"What's this?"

"A little something that I borrowed at the gala." She fired up the Racer and lifted it off the tarmac. "Can you upload it into the ship's drive?"

"I think so."

"Good. You strapped in?" She punched the thruster and steered the ship around the freighter. The sound of Carbrook crashing into something echoed up the open cabin.

"Guess not," she said. "Hold on." She'd been waiting for this moment since Lauden gave her the keys. Her palm slammed down the turbo-burn boosters and the docking bay shot past in a blur.

"Are you crazy?" Carbrook's voice came from somewhere aft.

"Just another day on the job." Lilline banked the Racer away from the orbital. Her eyes went to the board. Nothing in pursuit. The Preacher and her goons were probably talking to a very confused dock worker at the civilian port. One who was having a hard time remembering who authorized the re-location of the ship to a cargo bay.

"What happened to those Gej-ti?"

A smirk rose on her lips. "They met a cold-blooded killer."

Silence.

The joke was lost on him. Too bad.

"Anything on that thing?" Still no intercept on the screen. They'd have a clear run from the orbital for the jump back to Tavi-Prime.

"Nave's about to hold a virtual meeting."

"When?"

"Tomorrow. 4:00 Galactic Standard."

"Are there any names of who is attending?"

"Kinda."

She never liked that answer. "Carbrook, you're leaving me hanging here."

"Yes and no," he said.

That was more annoying.

"I mean, they're usernames," he said. "For what I assume are avatars to keep their identities secret."

From whom? That was the question. Not Nave, that was for sure.

"Are the identities attached to the usernames traceable?"

"I doubt it considering the level of tech we've encountered."

"Well, you'll have to try to crack it. Get Pin to help."

"You do realize that I'm one of the best hackers in the galaxy, right?"

Lilline checked the board. Three ships popped up, departing the orbital on an intercept course.

"Pin's area is clandestine tech and gadgets," Carbrook said, filling the silence.

"Gotcha." She set the FTL track to Tavi-Prime's jump perimeter. No need to bother him with the news about the approaching ships. *Celebrity Crush* spun up its drive like a top on Jivi-juice. They would be out of here before anyone could reach them.

"Can I ask you something?" Carbrook's voice had a strange tone.

Please don't get weird about the kiss. "Sure."

"How did you move the ship?"

She sighed with relief, happy to answer. "I didn't."

"You know what I mean."

"Credits, Carbook. They're a magical thing when working with freelancers." She banked the Racer left and the orbital fell away. Out of the cockpit, she took a last look at Nave's empire.

I'm coming back for that Ice Ranger.

"I bribed the dock master," she said. "Had him move the ship for us."

"Why?"

"Do you really need to ask?"

"I mean, how did you know to do it?"

"Instinct." She switched on the FTL drive for the jump to light speed. "It's called thinking ahead to control the board."

"I'm impressed, Renault."

The sincerity of the phrase was undeniable.

"Oh, hello there," he said.

"What is it?" Lilline waited.

Carbrook had gone silent.

"Suspense isn't killing me, Carbrook."

"There's an access code to the meeting. That means—"

"We can get in." She hit the FTL switch, sending them through the stars.

SIXTEEN

"I've got two dead Gej-ti and one more in rehab!" Nave picked up a game controller and hurled it across the office.

Ke ducked with practiced precision.

"Sir, she was one step ahead of us the entire time," the Rasp said.

"You're telling me she's that good?" He paced back and forth. "The Ganghuts I can understand. That makes sense considering her profession."

Nave eyed The Preacher next to Ke. Why did the Kreeli stand at attention like a statue? His temperature rose. He barreled over and halted inches from her, aiming his head up to lock eyes with the much taller killer. "And you and your security force?"

The Kreeli didn't move a muscle.

"She made you look like fools!!" Spit flew like sparks between his shouted words.

"There is devilry in her," The Preacher's deep voice said.

"Bah!" Nave waved a dismissive hand. The Kreeli's remark wasn't all wrong, though. Larkin played the rhetorical game well during their brief conversation on the promenade.

"First your Gej-ti fail to eliminate that professor, leaving a witness to what unfolded on Frebu out who knows where, roaming the galaxy." He waved his arms in a sweeping gesture. "You had one chance to plug that leak."

The Preacher bowed her head.

"You think she'll risk using her public transport ID again on another moon hop?" Like magma rising inside a volcano, the incompetence and insolence of his lessers would, as usual, force an imminent eruption. "After being chased and shot at? And, I might add, killing two of your elite guards sent to take her out?"

He turned to Ke, who shrugged.

"What kind of a 'professor' is this, anyway?" He burned a hole through the Kreeli's face. "You should have gone to Beisho yourself!"

The Preacher stood motionless before him.

"Instead of one problem, because of your incompetence, we have two."

"Larkin came prepared, like a sinner out to corrupt the converted." The Kreeli made a gesture of disgust.

"And what about her companion?" Nave turned to Ke.

"Small time," the Rasp said. "Has a startup company in gaming. Nothing there as far as I can tell."

"Nothing there?" Nave did his best to hold back the rising anger. "He mentioned my private tech designs, Ke."

The Rasp's neck sunk.

Nave turned to The Preacher. "And you failed to apprehend either of them!" His eyes glared at the Kreeli.

"Do some digging on this Carbrook, Ke. I want to know who he is and why he's talking about my AR and VR data cloaking systems."

"Yes, sir."

"There something going on here. I'm certain of it," he said.

"That was no ordinary expedition guide," The Preacher said, shaking her oblong head.

"Then who might she be, eh?" Nave poked his finger into the Kreeli's massive chest. "You think Larkin's working for someone else? One of my competitors?"

The band on The Preacher's head glittered with a pressure adjustment.

"You think she's a hired eye to gather information about me and my empire?"

The Kreeli gestured as if to say, *"perhaps"*.

"I have no worthy competition!" he shouted up at her face. "Those others are amateurs. Neophytes who copy my genius. Every one of their products is but a pale reflection of my innovation." Fury rose from his belly up into his throat. He wanted to smash something and watch it shatter in humiliation and shame, but nothing was within reach.

His gaze went to the Rasp. "And now we don't know where she is?"

"Her expedition company has her status as personal leave for two weeks. They have no idea where she would be, if not at her Domus unit," Ke said. "The one I spoke to at their headquarters on Tavi-Prime said she has a penchant for going off-network for holidays." The Rasp shrugged their stout shoulders in a gesture of futility.

"Of course, she does." Nave clenched his jaw and felt the veins on the side of his forehead swelling. He marched to the window and gazed at the freighters arriving and departing along the curve of the orbital. "'On leave' my ass," he said. "My empire and our ascendency will not be challenged."

Larkin's remark about playing games in the 'real' world came back to him. *She'll get a taste of what's to come if I don't find her first.*

"There is one possible lead, sir," Ke said.

Nave didn't turn. Nor did he respond.

"I just checked on something. I've pulled it up on the holo," the Rasp said.

Nave sighed. "I have no time for dead ends." He turned and froze. A familiar face among a group of portraits brought a flurry of memories rushing back. They battered and smashed all the pieces of the life he'd designed.

"You're sure about your sources on this, Ke?"

The Rasp's vocal flap vibrated, and their monocular head went up and down. "Without any doubt."

The lava in his belly cooled and hardened. He looked to The Preacher.

"Pack your bag. There's a heathen in need of penitence."

SEVENTEEN

GAM-OPS HQ | Planet: Tavi-Prime | Star System: Pesari-9, Galactic Core.

"Knee is all better, then?" Lauden stood at the office window, smoke rising from his pipe.

"Yes, sir." Lilline hadn't felt any lingering injury during the chase on the orbital.

"From your report, it sounds like you put the Racer to good use."

She had. And got it back in one piece without so much as a scratch.

"Your grandmother sounded well."

"Yes, sir. She's as spritely as ever."

Smoke wafted from the Gej-ti's gills. "How's her memory?"

He's concerned about something.

"Fine. She reminds me of my previous disappointments every visit, without fail."

Lauden nodded in earnest. The director was never one for humor, especially sarcasm.

"Now, about this meeting." He faced her. His silhouette glowed at the edges. Today the cravat had a touch of aqua that made it sparkle like sunlit ripples on a clear sea. "I'm hoping—"

"Excuse me, sir." Cazshi's voice interrupted him.

It always felt odd to her that Lauden allowed these abrupt intrusions. Though domineering and authoritative, even a bully at times, the director had no problem with his assistant breaking into his words over the intercom. GAM-Ops came first. Even he, as its highest officer, bowed to the company.

"What is it?" Lauden asked.

"Carbrook and Pin are here."

"Send them in." He strode to the desk and sat, tapping out his pipe.

Lilline shifted in her chair as Carbrook and Pin shuffled through the portal. The Oltari's wings fluttered as she hovered off the floor.

"So, where are we?" The Gej-ti sparked a fresh bowl of Queen Yaz Flake. The glow cast an orange light on his milky-skinned face.

Carbrook wiped his brow. He looked pale, almost flustered. She made a note to have a talk with him about meetings with the director. A bit of advice on what to expect and how to read Lauden's body language or lack thereof would go a long way toward easing his nerves.

"We're in, sir," Carbrook said. "At least, in theory. We won't know for sure until we sign on to the meeting but T8 should be able to observe without being noticed. I doctored something rather clever."

Good. This was the best kind of intel. Direct access to Nave without him knowing of her presence. No showing off about one's knowledge of wine. No banter with innuendos.

"And what of the attendees?" Lauden asked.

Lilline read the disappointment in Carbrook's face at the Gej-ti's lack of interest in his tech wizardry.

Carbrook turned to Pin, indicating she should answer.

He looked wiped. *Must be a lot for a lab rat to be in the field.* A quick turnaround in FTL, and then having to hack into the top galactic company's secret meeting.

"Sir," Pin clicked on a handheld holo-projector. A blue and green display made of squares in a grid manifested in the air. Lilline counted twelve. Nave's image and name occupied one at the top. The others were assigned usernames.

"I was able to re-route the computer's password breaker to decipher any consistencies between the usernames and known individuals of power, economically, politically, or otherwise on the GAM-Ops watchlist. The results were interesting." Pin thumbed the clicker with a finger on one of her short, uppers arms.

Five of the eleven squares rotated, revealing identities. They ranged across a variety of known species and occupations. Lilline knew them all. They'd been set to memory, the list revised and expanded based on constant updates to GAM-OPs intel. They all shared one thing: ties to the criminal underworld.

"Well done, Pin," Lilline said, giving her a plug.

"It's only a hypothetical but thank you. The computer is guessing, but there is a pattern."

Lilline caught Carbrook looking glum. Pin was turning out to be an excellent assistant. He needed to accept that she complemented him and wasn't a competitor. Another note to add to her pep talk.

"So Mavron Nave is gathering the galaxy's top criminal minds," Lauden said. He took a long pull on his pipe. The Gej-ti's gills fluttered like window blinds as he exhaled.

She stole a glance at Pin. The Oltari was faring better this time. She looked on the edge of bursting into a coughing fit but she was holding it together. When this was all over, Lilline told herself she'd take her to lunch in the Octagonal. A rite of passage at GAM-OPs for rookies and, with her work thus far on Operation Freestrike, well deserved.

"And Carbrook, you say we can get in unseen?" Lilline asked.

"I believe so, yes. I've designed an avatar that should pass unde-tected regardless of what the environment presents. We can route through the new computer rigged to the Hyper-Healer. It's got the juice to do it."

Lauden nodded and tapped a finger on his desk, pulling up a clock displaying Galactic Standard Time. "The meeting is at four GS. That's just under an hour."

"We're ready down in the lab," Pin said.

"Excellent. Dismissed," Lauden gestured with his pipe.

They both nodded and headed for the portal.

"And nice to see you again, Pin," the director added, shutting off the holo-clock.

Lilline held back a smile. *Definitely time to take her to lunch in the Octagonal.*

"T8," Lauden said after they were alone.

Lilline straightened in her chair. She knew this tone. Orders were about to be given.

"Pay special attention for any references to outlandish prophetic claims by Nave or..." he drew on his pipe, "thoughtforms in that meeting."

"Thoughtforms, sir?"

"Like the one you encountered on Frebu." He moved a hand in a way that indicated no further explanation would follow. A holo-screen popped up between them on his desk, filled with T# reports and associated star maps. "Get down to the lab and have Carbrook set you up. Good luck."

"Thank you, sir." She rose and made to go.

"And T8?"

Lilline stopped but didn't turn.

It never failed. Lauden always had a footnote.

"Leave the past to those who lived it."

EIGHTEEN

You enter the board room. The scent of evolution lingers in your nose. You are the apex. The apogee that will see the contributions of your predecessors reach glorious fruition.

It is imminent. Civilization will move to the next level. An empire will be gifted a new king.

All rise at your entrance.

"The Mind is the ultimate eye," you declare.

The lower Tier members respond as one, with like tone and cadence.

"Be seated." Your directive isn't etiquette. It's an order.

The water wall soothes your ears. The urban architecture out the window calms your mind.

You take your seat at the head of the table. "The agenda for this meeting has changed. I wish to address the incident at the gala, and to make an important announcement."

Avatars fidget. Virtual hands shift apprehensively on the table's surface.

Let them be wary. You observe the empty seat with sinister delight. A reminder of the price of insolence.

"First, regarding Frebu. Our freelance specialist has been well compensated. All tracks and evidence have been covered and concealed."

You wait and watch. None react.

They do not need to be told about the missing witness. Not now that you have all the links in the chain.

"As for the gala, it was nothing more than a minor disruption. We proceed as planned."

"And what of the one who escaped?"

You lock eyes with she who spoke. Her avatar, a tiger-hybrid, takes the form of a humanoid with the features of a cat.

"I have plans for that one."

"We are a collective, are we not?" she asks. "Do we not deserve to know of these plans?"

"No, you do not!" You slam your fist down on the table. The sound echoes louder than thunder. A seismic tremor shakes the building's foundation.

Hands grab for the table. Heads turn in all directions in terror.

You wait with smug patience as the effect settles at the precise moment you designed it to.

"Larkin is finished." You lower your voice but keep the particulars of why and how to yourself. This will be more satisfying than luring a Cronkhead to the bait. "She will not interfere again."

A GAM-OPs agent. How perfect. So smug and convinced of their organization's secrecy in the galaxy. She will be the ideal foe to challenge in open play.

"And what of our reward?" The voice comes from the end of the table. It is the one that looks like an owl.

"Each of you will be paid, as agreed. Five million credits." You rise from the chair and walk to the window, your back to the attendees. The view soothes your anger.

Such peace and order.

It is what the world needs.

"All of you will receive compensation for your expertise when we have the galaxy at our knees. Our Order will teach them all a lesson in humility. They will learn about our power and they will yield to it." You pause for effect. "Or they will die."

Magma rises in your belly. *But first, those who've wronged me need to suffer.*

"I have deposited one million credits into your accounts. The rest will arrive when the Ascendency is complete."

"What happens next?"

You recognize the voice as the tiger-human. *Give her a taste... give them all a taste.*

With thought alone, you activate the display. A glimmering speck hovers in the cosmos in two dimensions, replacing the wall of water. Avatars on that side of the table swivel in their seats toward the view.

"Frebu was a minor setback. It demonstrated the thoughtform's potential while exposing a weakness. That has been corrected."

You let the words sit in silence long enough to draw forth their desire. *They are the same as all the others.* Despite being a part of the Order, they are nothing but fools.

You zoom the screen in. Kilometers race past. The view jumps to the interior of a facility. A wall of electromagnetic static sparks and glitches, spectral shadows cast a haunting glow on the surrounding grey steel walls.

"Behind this barrier lies the ultimate challenge in a most dangerous game."

Avatars edge up in their seats. You thrive on their anticipation. What hides inside this shield is terrible and glorious. Your rivers and ecosystems, your gaming worlds, and even this private city that surrounds you – all express beauty through control and perfection.

But they remain sketches of an artist perfecting their craft. This weapon is your masterpiece.

"Phase Two begins now."

Yes, they are pleased, as they should be. Fools. Talented and clever, but fools, nonetheless. Their criminal minds and your brilliance have created the most challenging enemy ever faced. The ultimate game is set. Entertainment will become reality, and you will teach the galaxy an important lesson.

"I give you, the egregore."

None move. No gasps. Only the terrible and sublime shock and awe of silence.

Even you find its appearance, its aura and beauty, mesmerizing. Your thought, and that of these minions around you, has bred a being from the other side. Your brilliance and access to secret knowledge has broken a cosmic barrier that stood for millennia. All those in your hall of glory laid the path. Their faith in the occult and the potential of super intelligence pointed the way. You alone crossed the threshold.

You want to gloat at the expressions of your lessers around the table, but you cannot turn from it. The power, the pulsing energy is too all-consuming. And it is *you.* Your mind is integrated with these petty criminals, their talents forming a hybrid with your brilliance in competition and technology. The egregore thinks like you. It desires what you desire. And that—

A black dot on the projection catches your eye.

A glitch? Impossible.

There are no imperfections in your designs. You shut off the display. The water wall returns.

No words come from those in attendance. You stare at the speck. It moves, flitting about on the surface of the falling water as if two- and three-dimensions tangle.

"Meeting adjourned."

Those at the table look to you, stunned. Confusion fills their faces.

"But we haven't discussed the final ritual and—"

"I said meeting adjourned!" You cut off the owl before it can finish. Thunder bellows and the building quakes as it had when you slammed your fist.

One by one the avatars vanish. You, and the black speck defiling the perfection of your world, are all that remain.

You navigate around the table to the wall of falling water, homing in on the dot.

It darts to and fro.

It can't be.

A fly.

NINETEEN

GAM-OPs HQ | Planet: Tavi-Prime | Star System: Pesari-9, Galactic Core.

"Shut it down!" Lilline threw off the goggles.

Carbrook flipped the kill switch on the wall unit.

"Clear!" Pin shouted from down the line, the massive computer alive with carnival-like activity.

"What happened?" Carbrook asked.

"He made us." Lilline rubbed her eyes. The hangar filled with gadgets and experimental devices returned, slapping her back to the physical reality of GAM-OPs sub-level four. She breathed in a steady rhythm, cycling herself back from the virtual experience. "Can Nave track us?"

"I doubt it," Carbrook said. He took the visor out of her hands. "I activated the entropic software as soon as we cleared the connection."

"He'd have to start the trace within five seconds," Pin said flying over. "I don't think he had time to grasp what he was looking at before we were gone."

"What was it, Carbrook?" Lilline asked. "You called it a small eye."

"Nope. Better than that." He stood, biting his nails.

"Stop that."

He lowered his hand and spat a nail away. "You'll appreciate my creativity on this, T8." An eyebrow went up and down. "You were literally... wait for it..." Carbrook spun around and finished in a posture as if shooting in a game. "A fly on the wall."

"Clever." It was, she had to admit. "Somehow though, he saw me. Or, it."

"Well, I had to hack into the spatial configuration," he said. "So, it didn't fit seamlessly into the illusory dimensional matrix."

She didn't follow, but it didn't matter. It worked well enough and long enough to get vital information.

"Too bad I couldn't make him swallow it," Carbrook said. "If that happened, perhaps he'd..." He did Lauden's hand gesture.

The techie waited. Pin giggled.

Lilline wasn't interested. She was already opening a line to Lauden on her wrist comm.

"Go ahead, T8."

Carbrook halted his goofing at the sound of the director's voice.

"Sir, it worked," Lilline said. "I got into the meeting and..." she glanced at Carbrook and Pin, "hold a moment." She muted the comm. Her eyes searched the hangar and landed on the *Velociter Bullet*. "Is that open?" She nodded her chin in the direction of the mini-rocket.

"Well, yes," Carbrook said, "but—"

Lilline hustled over, ignoring the upcoming caveat. She hit the release switch for the cockpit window. The tubular pane on the bullet-shaped craft slid back with a whoosh. She dropped into the pilot seat and closed the transparent component over her head, re-sealing it.

"Apologies," she said, reopening the line. "I wanted this secure. Nave's got another entity."

"Where?"

Lilline's mind glitched. She'd caught no more than the reflection of this new manifestation on the office window. Even that had stirred her to horror. Memories of Frebu couldn't be pushed down.

"T8?"

"I don't know, sir. I didn't have a clear view, nor did I see any geo-data. No star or moons for scale, either."

"It must be one of his other properties," the Gej-ti said. The familiar click of Lauden's lighter came over the line.

"From Nave's comments to the other attendees, it sounded like there was a cover up on Frebu."

"Hacking? This 2112 perhaps?" Lauden asked.

"Could be. That would take care of the satellite and geological data."

"And the facility was lost in the implosion and collapse described in your report."

"Yes, sir. It's possible." It did make sense. Considering who she thought were the participants at the meeting, the degree of serious-ness was rising. "He's gathered some kind of collective around him. They were all cloaked by their avatars, but I'm sure they're top minds from the criminal underworld. I got the impression they were part of a secret organization, with customs and whatnot."

"So Pin got it right?"

"She did, sir. Their knowledge is being used by him."

"How?"

"I'm not sure, but he mentioned something about an 'Ascenden-cy'. It sounded like something big was going to happen."

Lilline waited for a response. Lauden was smoking and working through the intel.

"Did you get a timeline?" he asked, breaking the silence.

"No. Only that it's moving to Phase Two."

"Blast."

The word was a whisper over the comm. Lauden never did that. *Is he rattled?*

"Whatever it is, considering the evidence we've put together, my guess is he plans to unleash it as a sadistic game," she said.

"In *Freestrike*?"

"I don't know, sir. I think so. I keep coming back to something Nave said at the gala."

"Yes," Lauden mumbled, speaking the way he did when the pipe's stem was clenched between his teeth.

"Nave prodded me about the boundary between the physical and the virtual, and entertainment and the 'real world'."

"What did it look like, this entity? The same as on Frebu?"

"I couldn't see it clearly. Carbrook had me positioned on the wall used to display it to the group. I had movement but no flight through three-dimensional space. We were in a virtual corporate office. I didn't recognize the setting. It looked..." She searched for the right words.

"What is it, T8?"

"It looked too good to be true... almost utopian."

"The man's a lunatic," Lauden muttered. The clanking of his pipe being tapped on the ashtray sent static over the line, causing her to wince.

Tell him the word Nave used. Something about it made her stomach turn. The phonetics felt ominous.

"Sir," she hesitated. "He called it by a different name."

"Not a thoughtform?"

"No. It's a word that I've never heard before."

"Egregore," Lauden whispered.

He knows it. Her silence spoke for her, confirming the utterance.

"Get down to Intel, T8. Have the astronomers and astro-geographers work with you to try and identify that location. As soon as you have the most probable geo-data, get on a cruiser and get out there and check it out. We'll send the other T#s to the second and third possibilities."

"Wouldn't the Racer be a faster option?"

"It's in use."

In use? Who could need to get somewhere faster?

"Sir, what is it?" The question gnawed at her. "This thing Nave has created."

"Not created, T8. Summoned."

The tension on the line hung like lingering smoke.

"Something you don't want to believe," Lauden said.

The memory of the cave on Frebu returned. Like a vortex, that entity had sucked her life force away until almost nothing remained.

"You are no one." The words echoed inside of her.

"Sir, is this about revenge? Nave mentioned teaching others a lesson. It sounded like retribution."

"Mind your boundaries, T8. As I said, leave the past to those who lived it. I will address that aspect myself. Get down to Intel and off to the best guess location. I will contact you with more details when I have them."

"Yes, sir." Lilline cut the line.

She leaned her head back on the neck rest and closed her eyes. "Egregore," she whispered. The fury of Nave's temper was startling. And she had forgotten about what he'd told the attendees: that he had 'plans' for her.

She opened her eyes and focused on the *Bullet's* dashboard. Carbrook's upgrade mods and repair job gave the interior controls a whole new look.

Not only did Nave discuss her, but he mentioned plugging—

Her comm buzzed. She lifted her wristband into view. It was a GAM-OPs number over the secure line. Location: Beisho. She activated the call.

"Yes?"

"Renault?"

Lilline recognized the voice: former T# Agent Weo. They'd been assigned to check in on Granny once a week.

"What is it Weo?"

"Is Kissy with you?"

"No, why?"

"She's not at the retirement facility. According to the front desk, she left yesterday evening with a guest. And never came back."

TWENTY

Lilline pinged the retirement facility as she crossed from the parking tower to Tavi-Prime Exo-Central.

"Rolling Gables, front desk." The voice was the Rasp. The one she'd spoken to on her visit a few days earlier.

"This is Keely Larkin." She held her wrist comm close to her lips and made her way through the crowds of arriving and departing passengers outside the station. "I'm calling about my grandmother, Imani."

"Yes, Ms. Larkin. It's been very quiet and enjoyable here today."

She brushed past a group of Kreeli tourists, their oblong heads bent back, gazing at the skyscrapers. The family looked as if they'd never seen the dense air traffic and hustling pedestrians of an urban megalopolis.

Lilline crossed through security with a flash of a badge and entered the station. Throngs of travelers, of all species, milled about or hustled to departure gates. That was the one thing that bothered her about public transportation on ops. You never knew if someone was watching or following you in a crowd. The Racer, if it were available, removed those problems.

"I was told she checked out voluntarily?"

"That's right, yesterday evening."

"Alone?" Lilline scanned the holo-board floating in the middle of the three-story interior. Forty minutes until boarding. Her transfer shuttle would bump up to orbit for connection with the cruiser. From there, a long eighteen hours in FTL to the Kitarin system on the edge of known space. The plan was to drop in-atmosphere on a local transport to the remote planet, Eshi. Intel picked up a signal with a sub-frequency that was barely audible on GAM-OP's most sophisticated radio equipment. Without much to go on from the virtual infiltration of Nave's meeting, this was their best guess. Eshi was not unlike Frebu; an inhospitable planet in one corner of the galaxy. She would do the same thing again – rent an Explorer Pod and make for the southern pole. No guide this time. Not worth the hassle with the clock ticking.

Pin had given her a new piece of equipment that she hoped would help out. It picked up frequencies and transcribed their source based on intensity and direction by tapping into a geo-nav system linked to a planet's communication satellites. Would she meet something like she had on Frebu? Or, worse?

"No, Ms. Larkin. She left with a guest."

Guest?

"They must have signed in?"

"Oh, yes. I have it here. One moment."

Storefronts inside the station sparkled with holo-displays for *Freestrike*. Enticing teasers created a cacophony of advertising streams. Explosive graphics, vibrant color splashes, and dramatic music filled the interior. Nave's empire was everywhere. Not one shop was without a crowd. It was as if the imminent release of the next version of the game pulled at consumers with an involuntary and alluring hand.

"Here it is. A Kreeli."

Lilline halted. "A Kreeli?"

"Indeed. A preacher."

Her stomach dropped.

"Did you get a name?"

"Indeed, Ms. Larkin. She signed in as Teews Egnever."

Lilline was no fool. And she was a poet. It was a simple slap in the face. 'Sweet revenge' spelled backward.

What is Granny doing mixed up in this? "Were you on duty at the time?"

"No, I'm sorry. But Fin was here," the Rasp said.

The orderly. The one who tried to draw Granny's blood.

"Get him."

"He's in the middle—"

"Get him now!" A group of Dendari making for a nearby gate turned, their furry heads and bulbous eyes staring. "Look, this is an emergency," Lilline calmed her tone. "A family emergency. I need to speak with him."

"Hold please."

A group of Rasps eyed her. She shot them a look of death. Their necks swiveled, five single eyes twisting backward. She resumed walking and aimed for the bar.

"Yes?" someone said.

"Fin?"

"That's right."

"Kelly Larkin."

"Hello, Ms. Larkin. I am sorry for your loss."

"Loss?" Lilline shoved aside an AI-peddler trying to get her to buy travel insurance.

"Your grandmother told the front desk that this was a family matter. I assumed with the preacher picking her up—"

"Granny... I mean, Imani, said that?"

"Yes. She seemed quite calm considering... well, you know... her usual temperament."

"Did she say anything about where they were going?"

"No, Ms. Larkin. I guessed she would be meeting you for the arrangements and the service. Again, I am sorry."

"Thank you, Fin. Can you put the receptionist back on?"

Lilline halted outside the bar.

"Yes?"

"What time did my grandmother sign out?" She caught sight of the bartender inside, who knew her well from the constant travel across systems. He raised a High-Four glass in his human hand, asking if she wanted one. She nodded and watched him pull bottles down off the shelf.

The Rasp had said something.

"What was that? Sorry..."

"Just shy of twenty-four hours ago," the Rasp repeated. "Three minutes short to be exact."

"Thank you, if you hear from her will you ping me?"

"Certainly, and again, our condolences, Ms. Larkin. Remember your grandmother needs to be given her blood pressure medication every—"

Lilline cut the line. She needed a cocktail.

***

"Evening, Ms. Larkin. Where to this time?"

Lorre slid the High-Four across the bar. In the dimly lit establishment, the cacophony of marketing fireworks vanished behind sound-proof panes.

"Pretty far, Lorre. And cold."

"Ouch." He took a glass off the shelf and polished it with a well-muscled stroke.

Lilline followed the up and down motion of his bicep as he twisted the towel back and forth.

"Been all cold spots lately, huh?" Lorre put the glass back on a shelf and ran a hand through his wavy black hair.

"Unfortunately." She had to pull her eyes away from his flawless copper skin.

"What do these adventure customers want with snow and ice?"

"You know," she said taking a sip. No one made a High-Four like Lorre. "Glacier slides, Kuruk watching... that kind of thing."

"More like fleeing from Kuruk before they eat you."

She laughed. He always made her laugh. Pre-flight was the best part of her op runs. "It's an adventure company, Lorre. There must be adventure."

"And danger," he said, taking another glass down to polish it. "Something tells me you thrive on it."

"Do you like dangerous women?" They did this every time. She never tired of it.

"I'm just a bartender on Tavi-Prime. One who—"

Her comm pinged. She rotated her wrist under the counter. The source of the missive read *Imani Larkin*.

"I'm sorry, Lorre, I have to take this."

The bartender held up a hand. "Too much excitement for me already." He winked and strolled down the bar to another customer.

Lilline checked the time stamp. Exactly twenty-four hours ago, to the minute.

That was too perfect not to be intentional. It had to be a time bomb, preconfigured to send at a certain point after a trigger. Like Kissy not resetting its countdown.

She opened the message.

Lilli,

If you are reading this, one of two things has happened. Either I am dead, splayed out with a twisted and tortured look on my face. Cause of death: BOREDOM. Or, what I hoped would never happen has come to pass. If it is the former, make sure there are Dari cakes at my memorial service. FROM MALARDI'S. And give Helene back her diamond brooch in my drawer. (Don't ask – I borrowed it and hadn't gotten around to returning it yet. It's not like she needs it anyway, she sits and stares out the window like the others).

If the latter, then I need you to use your skills to do what must be done. This is important, dear. It supersedes whatever else you are engaged in and must be taken on at once. Otherwise, I, and more importantly you and the rest of the decent people in the galaxy, may not survive or be forced to live under conditions unimaginable.

A bit of poetry for you, dear. Possibly my last attempt to get you to find your own voice.

> *Meter is the measure.*
> *Use your feet, dear.*
> *Ignore the obvious route.*
> *Count on me.*
> *Decide.*
> *Alone.*
> *Trust your instinct.*
> *Listen with one ear.*
> *It's the only one you've got.*
> *What do you hear?*
> *They're all on borrowed time.*
> *But one is out of credit.*
> *And to most, has no credit.*
> *Last lines are never what they seem.*

With love,
-Kissy

p.s. I typed this on one finger, after writing it by hand. I know that I don't need to tell you why.

Lilline scrolled back to the verse. It was terrible. The meter, feet, and even the scansion made her eye's wince. Why would Kissy write her a poem with odd, borderline egregious, errors in form?

The first part of the letter, she understood. It was classic Granny.

Luckily, she wasn't dead. Even if the contents made clear that option was less dangerous. This was a message and not too cryptic. She was telling her what to do.

'*Use your feet.*'

That was easy. She wanted her to go somewhere.

'*Decide. Alone.*' Did she want her to ignore orders?

And the ear. What did the current situation have to do with that incident? Something about loss? Or listening?

This was like Carbrook's games. Why did everyone need to make everything into a puzzle?

Kissy always spoke her mind. So why not now? It had to be out of prudence. Whatever was in that message needed to be written in a way that only she could interpret it.

The station bell chimed, followed by an announcement that her cruiser was boarding. She knocked back the High-Four.

"Gotta run, Lorre. Thanks again." She gathered her things to go.

"Stay warm out there."

"They say in an emergency that bodies close together can keep each other alive, you know," she winked at him.

"Yes... well... um, that makes sense."

"It works well when the conditions call for it." Lilline could see by his face that he was melting right there on the spot.

"I would think so... especially when you're hot." He held up a hand and blushed. "I mean, when the bodies are hot... no, like because of the blood..." Lorre leaned his bulky frame against the bar and shook his head in defeat.

He was adorably vulnerable for a hunk. Someday maybe she'd pounce, but not until she was through making these hops around systems. She wasn't going to risk losing one of the few things to bring her consistent pleasure, even if it meant mere flirting sessions instead of the potential rewards of dating.

If she were honest, it was more than that. Who did Lorre find attractive? Keely the adventure guide? Was that who liked him back? What kind of relationship would be possible between them?

Problems like this were always the thorn in the side of GAM-OPs agents.

"I have to run, Lorre. I'm going to miss my transfer." She waved a hand and made for the portal.

Her mind flipped back to agent mode and the missive.

'Meter is the measure.'

Each stride took her further along through the station.

Meters... not physical distance. It's poetic.

'Use your feet.'

That was poetic, too.

Granny's writing beats.

'Count on me.'

Lilline halted amidst the throngs of passengers. She counted the number of words in each line of verse. Then the syllables. And beats. Her fingers entered the results into the comm.

A jumble of numbers. She dragged a fingertip over them, arranging them in individual sets: words per line, syllables per line, beats per line.

Wait.

She needed one number for it to work.

Her finger swiped the screen, back to Granny's poem. She counted each line, working her way down to the bottom: there were fourteen.

She switched back to the numbers and added the new one at the end. The pattern glowed explicit.

"It's coordinates," she said out loud. And she knew that quadrant. "Highlight sequence," she held her wrist up to her mouth. "Copy. Paste into geo-sat."

"Now boarding: transport shuttle, Flight 4876 to Kitarin system."

"Damn." She scurried towards the gate. Her eyes focused on the small screen on her wrist.

"Come on, what's taking—"

She bumped into a Oltari heading the other way. "Sorry."

The location point popped up on a cosmic grid.

Jackpot.

With a finger on the comm pad, she zoomed in and read the geo-stats.

"I don't believe it," she whispered. There it was, undeniable. An exact location that solved the surface of the poetic puzzle.

Oh, I hear you Granny. My one ear hears you loud and clear.

"*Final boarding call for Flight 4876. Doors closing in two minutes.*"

Lilline looked at the departure board.

'*Trust your instinct.*'

She took Kissy's advice.

TWENTY-ONE

The city of Hikesh lay like a string of jewels on green velvet. Once the sun rose, the curving sliver of land cut into the slopes of Yu-Shek, the looming volcano, would gleam over an endless jungle. What lurked below the plateau in the pre-dawn darkness was alluring and profitable, but also dangerous and deadly.

Hikesh's urban landscape climbed in organized tiers until it butted up against the cliffs leading to Yu-Shek's smoking peak. Colorful one and two-story residential structures and wide boulevards dominated its outer districts. Further back, the sleek spires of corporate buildings rose like the layered teeth of an aquatic predator.

At the city's eastern edge, the landing port was already alive with activity. Traders, negotiators sent to arrange resource extraction contracts, and tourists looking for adventurous getaways from their mundane lifestyles, crowded the entry gates leading into Hesh-9's lone equatorial city.

A secret agent posing as an adventure guide was among the early morning arrivals, one who defied orders to head to Eshi, a decision that she hoped she wouldn't regret.

Wrapped in a Sootari, the blood-red fabric traditionally worn by locals, Lilline strolled to the promenade hugging the outer curve of the city. At an elevation of five thousand meters, Hikesh presided over the jungle from the side of the volcano like an aerie over a majestic dominion.

Her finger pinched the onyx brooch at her shoulder to let out more fabric and loosen the folds at her waist. With the sun breaking the horizon, the humid air and heat would mean sweaty skin until it sank at dusk.

She reached the railing overlooking the jungle and leaned her forearms on the bars. The memory of her conversation with Nave at the gala returned, and with it, the reason she was here.

"People are looking for you," a voice said, words bubbling from a phlegmy throat.

She smiled but didn't turn. "What can I say. I'm desirable."

"You didn't give me much time on this one."

Out of the corner of her eye, Lilline caught the distinct black ringed patterns on green skin she'd hoped to see when she sent the message eight hours earlier. Long, six-knuckled fingers clasped together over the railing next to her, moist skin providing the amphibious human variant with an internal cooling system that kept their cold-blooded body free of the burden of excessive heat.

"Oh, come on, Gribb. You're happy to see me and you know it."

He gurgled phlegm from his throat. Lilline didn't speak Froo, but she got the general translation. Regardless of language, those raised in Hesh culture had a distinct fondness for irony and sarcasm. She'd worked with Gribb on and off for over six cycles, here and there in the galaxy, but only one other time on his homeworld. That mission had bonded them in a way that made it difficult for her to offend, even if she missed the mark on linguistic transcription.

"There's a single-driver AM-PHIB parked in the public slots to your left," Gribb said.

Lilline shifted her gaze down the promenade. A well-outfitted backcountry hybrid driver gleamed in the morning sun alongside commuter vehicles and small tourist shuttles. "Nice," she said and meant it.

"Wait until you get my bill," he gurgled.

"Fully loaded with my equipment list?"

"Everything but the sonic repellent. The supply chain is delayed. Bad weather on Xet. It's the mating season here and everyone on tours out of Hikesh wants protection. Even if they barely edge into the wild."

She hadn't expected Gribb to conjure everything on this short of a turnaround, but going into the bush without beast repellent? Lilline took in the endless jungle running to the horizon. Morning mist lingered in the seams between the rolling mountains. At the farthest observable distance, a vast yellow savannah broke the verdant land-scape. The edge of Lake Niknik shimmered on its far side, falling off the edge of the visible world. Hesh-9 was beautiful but deadly. She'd been called that once too, by someone right before she'd put a knife through their heart after a night of lovemaking. Sometimes the job required strange bedfellows, literally and figuratively.

"I need to go into the Red Zone, Gribb." She focused her gaze on the edge of the lake at the horizon. The coordinates uncovered in Granny's poem lay somewhere beyond it, out of sight. "What am I walking into?"

"It's the unknown. Radioactivity is lower, at least from the last figures I saw. The half-life has cycles to go still. Corporate interests are eyeing it for extraction already. Bastards always play the long game. It's still the wild. The entire area is closed to air traffic, as I'm sure you know since you requested the AM-PHIB." He gurgled. "That's a long ride. And uncomfortable."

"About nine or ten hours?"

"Maybe less, with that model."

"So, no one's been out there?"

"The Red Zone is what Hesh-9 would look like if all of us idiots didn't get in the way." Gribb's spotted green fingers unclasped and his padded hands dangled over the edge. She and Gribb had never made physical contact. As a Froo, he was off limits. Not that she wanted to touch him, or had reason to, but if she did, a component of his skin slime would cause gastrointestinal issues for weeks.

"If you are going to ask me to come with you, the answer is no," Gribb said.

"I knew better than to try."

"You do know what I mean when I say people are looking for you, right?"

Her eyes followed a tour shuttle made of transparent glass, leaving for a day cruise. The skiff descended a few thousand meters and vanished into the mists. "Yes, there's a mark on me. Under one of my aliases... with a high price. Five million."

"That's not what I am referring to."

She didn't respond. *What then?*

"Someone is making noise about an agent," Gribb said. "There's chatter about tracking. GAM-OPs may be compromised."

"Compromised?" It came out as a whisper.

His green hands disappeared from the railing. The crunch of gravel told her he was turning to leave.

"Be careful," the phlegmy voice said. "I'll keep my eyes open here."

"Gribb." That was also a whisper. And a breach. You didn't use names in meetups. "Thank you." Lilline did it because it mattered that he shared the intel.

"Ignition code to the AM-PHIB is in the pocket of your Sootari.

Nice job on the folds, by the way. You remembered after all this time." He gurgled.

She smiled. No one had hands like a Froo.

"And you're welcome."

Lilline kept her eyes on the jungle as the crunching of Gribb's foot pads faded.

TWENTY-TWO

The AM-PHIB's grill cut through the yellow grass as Lilline tore across the savannah. In the late afternoon light, the flaxen plain glowed with orange accents.

She eased her grip on the steering column. For the first time in five hours, she didn't have to concentrate on dodging potholes or slowing to make it through gutted tire trails and muddy stretches of rough roads.

The first two hours out of Hikesh were easy. The central highway sliced into the interior with laser-like precision, laid by the corporations and maintained by profits reaped from the planet's natural resources. Small villages and roadside kiosks offered pitstops and supplies to the many tourist vehicles that went to and fro on short jaunts, taking visitors just far enough so they left the safety of Hikesh without traveling into regions that required them to manifest self-reliance.

By hour three, the villages became less frequent. Then they stopped altogether. The paved road gave way to untended dirt. Routes split off in different directions and became more difficult to negotiate. Her speed was halved for an hour. The next two, it was quartered. She had passed one vehicle the entire trek, an older AM-PHIB with a Froo and a Rasp. She steered off-road to let them pass with the right of way as returning travel. The Rasp had eyed her suspiciously from the passenger seat as their AM-PHIB struggled, its three flex wheels spinning in the mud.

She knew the type. Poachers. In the rear cargo hold, they most likely had pelts and horns that would be off-loaded at an outlying village to enter the illegal market. From there, they'd be exported off-world to reach wealthy clients via an underground network throughout the galaxy.

Another ten minutes across the savannah and she would break the shoreline of Lake Niknik. She'd been waiting for the time zone window to open and for a comfortable enough moment to make the call. This was it.

She reached into her pocket and withdrew the communicator. Pin told her the range of the new gadget was guaranteed to be at least two thousand kilometers from the nearest tower. If that were true, this should be a breeze. The device would ping to Hikesh. From there, it should ricochet off-world and through galactic comm channels to GAM-OPs HQ on Tavi-Prime.

What had the Oltari called it?

"A remora in a network, jumping from signal to signal like going fish to fish."

Lilline flipped it on and programmed the HQ code, steering with one hand. Her eyes followed a herd of Pan-ti moving at their usual slow and steady pace across the grassland. The purple and white striped mammals, with their sleek frames and muscular legs, were the perfect complement to the palette of the grasslands. Gribb had a point, nature knew what it was doing without their interference.

"GAM-OPs HQ," the AI said.

Pin was something, that was for sure. The signal bar showed full green, and the AI operator sounded clear as a bell.

"T8 requesting access to GAM-OPs network, clearance number 098-35 Z."

"One moment, T8."

Her eyes went to the Pan-ti. The herd was making for the shoreline beyond a lone tree that broke the grassland's beautiful monotony. The AM-PHIB would beat them by a few minutes. That was good. Her presence wouldn't disturb them. There was poetry here, of a different kind. Something stirred in her belly but wouldn't rise. The words were close but remained held back, by what she wasn't sure.

"Clearance granted, Agent Renault. Destination?"

"ID 587."

"Transferring now."

The shoreline neared.

"This is Carbrook."

"It's T8."

"T8? I didn't expect—"

"Hold on." Lilline punched the throttle. The speedometer spun around the digital dial. She flung the comm on the seat next to her and used that hand to grab a handle overhead.

"Can you hear me?" she asked over the hum of the engine.

"Yes."

The AM-PHIB broke the shoreline and crashed into the lake. Water shot up and over the windshield. After so many hours of rough road, the smooth glide of the craft easing across the lake's surface felt weightless.

"What's that noise?"

"AM-PHIB." Lilline pushed the handle overhead to the forward position. The whirring sound of wheels retracting added to the vehicle's mechanical music. She reached for the outboard extender and yanked it.

Clunk.

The green light indicated full release. The speedometer switched to a second digital readout indicating knots.

"AM-PHIB? On Eshi?"

Lilline pulled back on the throttle. The lingering water on the half-submerged craft blew off the windshield as the bow rose in the air.

"Not on Eshi." This thing was fast. If she maintained her rate of speed across the lake the crossing time would be cut in half.

"Where are you?"

"Hesh-9."

"Hesh-9? Why?"

"Need to know, Carbrook."

It felt good to get that in there, and even better to know he was sitting back at HQ and not in the seat next to her.

"I need you to do something for me," she said and aimed the AM-PHIB towards the far shoreline.

"But Pin gave you the radiometer, and I arranged for the—"

"Listen. You need to understand that sometimes in the field there are surprises. That means making decisions on the spot. Based on instinct."

Why am I bothering with this? He isn't an agent.

"Is Pin there?" she asked.

Niknik's surface passed like silvery glass. The AM-PHIB cut through the water like a blade fresh off the sharpening stone.

"Yes, why?"

"Put her on."

"I'm her boss," Carbrook said, *"Shouldn't I—"*

"Put her on, Carbrook!"

"Okay, okay."

Lilline checked the navigation board. The digital map showed her halfway across the lake. She'd be to the other side in three minutes.

"This is Pin."

Thank God. Even Pin's voice was a relief.

"Your comm works great."

"Thank you, T8. It sounds clear here, too. I am impressed, considering you're all the way out on Eshi."

Lilline shook her head. "Not on Eshi." *Techies. Next time I'm calling Katar.*

"I need you to do something for me, Pin."

"Okay."

"I'm following a lead on Hesh-9."

Carbrook's voice in the background came through, garbling the line.

"Tell him to shut up. I can't hear you."

"She says be quiet and to listen."

Lilline couldn't hold back a smile. The way Pin said it was priceless. The Oltari had a pair of wings on her.

"I need you to keep me dark for twenty-seven hours. No updates until I contact you again. Can you do that?"

"I guess so. Am I in violation of GAM-OPs protocol if I do?"

This was the delicate part.

"Not exactly. If Lauden contacts you and asks for an update, then you tell him what I requested. And that I ordered you to do it."

She wouldn't risk sharing what Gribb had told her about GAM-OPs agents being compromised, not even over this line. Until she knew more, she wasn't telling that to anyone. Not even Lauden. First, she needed answers. Ones that she hoped to get at the coordinates hidden in Kissy's poem.

"Hoo."

Lilline did a double take at the comm on the passenger seat. "What is it, Pin?"

"That shouldn't be a problem. Lauden isn't even here."

"What do you mean he's not there?" The Gej-ti was always there. That office was like his fishbowl.

"Cazshi said he took the Racer."

Lauden took the Racer?

"Where to?"

It was a useless question. She knew it as the words left her mouth, but they burst out more from shock and confusion than an expectation of an answer.

"I certainly don't know," Pin said. *"Do you, Carbrook?"*

A muffled reply came over the line.

"Neither does Carbrook. All we know is he hasn't been in the office all day. He can do that, right?" Pin asked. *"Just leave and take the Racer?"*

"He can," Lilline said, staring at the passing water out the windshield. "I mean... he's the director." But Lauden wouldn't unless it was vital to GAM-OPs. Even he bowed to the company. He always had.

His words in their last conversation returned. *"I will address that aspect myself."*

"Pin, keep me dark. If Intel or Cazshi want to know where I am or if I've pinged, make up an excuse."

"Well, it wouldn't be my comm not working."

Classic Oltari. Time to re-route.

"I know, that's right. Use the angle of the pole on Eshi. That's good enough."

"But you aren't on Eshi."

Between the two of them, Lilline was ready to explode. This was more difficult than infiltrating enemy territory and getting out alive.

"You're right, Pin. What might cause even your device to be unable to work effectively?"

"Maybe a CME."

"Perfect, so a large solar storm caused a Coronal Mass Ejection somewhere between Tavi-Prime and Eshi, disrupting transmissions. Tell them you expect it to return to normal in about twenty to thirty hours."

"Okay," the Oltari said.

Lilline heard the uneasiness in her voice.

"But Pin, you and Carbrook don't need to say that unless they ask for a reason. Otherwise, 'not yet' is fine if someone asked if I've checked in. I'm out of touch a lot in the field. It's not uncommon."

"Got it."

The shoreline to the Red Zone approached. Lilline throttled

down and the bow dipped, revealing an expanse of jungle. Another hundred meters and she'd break land.

"There's one problem, though," Pin said.

Isn't there always?

Lilline readied to transfer back to wheeled travel over land. She cut the outboard and let the AM-PHIB coast to the shallows. "Give me a second, Pin." She retracted the motor. Her hand went overhead while she watched the depth reading. The light went green at half a meter, and she yanked back the handle. With a whirr, the wheels dropped. She throttled up, driving out of the muck onto dry land.

"Okay, now what is it?"

"We don't have twenty-seven hours. We have twenty-two," Pin said.

Lilline knew the answer but had to ask. "Is it *Freestrike?*"

"Yes. Mavron Nave was just on the feeds. He announced it himself."

"Can you send it to me?"

"I think so. It will take me a few minutes to set it up and then about five minutes to get to you," Pin said.

Lilline programmed Kissy's coordinates on the AM-PHIB's nav system and made her way through the low shrubs, steering left and right to avoid obstacles as she entered the thicker underbrush.

It was late. No more than an hour of light left. The nav system indicated eleven minutes to the coordinates.

"You have ten minutes, Pin. Get on it."

TWENTY-THREE

Lilline halted the AM-PHIB a thousand meters shy of the coordinates and killed the engine. Dusk neared. Out the windshield, the jungle formed pockets of darkness. Dense foliage and razor-edged ferns vanished into the shadows ahead.

Pin's comm pinged.

Right on time.

With a finger, Lilline tapped the micro-screen and started the stream.

A *Freestrike 3* icon introduced the company's announcement. Suspenseful music followed. Nave appeared, standing on the same promenade where they had verbally sparred over a glass of Gondau.

"Citizens of the galaxy, the moment you have all been waiting for arrives." The entrepreneur gestured his arms wide. *"In twenty-four hours, the next version of the most popular entertainment takes us to the next level."*

His emphasis on the final word didn't sit well with her.

"What is a game?" Nave strolled along the promenade. *"Escape? A way to live vicarious lives that we wish were our reality?"*

She marked that line for later.

"Or do these entertainments provide a way to challenge our faculties, to push ourselves to new heights of achievement personally and with our peers?" He nodded as if affirming the answer to his question.

"These are all its purpose." Nave stopped and smiled at the camera. *"Until now."*

Clips of previous versions of *Freestrike* replaced the entrepreneur. A fast-paced collage streamed past, edited to emphasize the game's excitement and action.

"Freestrike is all of these and more." Nave's voice spoke omnisciently over the running image stream. *"And starting at this time tomorrow..."*

The screen went blank. The audio fell silent.

"Two parts of our lives will be separate no longer. A new challenge awaits. One you've all been waiting for but never expected."

Nave's figure re-formed.

Lilline's eyes went wide. He was in the virtual board room. The one she'd infiltrated undercover as the fly. Arms clasped behind his back, the entrepreneur stood at the window overlooking the urban landscape she'd described to Lauden as *too* real.

"The world we dream is at hand. The countdown begins..." Nave turned to face his viewers. The entrepreneur's lips curved into a sinister smile. *"Now."*

Dazzling red beams overtook his image. They danced in circular patterns in front of a backdrop speckled with distant stars. She had to admit, the effect was hypnotizing. Lilline found herself following their rhythm and movement with full attention. Even on a tiny screen inside an AM-PHIB far away from his empire, she lost herself in the magic of the image.

The serpentine beams slowed. One by one, they settled. As they did, the individual parts synthesized to form a single symbol. The same one Pin had conjured through cymatics in Lauden's office.

"Freestrike 4!" Nave's voice echoed as if resonating across the galaxy.

The stream ended.

Lilline noted the timestamp in the corner of the screen. Just under three hours ago. She set the comm on a countdown and stared as the seconds ticked away. Had diverting been a mistake? Did Nave bait her away with Kissy so she could not stop him in time? If she was on Eshi, instead of Hesh-9, would she have already discovered the source of his plans and be on the road to halting his madness?

There was nothing for it. She had to trust her instinct. It'd never let her down in the field before.

Except...

Her eyes shifted to the jungle out the AM-PHIB's windshield.

Hesh-9 had been the one place where she'd been bested.

"Not this time," she said and geared up. Granny wouldn't steer her wrong. Kissy and Lauden were involved in this – there was something they weren't telling her. These coordinates were her first objective, whether they were the location of Kissy, if she was being held somewhere, or if they had something to do with Nave's plans.

She kicked the door open and got out.

A hand reached for Pin's radiometer. Signals flew in all directions, the readings an illegible mess. Radiation was the one steady reading: low but outside safe levels. That wasn't a problem. She didn't intend to stay long, and she'd downed an iodine tablet from the AM-PHB's First-aid kit.

The small red dot on her wrist comm pulsed. Her nav-system indicated a course forward and to the west. Other than the usual animal noises, her ears picked up the faint sound of falling water.

Hesh-9's jungle loomed as an ominous sight. Darkness in the wilds would make anyone uneasy. Add to that no sonic-repellent and you'd send everyone on a fast-track back to Hikesh. All except a GAM-OPs agent. Where others walk away, they walk in. Lilline started off on foot through the rainforest.

Bird calls diminished. Unknown sounds replaced those of daylight hours both near and far. Lilline drew the blaster from her hip. Gribb came through with the model she requested. It had an IR beam, but she didn't want to use it. Not yet. There was still enough light for her eyes and it would do more harm than good, screaming out to predators that something made of flesh and blood walked alone in the Red Zone.

For over two hundred cycles, a five-thousand-kilometer grid of jungle had been rendered uninhabitable. A nuclear waste carrier heading to Hikesh from an energy facility on the far side of the planet crashed, rendering the area off-limits until radiation half-life reached safe levels. The Red Zone, as it was dubbed, had been a zero-entry point ever since. Rumors of mutations to whatever survived the bloom added disturbing flavor to popular myths and folklore about the jungle.

The flashing dot on her wrist comm pulsed. A hundred meters and she'd be there. She waded through tall ferns and navigated around massive Kee-i trees that towered to the canopy fifty meters above. Long mossy leaves dangled amidst creeper vines, their elegant purple and red flowers decorating the empty spaces between branches in the understory. Lilline knew from past ops that their scent killed if inhaled close to the petals.

Hesh-9 was a unique planet.

Beautiful but deadly.

That was a poem title if she ever heard one. Maybe even the title of a collection.

Her wrist comm vibrated. Twenty meters ahead lay the coordinate point. Somewhere off to her right, not more than a hundred meters, the steady rush of pounding water on rocks filled the growing silence.

Lilline kept her blaster up and aimed forward. Her free hand wrapped around a razor fern and shifted the leaf aside. She peered ahead.

Low grasses ran at knee height in a clearing that broke the verdant surroundings. Nothing else grew in the roughly hundred-by-hundred-meter square plot. She stepped out from the underbrush and crept to the spot indicating the coordinate point. Not surprisingly, it lay dead center in the field.

"It's empty," she whispered.

Kee-i limbs extended over the grassy boundary, but at ground level nothing intruded over a purposeful threshold.

This isn't natural.

Her eyes made out nothing in the near darkness and yet, the hairs on the back of her neck rose.

Someone, or something else is here. I can feel it.

In the crepuscular light, the twinkle of stars dappled a purple and pink sky. Was she looking towards the Core? Or outward to where Eshi, or even Frebu, rotated around a remote star? Distances could be so deceiving in a world with faster than light travel, especially in her profession. It was easier getting from star system to star system than making your way eight hours over a planet's terrain. Using your feet had become—

The poem.

Lilline scrolled through the comm and pulled up Kissy's verse. A growl echoed from the jungle. She spun; blaster aimed. It had the rhythm of a big cat but the deepness of something larger.

She ducked down in the grass to shield the light of the wrist comm.

> *Meter is the measure.*
> *Use your feet, dear.*
> *Ignore the obvious route.*
> *Count on me.*
> *Decide.*
> *Alone.*
> *Trust your instinct.*

She had checked off all of these getting here.

> *Listen with one ear.*
> *It's the only one you've got.*
> *What do you hear?*

That was Hesh-9, at least the reference to her anatomy and history with the Bukki tiger.

Kissy, what are you telling me?

Another growl. Small shrubs and ferns cracked and rustled in the darkness as something pushed its way closer.

Think.

The clearing was here for a reason. She bent her head back and took in the growing night sky.

A landing area? But how did it not grow back after so many cycles? Unless...

That was it. Nothing with large roots grew here.

With a mighty roar, the beast burst through the brush. Lilline caught sight of a massive shadowy form bounding toward her.

'Listen with one ear'.

She dropped down in the grass. Soft stems pushed against her cheek as she put her ear to the ground.

Yes!

Pounding feet rushed through the grasses.

She yanked out a clump of grass. It came out with ease. Her eyes went from the approaching shadow to the exposed dirt.

A hatch.

TWENTY-FOUR

Lilline slammed the steel door shut. Claws scraped against metal, echoing down the stairwell. She thanked whoever built the thick, multi-layered spin seal lock. Nothing would get through it without serious hardware or explosives and by the size and look of its thickness she wasn't sure that would be enough.

The place had the specs of a bunker. Walls of concrete, with venting and cooling tubing, descended into a dim abyss. No signage appeared anywhere in the red light cast from sconces running along the ceiling.

Other than the humming of the ventilation system when she put her ear to ground above, the interior was silent. She checked her blaster.

Time to get it on.

Would she find Granny or something dangerous below? Whichever, she needed to be fast. Time was running out.

Back and forth down alternating sets of steps, she made her way into the depths. At the top of the fifth set of stairs, she paused. The descent ended and the space widened.

Bent low, she creeped down to the bottom. The tubing along the walls pinged and hissed with pressure adjustments. She gazed ahead, blaster at eye level in a two-hand grip.

Capsules, in two parallel rows with a wide central aisle, ran into the distance. She guessed their number to be at least fifty, maybe more. Wires snaked from each pod to the walls. Lilline scanned left to right, up and down, blaster and eyes moving in unison, for any sign of another presence. If anything popped up from behind, or inside, the capsules her muscles were on standby to mark and fire.

Hiss!

She swung around, finger squeezed on the trigger. A rush of steam discharged from a vent down the chamber.

Kissy, where did you bring me?

With silent footsteps, she crept down the central aisle to a small control station. On the simple pedestal, buttons and switches blinked. Needles hovered inside dials. She reached for the illumination icon on its side and switched it on.

Cold white lights flickered and came to life.

It was a crypt. These were coffins.

"What is this place?" she said.

"Knowledge." The voice echoed through the chamber.

In the darkness ahead, beyond the range of the ceiling lights, came the familiar click of a lighter. The tall and gaunt figure of a Gej-ti strode into the light, followed by a trailing stream of smoke.

"Lauden? What are you doing here?" Lilline kept the blaster aimed at him.

"Saving the galaxy. A second time." He took a pull on his pipe. The orange embers of Queen Yaz Flake glowed. "You were supposed to go to Eshi," he said, starting forward. "You defied my orders."

"Kissy's gone missing. A time-bombed message triggered... in code. It contained a poem with these coordinates."

He shook his head. "Why am I not surprised?" The Gej-ti inhaled and let the smoke flutter out of his gills. "Still as clever and cunning as ever."

"I'm not following, sir."

"Put that thing away," Lauden gestured to her blaster with his pipe and continued approaching. "So, she wanted you to know."

"About what?"

"Our secret weapon."

Lilline looked at the capsules. "Who are they?"

"They are history unchained."

"Kissy isn't here?"

"Certainly not. She diverted you because she knew it was time to wake the one who can stop this thing."

Lilline lowered her weapon.

"Nave has her, clearly," Lauden said. "My guess is he plans on using her to lure you to him. If he managed to locate your grandmother, then he knows you are a relation."

"I think he may know more than that," Lilline said and stepped around from the pedestal. The nearest capsule caught her eye. She read the nameplate at its head.

Tuh-met Akketo: Cyro date: 4790. Voluntary.

Akketo? The mathematician who broke the mionumeric code?

"What makes you say that?" Lauden's earnest tone snapped her back from the distraction and confusion.

"A contact I trust said there's talk of an agent in the stream chatter. He thought GAM-OPs was compromised and warned me."

"Your contact is correct." His gills blew out smoke. "We think it is 2112."

"The hacker?"

Lauden nodded. "Whatever Nave intended has now taken a more personal turn."

"Kissy was involved with his parents?"

Lauden laughed. "That is a polite way of putting it."

She assassinated them.

"And this is his form of retribution?" Lilline asked.

"It's much more than that, I fear."

"The egregore," she whispered.

Lauden motioned for her to follow him down the aisle.

"For over five hundred cycles galactic citizens with specialized knowledge have sacrificed themselves for the future. Most made a choice and came along willingly, others were coerced. Some taken against their will."

Something stirred in her belly. She didn't like where this was going.

"You recognize many of these names, I am sure." Lauden gestured at the plates in front of the capsules. She did. Well-known intellectuals, philosophers, inventors, military leaders... Kreelis, Rasps, human variants, Oltari... it was like a history book of the last five hundred cycles molded into a mausoleum.

Lilline's biographical knowledge of the individuals she passed struggled to raise a pattern. Deaths, either natural or accidental. Mysterious disappearances. It ran the gamut.

"We are matching the intelligent mind to its purpose, its chosen destination in history. Like arranging a duel, a battle between a warrior trained to fight a foe they might otherwise never confront because of random chance and historical fate. Now, we make that encounter happen, and with the result that we protect, save, and maintain peace and order in the galaxy."

"This... they're preserved?"

Lauden nodded. "With a secret technology. Suspended in time until history calls them back."

"But some of these... are you telling me they were taken without their consent?"

Lauden stopped and faced her. "For the greater good."

"But that's no better than murder."

"How many individuals have you 'eliminated' to save the collective?"

The director's question wouldn't settle. "Yes, but—"

"These participants are not dead. They are suspended until they are needed."

"And if that day never comes?"

"Let us hope, in most cases, it does not. But think of the satisfaction for those who will return. Scientists and theorists who can one day awaken into a future capable of carrying out their ideas to purpose. The struggle to fulfill a dream may one day come for some. As for the others," he raised an eyebrow, "they are on retainer."

Lilline took in the landscape of capsules. *How is this possible?*

Lauden gestured to the capsule next to her. "The newest addition. A half-cycle ago."

Her eyes went wide.

Den-shi: Cyro date: 5011 Voluntary.

"Words can be a most powerful weapon," Lauden said, puffing on his pipe.

"They disappeared," she said.

"Yes, Den-shi wanted allure and mystery to surround their voluntary exit." Lauden laughed and shook his head. "Poets. Your grandmother—"

"She knows?"

"Of course, she knows."

> *They're all on borrowed time.*
> *But one is out of credit.*
> *And to most, has no credit.*

That meant Kissy was directing her to a particular capsule.

"How does this point back to my grandmother and Nave's parents?"

"He holds her, and GAM-OPs, responsible." Lauden's face shifted.

"For what?"

"His mother and father were developing a dangerous weapon. We knew they were growing into powerful influencers in a dubious organization. Something needed to be done."

"It was your call," Lilline said, putting it together. "To eliminate them."

Lauden smoked in silence.

"And Kissy carried it out."

"Are you surprised? This is what we do."

"And Nave knew how? He would have been a child at the time?"

"He was a teenager, already at the Academy because of his brilliance. We'd considered recruiting him for GAM-OPs. Started the vetting process as we often do with those who demonstrate prodigious abilities. He was far enough along at the time to put it together, I am sure."

Lilline felt it coming. She shook her head as if to deny it.

"You ordered him to be—"

"I did not. Your grandmother and I debated whether we needed to close the loop."

Granny? Was she that ruthless?

"Don't be too quick to judge, T8. I am sure you've chosen similar courses of action in the field."

"But Nave wasn't old enough to—"

"It doesn't matter," Lauden held up a hand. "I forbade it. We both agreed to turn our backs and hope for the best. His temper was an issue even before the problems with his family arose. Whether or not it was a mistake to look the other way is a debate for another time." He walked over to another nearby capsule. "What matters now is that we do what we can to stop a madman."

Mad? For certain. But at whose bidding? Fault and blame swirled in a vortex of misshapen morality.

"He must have made Kissy somehow. After my visit on Beisho."

"I told you to rest your leg, but you decided to make inquiries. Do not put too much of this on yourself, T8."

She almost faltered. Lauden had never eased away from scolding her for stepping out of line.

"We have all been hiding in the shadows," he said and pushed a series of buttons on the capsule. "And now, it is time to bring one back into the light." His black eyes looked to hers in earnest. "I started the re-entry process a few hours ago."

Lilline read the nameplate on the capsule.

'Inti Two Star: Cyro date: 4981. Voluntary.'

That was three ten-cycles ago, the same time as when Nave's parents were eliminated. This was the one Kissy wanted her to reach in the poem's instructions. At least it was a voluntary cyrosleep. The last thing she needed was an individual waking to learn they'd been forcibly admitted to the 'program'.

But one is out of credit.
And to most, has no credit.

"It shouldn't be long," Lauden said and tamped his pipe with a tool from his pocket. "Just a few more minutes."

"How did you get here?" It came out as a whisper. Her mind was racing, chasing after the history of the crypt and everything related to it. She didn't know this person's name, the one in the capsule.

"Racer." Lauden's face was as hard as milky quartz. "I assume you didn't bump into it?"

Lilline cocked her head, confused.

"You came through the hatch. I set it down in the clearing. The cloaking feature duped even you in the light of dusk."

That was the 'felt' presence.

"The Racer exists for this purpose first as a GAM-OPs asset. Both for its ability to rest unseen and for its advanced frequency jamming to enter atmospheres like Hesh-9 undetected. The previous ship we used was good, but not nearly this good."

The ultimate investment. With a return beyond monetary value should the unthinkable happen. And it just had.

"I let you take it less for its impressive status symbol and more to make sure you'd flown it in case we ended up here." Lauden looked around the crypt. The nerves and muscle fibers in his neck twisted as he craned his head back and forth. "And we have."

"But the clearing was undisturbed? How did you get in?"

"There's an entrance behind a nearby waterfall. In a rocky

cavern. It's invisible to the naked eye and requires knowledge to find. And a code to open."

"How many know about this?"

"Always two," Lauden said. "Until now."

What does that mean?

"Because of the circumstances at play, and the uncertainty of your grandmother's safety, I am giving the code to you."

"To me?"

"You seem surprised?" The Gej-ti raised an eyebrow that wrinkled the translucent skin on his forehead.

Lilline felt the weight of the galaxy that she carried as an agent shift. On an op, she bore it briefly in crisis. Her job threw the pressure onto her, and she got it off as quickly as possible by succeeding with the mission. This? It pushed down on her already. The haunting persistence of responsibility it brought was—

"Changes things, doesn't it?" Lauden drew on the pipe and exhaled. "Perspectives, for one."

In the space of mere seconds, even the Gej-ti appeared different. What he represented, how he managed it, and his choices and demeanor all made sense.

"This facility has been moved several times. The accident that created the Red Zone on this planet was manufactured to provide a location and time to extend our operation. Radioactivity is a strong deterrent, even for poachers and other suspicious and prying eyes."

A gentle bell chimed. Lilline turned to the capsule.

The green light blinked, and a message appeared on the small screen:

Cycle complete. The capsule is safe to open. Occupant stable and conscious.

TWENTY-FIVE

"Who is this?" An elderly Rasp lay prone in the opened capsule, its single eye focused on Lilline.

"That's T8," Lauden said.

Lilline nodded in greeting.

The Rasp's eye narrowed. "Eight is a good number. Not arrogant, like ten. But more modest than nine, which veils its self-importance."

"I've always liked it," Lilline said. This was a little too deep for her, but so long as he helped them stop the egregore she didn't mind eccentricity.

"Better than seven," he said. "That one teeters unsure if it is part of the premiere or the mediocre."

Lilline turned to Lauden who raised an eyebrow.

"T numbers are assigned arbitrarily, from one to ten," the director said, "as they open up."

"Nevertheless," the Rasp said.

"I'm less interested in symbolism and more in sound," Lilline said. "I've always felt that single syllable numbers work better in T-designations." She shrugged.

The Rasp smiled. He rolled his small head towards the director. "She'll do."

What does that mean?

"I imagine you haven't awoken me for a dinner invitation," the Rasp said.

"Unfortunately not." Lauden reached out one of his translucent, milky hands and helped the Rasp raise its upper body inside the capsule. "We have work to do, Inti. Of a kind that only you are capable of guiding. T8 will be your feet on the ground." Lauden's other hand with the pipe pointed in her direction. "I, as usual, will be working from the shadows, providing whatever you both need."

"It is as we feared then?" Inti nodded to the edge of the capsule by his feet and Lauden pushed a control. A small set of stairs retracted.

The Rasp extended a thin, clay-skinned hand in Lilline's direction. "Give me a hand, T8, if you would."

She clasped it. He slid down the length of the tube and stepped down to the floor. The pads of his fingers felt like desert rocks rubbed with gritty sandpaper. Inti let go and re-arranged his white robe. The loose-fitting cloth fell from a tight collar around his serpentine neck down and over his stout torso to above the ankles of his three-toed feet.

Lauden reached into a compartment on the module and handed the Rasp a pair of sandals.

"So, Agent Number Eight—"

"Renault," Lauden said, interrupting. "Lilline Renault."

So, Inti was privy to the intimate secrets of GAM-OPs and their agents. He hadn't addressed Lauden by name. Not yet at least.

"Agent Renault," Inti said. "Do you know what a cryptoxenologist is?"

She didn't know the specific term but took her best guess. "Someone who studies unsubstantiated life forms beyond those of the known galaxy, I imagine. But using methods and evidence or making claims that others in established disciplines of science would consider..." she paused and looked at Lauden. He gave her nothing. "Suspect."

The Rasp's single eye blinked. "'Established disciplines'," he repeated, nodding. "Well put, Agent Renault." Inti turned to the director. The vocal flap along his thin throat fluttered. "Well Asher, if what I think is happening, it may be time to remove the 'crypto' from my specialization. That is if we can do what needs to be done."

"And in time," the Gej-ti added.

These two were on a first-name basis. Her anxiety about the Rasp knowing her real name eased, but the intimacy established a new layer of mystery. *Does Inti know Granny as well?*

"What is it? If I may ask?" Lilline said.

"That's something Inti should explain on the Racer," Lauden said, closing the capsule. "We should get out of here while we—"

Lilline's wrist pinged an alert.

"What is it?" Lauden asked.

A message ran over the mini-screen. It was from Gribb.

Five AM-PHIBs heavily armed heading your way on a transport. Guns for hire. Whoever set it up has connections and credits to burn. Bypassed airspace regulations. Left thirty minutes ago. My contact says the drop point is the south shore of Lake Niknik.

"We have company," Lilline said. "Five AM-PHIBs. My guess is they're dropping into the lake any minute."

"Come on Inti. This is going to be a bit rough on you, but we have no choice," Lauden said.

"Sir, I can go ahead of you," Lilline said, "and get to the lake on the AM-PHIB. That should buy you the time you need to get Inti to the ship. I took an iodine capsule when I departed Hikesh so I'm good for—"

"Negative, T8," Lauden said as they made their way to the stairs.

"It's a bunch of poachers for hire," she said, pushing back. "I can lead them off and you can pick me up when I swing back or after I take them out."

"I said, negative," the Gej-ti helped Inti up the steps.

Lilline took the stairs two at a time ahead of them. She turned at the top of the first landing.

Lauden halted a few steps from her. The director's face had a look she hadn't seen before. What was it?

Pathos.

"T8, help Inti the rest of the way." Lauden left the Rasp and climbed to the top. "Get him in the Racer and get off the ground," he said, dropping a ship remote start in her hand and hustling to the next set of steps. "Pick me up after I lead them away and buy you time."

"But the radiation—"

"That's an order!" he yelled back. "And cover the hatch before you take off."

Lilline took Inti's arm and helped him to the top. She and the Rasp continued up the four remaining flights. The squeaking of the hatch opening, and thudding shut, echoed down the steps as Lauden exited the secret facility.

"Come on, Inti," Lilline said, a hand on the Rasp's frail arm. "We need to hurry."

"You are like your grandmother," he said, between gasps of breath. "Don't like not being in the limelight."

"You knew Kissy?"

"I know many things that are not spoken," the Rasp said.

They reached the corridor leading to the hatch. Lilline ran ahead and spun it open. She climbed up and out. In the pitch of night, Lauden was nowhere to be seen. She leaned back in and pulled Inti up and through.

"Hesh-9," he said, gazing around in the darkness. "That makes sense." The Rasp wiped off his robe and twisted his neck in every direction. "Please tell me the ship isn't far."

"You may know many things that aren't spoken, Inti. But some things hide in plain sight." Lilline activated the de-cloaking system. The outline of the Racer manifested out of the backdrop of the dark jungle.

She felt the Rasp's three fingers clasp her wrist. "There's something else out there."

"Come on." No sooner had she turned and started towards the ship than a familiar shape emerged into the clearing.

This time it didn't growl. It roared.

Lilline knew the sound: Bukki tiger. Something wasn't right, though. The volume and tone were deeper and more disturbed. And the scale was wrong. This thing was the size of a small transport pod. Maybe the legends about radioactivity and mutations weren't so far-fetched.

A hundred meters ahead, the ship cut a faint shadow against the darkness behind it.

"Inti, make for the ramp to aft. It will illuminate and auto-open when you are within two meters. Get inside. I'll be right behind you."

The Rasp shuffled off in the direction of the Racer.

Lilline drew her blaster and pulled out two flash charges. *Damn the high season and all the tourists.* Sonic-repellent would make this easy. One sounding shot in the beast's path and it would take off and flee. It didn't matter if it was a horrid mutant or a standard beast. Now she was going to have to try and deceive this thing and buy enough time to get to the ship.

The hum of an AM-PHIB heading away to engage the poachers-turned-mercenaries for hire echoed in the distance.

Back in the field. Let's hope Lauden still has it.

She tossed a flash charge at the looming shadow and shielded her eyes with an elbow. The beast screamed with a tremendous roar. Peeking through the crease of her arm, she caught sight of it rearing up in the meadow, stunned by the blinding light. She bolted for the ship.

Green and red ramp orbs broke the night's pitch. Inti had reached the Racer.

Another roar, closer. The thudding of feet trampling behind her filled her ears. The hair on her neck rose.

So did the words.

Beast bounding.
Fear flash.
Gore.
Dripping anger.
Drooling.
Roar. Rage. Night.
Fight or flight?

She'd never used such a brute syntax before and she hoped not to ever again. The Carka cut-up style left the lines disfigured, as if the verses were slashed with a knife. The vulgar form fit what she assumed was a mutant and grotesque creature chasing her.

Fifty meters at most to the ramp and she would be safe in the Racer.

Maybe it will be easy this time. I could—

Her body left the ground and a searing pain ripped through her side. She landed fifteen meters away, rolled up with her blaster ready to fire. A finger switched on the IR beam.

The beast turned to face her. A half Bukki, half amphibian monstrosity rose and towered over her. Through the beam's green light, five cat eyes, two jaws complete with fangs, four good legs and one-half leg sprouting out of its spine shone, held together by a slimy frog-like torso. It was a radioactive horror, at least triple the standard size Bukki.

The creature roared and stood on its hind legs.

A tiny body with a long neck and small head appeared and blocked the IR beam shining at the beast.

Inti.

Lilline felt warm liquid trickling down her side. How bad the wound from the claw swipe was, she didn't know.

What is he doing? Before she could shout, the Rasp raised a hand. Lilline's eyes went wide.

Inti stepped forward. The creature, still rearing up on its hind legs, dropped to all fours. The Rasp touched it between its two snouts.

The beast snarled and flinched. Inti kept his hand out. The Bukki mutant purred.

The Rasp released his hand and the monster strolled away.

"Inti!" Lilline ran forward, blaster targeting the beast as it lumbered into the jungle, crushing and breaking brush and small bushes. "Are you alright?"

Inti turned his fist-size head, without rotating his body. His eye blinked. "Yes. We should go." He started back towards the Racer.

"What did you do?" Lilline asked, holding her side and catching up.

"Thought. Expressed as feeling."

***

"Is that a gift, what you did with the Bukki?" Lilline wrapped her side with tape from the ship's med kit.

"It is another way of speaking," Inti said. "A language beyond words that is all around us."

She was half-listening. The wound was bad, but with the quick-burn to cauterize it and the hyperheal antibiotic she would be almost one hundred percent in twenty-four hours.

"Well, I'm impressed." She tied off the tape, wincing.

"If you are anything like your grandmother, I imagine you are more than that."

Lilline tossed the tape aside and barreled up the central aisle to the cockpit. "What does that mean?" She reached overhead, activated the engines, and lifted the Racer off the ground.

"It means—"

"Damn," she said, interrupting him. "The hatch. We have to go back."

Inti was next to her, peering out the cockpit.

"I have to cover it up." Lauden couldn't hold off five AM-PHIBs for long, and he was out there in the radioactivity, but this usurped his safety. It usurped almost everything, considering what rested underground.

"I agree," Inti said. "It must be done."

Lilline lowered the ship. She bolted aft, snatched up a flash charge and hustled down the ramp and out into the clearing. Her hands cut the air like blades as she tore through the meadow to the hatch. In under a minute, she had fresh dirt around the exposed area and clumps of grass transplanted. So long as it rained soon it would re-grow.

No Bukki mutant. *Finally, a break.* She turned to start back but froze.

The unmistakable hum of an AM-PHIB's engine broke the silence. She marked its direction to the south, from the lake.

Is that Lauden?

She snaked her way through the grass towards the Racer. A set of headlights crashed through the pitch foliage.

Bam! Bam! Bam!

Shots whizzed by her head. She rolled, unlatching the flash charge from her belt in one swift motion, and threw it as she came back up. It arced toward the AM-PHIB making straight for her. Her blaster was out and unloading rounds before the charge landed. In red light from the bolts, she made out the large head of The Preacher, inside a hazard suit, leaning out the passenger window, weapon aimed.

Lilline took off toward the Racer, marking the ship's position with her mental memory. She closed her eyes to avoid the charge's blinding flash. The Kreeli's shriek was so loud it came through their hazmat suit. The crunching thuds of the AM-PHIB crashing and rolling followed.

A familiar roar boomed from the nearby jungle.

Lilline opened her eyes but didn't look back. "Alright!" she yelled and ran up the ramp and through the aisle to the cockpit.

The Bukki mutant's howl was cut short as the ramp sealed

behind her. The Preacher was in for a horrifying surprise if she survived the vehicle's crash.

"Here we go." Lilline yanked the steering column, lifting the ship off the ground. "Let's see what this thing's got." The Racer soared skyward. Out of the cockpit, an orange glow reflected on the jungle edging the clearing from the flaming wreckage of the AM-PHIB. Lilline turned on the exterior lights and tipped the bow. The Preacher pulled herself from the crumpled AM-PHIB. The Bukki mutant approached and reared up on its hind legs, blocking her view of the vehicle.

"Time to meet your maker," she said and reached for the firing button. The familiar sandpaper grip of the Rasp stopped her from reaching it.

"No. Not if it will kill them both."

Lilline followed Inti's free hand that pointed at the Bukki. She thought of the Ice Ranger on Frebu. Her hand softened and the Rasp released his grip.

Lilline hit the throttle. The Racer shot forward towards the lake. She banked the ship to port and caught sight of the Bukki tearing the AM-PHIB's driver in two with its double mouth. The Preacher, limping away, stopped and gazed up.

The Kreeli screamed something inside the suit and threw both hands up in the air.

"Have fun trying to get back to Hikesh," Lilline said and made for the lake. "Hit that switch, would you?" Lilline gestured with her chin at a green button over the passenger seat. Inti activated it. A screen descended over the cockpit window. The view outside displayed a range of heat signatures as they soared over the jungle – small life forms, most likely Tenki monkeys, clustered in trees for the night. Other beasts walked or ran under the foliage.

"A language beyond words that is all around us," Inti said.

"Present but unseen." Lilline smiled.

The clean edge of Lake Niknik's shoreline ran north to south, cutting a distinct line in the landscape.

"I've got him," she said. "He's leading them offshore."

She pointed at five blips, four in a V-formation trailing a fifth that she assumed was Lauden making a run for it. *Good thing Gribb scored the top-of-the-line model.* The standard AM-PHIB outboards didn't have the engine capacity to keep up.

They were, however, able to reach him with their weapons. Blaster fire rained across the lake. Lauden's evasive pattern rang familiar in her eyes.

GAM-OPs agent, indeed.

It was helping, but not enough. There must be a range of species in the AM-PHIBs because some were doing better than others at firing on him.

"May I?" she asked. It was more for rhetorical amusement than permission. The Rasp nodded.

Lilline sent off two Serpent missiles. They shot down ahead of the Racer's bow, showering white sparks through the night sky. In seconds, the projectiles reached the lake and two of the four AM-PHIBs exploded in bursts of orange.

"Can we get him?" Inti asked.

"We can if you can hold us steady."

"I have flown before."

Lilline activated the Spiral-Tak nose cannon and sent a blazing line of fire between Lauden and his pursuers. The two AM-PHIBS veered away.

She dove the Racer down to fifty meters, aiming them on a direct line between the two pursuers to Lauden.

"You see the pattern he's using?" she asked. "It's numerical if you prefer to—"

"I understand it, go," Inti said and gestured for her to rise.

"Keep us aimed at him!" She made for the starboard side of the ship and dropped through a down portal tube to the sub-level. "Lower us to thirty meters when you get close and hold there!" she yelled up the hole and activated the winch and cable.

This was going to be fun, so long as she didn't get shot.

Lilline pushed a button and the cargo ramp opened aft. The glass surface of Lake Niknik reflected white light cast from Hesh-9's single moon. She strapped into the belt system and hooked the carabiner to her waist. Step by step she walked down the open ramp.

"Leap of faith," she said, thinking of The Preacher who she hoped was being gnawed to death by a hungry Bukki monstrosity, and leaped out.

The winch did its job. Arms wide, she fell at a steady rate. The cool night air of Hesh-9 rushed over her face. Through the goggles, she made out Lauden's AM-PHIB dead ahead.

Bam!

A shot nicked her heel. She opened up on the AM-PHIB to her right with her blaster, sending it steering away.

Lauden stopped swerving. He got the message.

The Racer increased speed. Inti was bringing them up to get him.

Bam! Bam!

More fire came up and whizzed past her.

Lilline fired back. *Bastards are getting in my way!*

Lauden appeared on the bow of the AM-PHIB, struggling to hang on at high speed. He hurled something off the side to port. A plume of sparks blew up on the surface of the water in front of an AM-PHIB. It ran right into it and flew up and through the air, exploding.

Whoosh!

The fiery mass passed by Lilline no more than a few meters away.

He's crazy!

Inti barreled the Racer forward. Lilline swung back and up from the momentum. She fired off more rounds at the one remaining AM-PHIB. Lauden stood and balanced on the bow.

She wasn't low enough.

"Lower!" she screamed. Her voice was lost in the wind. "Lower me down, Inti!"

Ten meters. Five meters. Three...

Lauden jumped.

She felt his hands grip her ankles. Lilline twisted her hips. They swung around. She fired at the remaining AM-PHIB. It exploded in a burst of red and orange.

The Racer climbed over Lake Niknik. She activated the winch and felt the tug as the system kicked on to pull them up.

"Miss the field, sir?" she shouted.

"I much prefer my office and a pipe," Lauden yelled through the rushing air.

"What now? The agency's been compromised and we've got twenty hours until *Freestrike*."

"Now you learn why we put Inti on ice," the director shouted.

TWENTY-SIX

Paragon Galactic, Inc. | District: Executive Estate | Star System: Sesstari, Galactic Core.

"Enjoying your accommodations on my orbital, Ms. Larkin?" Nave smirked as his fingertips worked the fishing thimbles. He didn't turn around from the view of the stream. "Or should I say, Agent Kissy Renault?"

No response.

"Retired, of course," he added.

He sent the lure downriver to where he intended to drop it underwater. The Cronkhead would be lurking in its morning spot underneath the big rock.

"I hope you are enjoying the Gondau I left for you in your quarters."

"I prefer the pre-Roncheau."

His fingers halted.

"Oh, so you didn't know?" the voice said behind him. "I assumed you'd refilled the bottles yourself. Your knowledge of wine is slipping, Mavron."

He lowered a hand and balled it into a fist.

"I see your temper is still an issue. Such a shame. You could have been on our side if you'd learned to control it."

Blood boiled in his veins.

"Let me guess, you outbid all the others for that 'lost case' that showed up on the market? Even deals like that reach the ears of little old ladies on insignificant moons, especially the one that has the best cellar in the galaxy."

I will have that sommelier drowned in the stuff.

"And no, I am not enjoying the accommodations," she said. "They express an excess of... how should I put it?"

He waited.

"Control."

"You made it easy, choosing to come along willingly." He ignored her follow-up jabs. "Thank you for your professionalism."

"I make my own decisions," she said. "Always have."

"Well, it wasn't like you had much choice since you care so deeply for others in your organization. Especially your loved ones."

"As I said, I make my own decisions."

"You will have to make a difficult one soon, Ms. Renault." He waved a hand to his guards without turning. "Take her away."

The former agent wouldn't risk fighting back or trying to escape. Not with what was on the table. The sweetness of control was so much more delicious than brute strength or martial skill. It was like an invisible force that bound an opponent with nothing more than words. Put the right ones in their mind and they buckled. That was something the rest of the galaxy would soon learn, and he would have vengeance and satisfaction.

It is all coming together. Finally. He plunged the lure underneath the water.

"Sir."

Nave kept his attention fixed on the Cronkhead in the holo hovering at eye level. *Why won't you take the damn lure?* He was doing everything according to the revised formula. This was going to be the one that would crack the code. The fish would have no choice but to submit to temptation.

Nave moved his fingers over and over, following the pattern. *Come on.*

"Sir?"

"What is it, Ke?"

"The Preacher is on the line. From Hesh-9."

He turned. Ke held up a small mini-comm the size of an apple. Bright morning light dimmed as a cargo freighter passed over the meadow. Like a brief solar eclipse, night swept over the orbital. Daylight returned as the ship moved out of the rays of the nearby star and on to its destination at the station's spoke.

"Yes, yes. Bring it over." He indicated for the Rasp to approach with a nod of his head and went back to fishing.

"Linking now," Ke said, stopping next to him and holding up the comm.

"This is where the damned go to die." The Preacher's deep voice carried the tone of a sermon. "Ye verily do I walk—"

"Cut the rhetoric and report," Nave said. Religious zeal and performative speechmaking had their place in company marketing and their secret Order, but not here.

"I was unable to—"

"You what?" Nave swung around. The Kreeli's eyes and fore-head, visible through a transparent visor on a hazmat suit, filled the screen in Ke's outstretched palm.

"The target got away."

"She's a GAM-OPs agent, not a superhero. Five of you couldn't catch her?"

"There were others aiding her." The Preacher's massive fist clenched in front of the cam. "Heathens!"

"What are you talking about?"

"Larkin was not alone."

"Her name is Renault you fool! Agent Renault." Nave swung to face the stream. He focused on the floating holo and went back to working the thimbles. "Why won't you strike! Stupid fish!"

"There was also a beast... from the jungle," The Preacher said.

Nave turned and ripped the mobile-screen out of Ke's hand.

"Now you listen to me." The words came out through gritted teeth. He wanted to reach through the device and wring the Kreeli's neck. "On second thought, you are useless!" Nave tossed the mini-comm in the grass.

Chest heaving, he paced in a small circle. "Idiots! All of you!"

"Sir, your temper."

Nave fumed but his assistant's words got through.

Breathe. His heart was not appreciative of his rise in blood pressure. Nothing made him happier than allowing the malice and anger to rise, but his physical health risk had to be acknowledged.

He motioned to Ke to pick up the comm.

"Question," he said, loud enough for the Kreeli to hear.

"Yes?" The Preacher said.

Nave settled his mind and strode over to the Rasp. His assistant held out his palm with the comm as if nothing had happened.

"What do you mean she was not alone?" he asked.

"She crossed the Red Zone by herself in an AM-PHIB. But there were at least two more who arrived by ship."

"Two more?"

"A Gej-ti. He took her AM-PHIB and set chase, posing as Lark... I mean, Renault."

A Gej-ti? The one from three cycles ago? Nave stared at the small image in Ke's palm. "And the other?"

"A Rasp," The Preacher said. "It was dark but I caught sight of them in the ship. The same Racer that evaded us on the orbital."

His eyes narrowed. *So, GAM-OPs has been toying with me.*

"You found nothing on site?"

The Kreeli shook her head. "A field in the jungle, where they landed. Probably to pick her up."

Why would Renault ride out there? To the Red Zone, no less. He made a note to get 2112 to uncover more information. Now that he had the hacker by a string, it wouldn't even cost him anything. They worked for him now, whether they liked it or not. Their anonymity depended on it.

"There are creatures out here... works of dark Gods."

The Preacher's words barely registered over his racing thoughts.

"This is the last time I will tolerate your failure," Nave said, eyeing the Kreeli's holo-face in Ke's palm.

"Yes, Lord."

"Oh, stop with that!"

The Preacher lowered her head in the suit and gestured with hands clasped.

"Get your sorry Kreeli ass back to Hikesh and await my orders."

"I'm surrounded by demons here," she said. "It will be difficult. I am walking through the valley of—"

Nave reached out to the Rasp's palm and cut the line. "Contact 2112, Ke," he said. "Tell them I want Lilline Renault."

TWENTY-SEVEN

Ship: *Celebrity Crush* | Planet: Hesh-9 | System: Messo-23, Galactic Core.

"I can't say I miss the old days," Lauden said and climbed the tube to the Racer's main cabin.

"Well done, sir." Lilline followed him up and through. "Apologies for the delay getting to you. We had a bit of excitement outside the hatch."

"Is it secure?"

"Yes, I covered it well. Nave's enforcer is going to have a heck of a time getting through the jungle alive. We took out her AM-PHIB and," Lilline turned to Inti approaching from the cockpit, "something else made a meal of her partner."

The director pulled out his pipe and packed it. He lit the bowl and puffed. Waves of smoke passed through his gills. "There's nothing like a pipe after time in the field." The Gej-ti sat at a circular table. "That," he pointed the pipe stem at Lilline, "I do miss."

"I set a cruising course," Inti said. "I think the jamming system is set correctly." His three-fingered hand gestured down the cabin to a pair of switches above the pilot seat. "Orange and green twins?"

"That's it," Lilline said. *Celebrity Crush* would be undetectable in Hesh-9 airspace.

"T8, walk Inti through it. Get him up to speed. Everything you have so far." Lauden reached for his travel bag. He pulled out a towel and wiped the sweat off his brow. The Gej-ti's skin pulsed with pinkish waves from heat and post-adrenaline endorphins. With the added nicotine, his bio-system through the translucent skin was alive with activity.

Lilline recounted everything since the first encounter on Frebu: the discovery of the connection to *Freestrike* through cymatics, the cycle chase on Beisho, the gala and the data drive that led them to Nave's virtual meeting and the unveiling of the entity, the bounty on her professor alias, Kissy's departure from the retirement facility with The Preacher, how she'd been tracked, and Gribb's intel that GAM-OPs might be compromised. And finally, Nave's announcement filled with disturbing innuendos and the ticking countdown to the release of *Freestrike 4*.

"The cymatics you mentioned. Can you pull them up?" Inti asked.

Lauden swiped a hand to activate the table's holo-screen. The stills from Pin's demonstration hovered in a linear sequence.

"You are on to something here," the Rasp said. "This is a sigil." He pointed a finger at the icon for the soon-to-release version of *Freestrike*.

"As in magic?" Lilline asked.

The Rasp nodded. "Indeed. A pictorial symbol containing an intention from its maker." His eye scrutinized the image. "Its meaning isn't entirely clear to me. These," he directed his finger to a series of lines in the diagram, "are symbolic references to technology.

And this," the digit followed a curving boundary, "speaks of a 'game as reality' and something related to revenge."

"Mysticism and technology?" Lauden asked.

The Rasp nodded.

"It's as we feared then," the Gej-ti said. He held his pipe in front of his mouth as if carved from stone.

Lilline wanted to ask for clarification but knew better. If Lauden wished to share his thoughts or something from the past, he would.

"Tell me about Frebu," Inti said and took a seat.

Lilline recounted what had transpired in the ice cave. The Rasp nodded several times as she described the internal psychological battle with the violet-hued wraith. The basics had been shared in her report to Lauden, but that account was cold and clinical. This came out with affect and subjectivity. It felt good to share it. The one thing she didn't include was the haunting inner thought that ripped at her core: *you are no one.*

"What you encountered sounds like a servitor, a lesser manifestation of the Astral Mind," Inti said.

"Astral Mind?"

"An immensely powerful thoughtform, second only to the purported godforms. An entity manifested through the communion of psychic intelligence amongst a group that, when connected to an outside life force, is willed into existence. Summoned, if you will."

This sounded out of bounds to her scientific borders. That made sense for Inti, she supposed, being a cryptoxenologist.

"Compelling accounts are documented in texts by galactic historians, but none in recorded history have encountered one," he said. "Although..." Inti paused, "substantial evidence did recently come to light."

Lilline followed the Rasp's eye to Lauden.

"Proceed, Inti." The Gej-ti nodded approval.

"I am here, Agent Renault, because this is not the first time that your agency has confronted a threat of this kind. My choice to be put into stasis in the crypt related to credible evidence that legends and accounts relegated to pseudo-science may be, in fact, legitimate."

"Or, as close as possible without tangible evidence," Lauden said. "Close enough to set off a chain reaction that has led us here."

"Nave's parents were involved with Mind Eye," Inti said. "Have you heard of it?"

"The so-called cult?"

The Rasp nodded.

"I know the basics." Passing references to the group appeared in the material she'd read in FTL en route to Hesh-9. "A secret society rumored to have been here since the ancient days, with hidden knowledge related to a cosmic 'awakening.' Members claim to have a privileged understanding of esoteric teachings on how to connect with larger forces in the universe."

"With the political intention of rising above the masses to rule as 'enlightened' ones," Lauden said. "Usual world domination program you see with many off-shoots of legitimate societies. This one grew from benign forms of worship in early history with less dubious motivations."

"Nave's parents were members?" Lilline asked.

"Yes, in the highest levels of the organization," the director said. "His mother had a background in archaeology and his father in astrophysics. An interesting combination, in this case. On an expedition to Zeret, they located an ancient text that they claimed justified and explained the methods and teachings Mind Eye promulgated."

She knew that desert planet and the sect: philosopher-poets who'd been isolated for hundreds of cycles, and the rediscovered source of the modified version of the Cinquain system she had used for her favorite poem, "A Lifetime in Villain."

"With that in hand, Nave's parents were able to unify several fringe sects with similar intentions under their leadership. They pursued additional recruitment in earnest inside criminal sectors. By the time GAM-OPs and the GM's cabinet got wind of it, Mind Eye was in the planning stages of a public action. That is when your grandmother uncovered evidence of something disturbing and potentially deadly."

"Kissy?"

"Yes," Inti said. "Mind Eye was seeking a 'doorway' spoken of in ancient texts, one through which a legendary cosmic entity may be summoned. Your grandmother witnessed enough to prove they were close."

"The Galactic Minister insisted we reach out covertly and invite them to the table. It was an opportunity for great scientific advancement." Lauden's gills fluttered as he released plumes of smoke. "They refused, of course. Instead, issuing a not-so-subtle threat that we would be the first to learn what true power was." Lauden tamped the bowl of his pipe. "You know the rest from there."

Kissy eliminated both. "And what of this text?"

"Nave's mother wouldn't let it fall into other hands," Lauden said. "She destroyed it."

"Lost forever, or so we thought," Inti said.

"As it turns out we may be wrong." Lauden's tone carried a rare edge of regret.

"So, you think Nave has it?" she asked.

"More likely, a copy made at some point. And now he's found this 'doorway'."

"To what, exactly?"

"Power," Lauden said. "Mind Eye appears to be taking on a new face under Nave's leadership. It's evolved into a techno-spiritualist criminal organization. Insidious at best, deadly at its worst. Nave is coercing the masses in preparation for some sort of sadistic action. My guess is his end goal is retribution against those who he sees as having wronged him, while also overthrowing the political structure of the galaxy to become its supreme leader."

"A technocratic theocracy," Inti said. "A mutated form of the original prophecy of Mind Eye."

"A means and excuse for world domination by criminals, to put it bluntly," Lauden said.

The two held such differing perspectives on the case. Inti, seeing the philosophical and spiritual backbone and Lauden laying bare the motivations to use it to purpose.

"Mind Eye promotes a revival of ancient beliefs for the modern age," Inti said. "A cosmology where secular and spiritual meet in a Futurist Galactic Order."

Mind Eye. The gala, and the augmented reality, as well as the virtual board room, floated through her thoughts. "Nave's move to augmentation and virtual spaces," she said, "I suppose that relates to 'seeing' inside the mind?"

Lauden nodded. "I'm sure he and his evangelists believe that our current technological capabilities are a final stage of some kind of evolutionary 'awakening'."

"The irony is, they may be right," Inti said. "It's the intent that appears to be misdirected. I fear that the forces they are summoning are beyond any of our species' intelligences. We have no idea what they are inviting into our reality."

"None of us thought this would return during our lifetimes," Lauden said. "When and if it ever did, a more diplomatic entry into whatever larger world out there was our hope."

"So, you volunteered to be put in stasis?" Lilline asked.

The Rasp nodded. "I will not deny that I did it as much for personal and selfish reasons as those that were more philanthropic. If a day came when my discipline and life's study might be validated, I wanted to be there." The Rasp's long neck fell. "My hope was it would be an evolutionary moment of immense intellectual significance. Instead, it turns out my awakening was not to confront a cosmic expansion for our civilization but to stop its abuse."

"That should get you up to speed, T8," Lauden said.

"And Kissy witnessed this?" she asked. "I assume Nave wants her as revenge for killing his parents?"

"Your guess is as good as mine, but that would be logical," Lauden said. "The problem is, Nave, and many members of Mind Eye don't always follow that line of reasoning. These are criminals, intelligent and driven by goals that defy the boundaries of what you and I serve to protect."

Lilline couldn't ignore the irony. *And yet, we too deal in murder for the so-called collective good.*

"Kissy went willingly for a reason, of that I am sure," the director said. "You know as well as I do that if she didn't want to be taken, there would be a mess to clean up on Beisho."

"And now, we have the second stage of a problem that was left with loose ends three ten-cycles ago," the Rasp said. "The crisis here is very real."

"What is it, Inti..." Lilline said, "this Astral Mind?"

"That is their Order's name for it. The common and accessible term used to describe it is egregore. A cosmic intelligence pulled forth from unknown reaches of space and time. They are birthed from enough collective thought willed into being – the energy is alien and extra-dimensional. Most species refer to it in existing records. We've all sensed a larger world, though our ranges of inter-activity with nature haven't given us the means to properly 'know' it."

Some of this was familiar. Ancient poets she had read spoke of such things, albeit in more abstract terms.

"You know, I am sure," Inti turned his eye to her, "that a much wider spectrum exists than what we perceive with our senses."

"Without question."

"Technology, whether a simple telescope or a sophisticated spec-tral reader, aids us in expanding our vision, 'seeing' these broader spaces and communication channels," Inti said. "Nave has discovered a route inside using some new innovative technology."

"Into what?"

"Some think that the Astral Mind is a bridge, a portal for us to break out of a limited condition. Entry into the greater cosmic order through awakening to higher dimensional intelligence." The Rasp spread his thin, dry-skinned arms wide in a gesture of sublime expansion.

She could sit and talk with him about this for hours. Unfortunately, they didn't have time to spare.

"So, what is the plan?" she asked, returning to the view from ground level. "If we take out Nave, or as many of the other criminals who have generated this thing as possible, the entity dies with them, right?" It wasn't the most efficient approach, but it was logical. "Sir, we can get all the T#s to go after the ones we identified. Pin had about two-thirds of them ID'd."

"Not quite," Inti said, shaking his head. The skin on his snake-like neck crackled with the twisting tension.

"An Astral Mind doesn't vanish, from what we know. Well, not right away, according to the texts that survive."

"So how do we make it leave?" Lilline asked.

The Rasp sighed. "That is an answer we still seek. There are ways to summon these entities, which means there may be methods to send them back."

She examined the weathered face of the Rasp. *He doesn't know?*

"This isn't something blasters and daring maneuvers can stop," Inti said. "This is a deeply complex matter, beyond the borders of known physics. My studies are 'out of bounds' as a cryptoxenologist. You will need to let go of skepticism to have any chance of stopping this."

Lilline looked at Lauden. A plume of smoke rose over his face. As it cleared, the Gej-ti's expression emerged as earnest as when he gave orders in his office at HQ.

"Sounds like a paradox," she said.

"More like a trap," Lauden said, puffing away. His nerves and inner systems shifted hue as comfort returned after the trials of the recent chase.

"I sense you are thinking too clearly, my old friend," Inti said.

The cryptoxenologist's statement struck a chord. He had not said, "*I think you are thinking too clearly.*" He had said, "*I sense you are...*"

What was it he had said after communing with the Bukki mutant? "Thought expressed as feeling."

"All the sentient species in the galaxy hold the means to break out of our limited condition," the Rasp said. "It's a different approach to intelligence. We call it many things. A 'hunch' or our 'gut' telling us something."

"It's instinct," Lilline said.

Inti nodded. "We have it for a reason, but we have never tapped its full potential. It forces its way through at times, fighting against rational blindness. But until we learn to let it speak freely, we will remain alone among a much vaster cosmic order."

"And Nave has managed to connect us to it," she said. It made no sense. *A criminal entrepreneur broke galactic civilization through an existential boundary unreachable for millennia?*

"Some new technology has provided a gate, which isn't a bad thing," Inti said. "It comes from a place of innovation. The issue is the minds that form its core outlook, which in this case are individuals with criminal intentions." The Rasp's long neck lowered and his eye closed. "What purpose he has for it, I cannot imagine."

"There's something you two need to see," Lauden said. He stood and pulled up a new holo-screen.

A prompt manifested, requesting a special access code.

"This is of the highest classified intelligence. What you recounted, T8, along with the following exchange I am about to play, is what brought me to Hesh-9."

Lauden tapped the air with a fingertip, entering a set of numbers.

Nave appeared in his virtual board room.

"Good evening, Galactic Minister, and respective quadrant ambassadors," the entrepreneur said. "Do you like to play games?"

TWENTY-EIGHT

The galactic minister and her cabinet sat in the executive suite at Ministry Headquarters on Tavi-Prime. Lilline's attention was on the GM at the head of the table. Her Kreeli headband was alight with activity.

A projection wall ran along one side of the government meeting room. In it, Nave stood inside the skyscraper's virtual office. The entrepreneur crossed to the floor-to-ceiling window, turned his back to the GM and galactic ambassadors, and gazed out at his too-perfect city.

"What is a game?" he said. "For some, its purpose is play and amusement based on skill, ability, and luck. For others, its sole function is to foster competition and determine winners and losers."

He swung around to face his audience.

"You like to play games with people's lives, don't you Minister? To make decisions and weigh outcomes, challenging your abilities to succeed or fail? Governance is a game, is it not?"

"Is there a purpose to this meeting, Mavron?" the GM asked.

"I like to play with people's lives in augmented and virtual worlds. My company provides the public with a much-needed service. Our products save them from boredom and monotony in a galaxy controlled by you and your limited vision." He spread both arms wide. "I offer escape and pleasures unattainable in your moral prison. Now, it is time for my world and yours to meet. The galaxy will be set free from your arrogant rules. There can be only one winner."

"What are you talking about, Mavron?" The GM said. "It's a busy time here and—"

"Allow me to give you a demonstration."

Nave waved a hand and the screen split. Next to the entrepreneur, the vault Lilline had seen during the secret meeting appeared.

The Astral Mind.

"Your days of making the rules are over. Now I control the board."

Nave switched the view.

Lilline grabbed the edge of the table. Even though the recorded transmission displayed earlier events, it still shook her.

"The Astral Mind," Inti whispered.

"Mind Eye is very real, and I am its supreme leader. We have summoned a power greater than any in galactic history. For millennia, we have put our faith in the capability of integrative intelligence to achieve ascendence. Mind Eye has worked in the shadows while you have touted so-called 'progress' to the masses. Now, our achievements will be the reward for those superior and destined to rule."

The entrepreneur switched the feed. A fleet of attack ships stood against a backdrop of distant stars. In a burst of light, the Astral Mind manifested, blocking their path through the void.

"No physical material can halt it. No weapon can harm it," he said. "It can crush and consume anything in its way. But that is not its greatest power. Its mind is capable of horrors beyond your imagination."

Lilline felt the sting of Nave's words. Even her encounter with the prototype had harrowing effects. That wraith on Frebu was nothing in scale nor scope compared to what stood before the eyes of the GM and her ambassadors.

"It's bigger than I imagined possible," Inti whispered.

"What do you want, Mavron?" The GM's tone was cool and collected. Lilline remembered that the Kreeli was the leader of the entire galaxy for a reason. "I empathize with the fact that your family was the victim of a government-sanctioned action, and this news has reached you, but you need to keep in mind we—"

"What do I want?" Nave interrupted her and switched off the parallel feed. He walked a few steps closer to the cam. "You are thirty cycles too late in asking that."

So, this is about revenge.

"Then, I imagine you wish to provide us with a list of demands related to techno-commerce for your company?" the GM said. "As well as a seat at the table as we work together to learn more about this discovery?"

Nave laughed. His neck went beet red. "I have no demands!"

Several ambassadors jumped in their seats.

The entrepreneur adjusted his sleeves and collar, recovering from his outburst. "I have only one wish," he said through gritted teeth. "And that, Galactic Minister, is to play a game." He waved a hand and the *Freestrike* icon, with the familiar sigil, appeared on the split screen. "It starts in forty-eight hours." Nave moved closer so his face filled the holo's frame. "Any aggression towards my orbital or other properties in the galaxy will accelerate my timeline and provide the excuse for an early demonstration. That would be, as you have seen today, most unwise."

He stepped back. The virtual office exploded into a cornucopia of *Freestrike* icons. They swirled against a backdrop of the Astral Mind. "Let the games begin!" he exclaimed with arms wide.

The transmission ended.

"Get me a line to the director of GAM-OPs," the GM said to her assistant.

The Oltari nodded and flew off to carry out the order.

"He's insane!" a Dendari ambassador said.

The room erupted in boisterous conversation.

Lauden cut the feed.

Lilline turned to Inti. The Rasp stood, frozen.

"This is the largest and most dangerous threat to the galaxy in modern times," the Gej-ti said. "Now you have the full picture of what—"

The ship's alert system pinged. Lilline recognized the tone: incoming call. She turned and made for the cockpit.

"It's from Carbook, sir. Source is HQ."

If GAM-OPs was hacked, then responding would give away their position.

"Answer it," Lauden said. "Put it through on overhead."

"Carbrook, this is T8," Lilline said. Out the ship's window, flashes of lightning illuminated thunderheads thousands of kilometers below as a nightly storm drenched Hesh-9's rainforest.

"T8, you need to know that—"

"Stop talking." Lauden's voice carried the authority of his post as director.

"It's Lauden," Carbrook's muffled voice said to someone in the room.

Idiot! Lilline turned, waiting for an order from the director.

"Listen to me," Lauden said. "Cut this transmission. Re-connect from Station Zeta."

"But, sir. It's—"

"Goodbye, Carbrook." Lilline reached for the button on the dashboard.

"I cleared the system! We were hacked," Carbrook spat out.

"Wait," Lauden's voice halted her finger inches from the controls. "Go ahead."

Lilline looked back at the Gej-ti. He motioned for her to return to the table.

"*Sir, I can't believe it, but GAM-OPs was hacked. It had to be 2112. No one else could pull this off.*"

"And we're secure again?" Lauden asked, lighting his pipe.

"*We are. Whoever it was, they got in through the new Hyper-Healer computer system.*"

Wow. Lilline kept it to herself but she was impressed. That was no small feat. Carbrook had built that machine from scratch. Whoever this 2112 was, they bested the best of the agency.

"*They installed a 'push space' inside the system, sir. Not unlike the virtual vault on the drive that T8 lifted at the gala. I'm on to them now, though. Whoever they are.*"

"How did you know?" Lauden asked.

The scent of Yaz Flake wafted across the table.

"*Well, I didn't but then once we—*"

"*I found it, sir,*" a familiar voice said.

Lilline put a hand over her mouth. Lauden's eyes caught her hiding the smile.

"Excellent teamwork, both of you," the Gej-ti said.

"*Thank you, sir,*" Pin said.

Carbrook didn't respond. It had to be difficult on him, but the fact was, he got the hacker out. That was a feat unto itself, Lilline was sure.

"Good thing you were able to clean the system, Carbrook," she said. "That must've been tough."

Lauden nodded approval of her gracious compliment.

"*Thanks. It wasn't that hard. I ended up using a—*"

"Anything to report from Eshi or the other sites?" Lauden asked, cutting him off.

"*That would be me, sir,*" Pin said. "*The news isn't good. Eshi is emitting a strong frequency.*"

Damn. Had she done the right thing following Kissy's lead to the crypt? Would this already be over if she had followed Lauden's original orders?

She looked at her boss. The Gej-ti didn't flinch a muscle.

"But no stronger than several other locations," Pin said. *"The issue is, I'm picking up sub-frequencies."*

"Where?" Lilline asked.

"Everywhere."

TWENTY-NINE

"What do you mean, everywhere?" Lauden asked.

"*All over the galaxy,*" Pin said. "*They're popping up on network satellites along the populated star chains. Even Tavi-Prime. You'd only find them if you're looking. Whoever is transmitting them is cloaking the signals.*"

"These are the systems where the most consumers are?" It was Inti.

Pin didn't respond.

"Answer the question, Pin," the director said. "Don't worry about introductions or who is here."

"*Yes, sir. And 'yes' to the question.*"

The Rasp's eye closed.

"What is it?" Lauden asked.

"He must be setting it up to connect to the game," Inti said, opening his eye. "It will be able to link with every player."

"To do what?" Lilline asked.

"Feed," the Rasp said. "The thoughtform thirsts for psychic energy. It will drain them to manifest the cruelty and malice Nave has placed inside its core. If that happens, its collective power will be unstoppable."

"*Sir, it's chaos everywhere across networked systems,*" Pin said. "*I've never seen anything like it. Everyone is waiting for the game to drop. The streets are filled. Freestrike evangelists are holding rallies all over Tavi-Prime and other urban planets. It's getting all the attention on media channels. It's like—*"

"Mass worship," the Rasp whispered.

"*Yes,*" Pin said. "*It's very creepy.*"

"He's drawing them together through a collective spirit."

"Based on what?" Lauden asked.

"Consumerism," Lilline said. "Nave has built a quasi-religion around his entertainment. The Preacher and her 'apostles' spread the gospel."

"It sounds like nonsense," the director said.

"It's a means to an end," Inti said. "A bond that provides the unity needed to tap into a collective intellectual spirit. We have become increasingly secular over the cycles. All species who are part of our galactic civilization have within them a need for connection, for a sense of their place in a greater whole. Nave is tapping into that. The irony is, he has found a portal. One that may prove what so many of us have persisted in believing exists."

"It's been there, right before our eyes and we never saw it," Lauden said, rising and examining the sigil. "Nave's been building up an army of followers."

Lilline tracked Lauden's hand as it scrolled through the various versions of *Freestrike*.

"Millions, perhaps billions, across the galaxy have been playing *Freestrike*. These sigils are embedded in their collective psyche. To them, they're pop culture icons," Lauden said. "It's madness." He shook his head in frustration. "And now he's ready."

All three stared at the holo over the table. Neither Pin nor Carbrook made a sound over the comm.

"What about the game?" Lauden asked. "Where is that run out of?"

"Nave's company orbital," Pin said. *"It works off a super-computer at the central spoke."*

Lilline knew where Lauden was going. GAM-Ops' mission statement: protect the citizens first and foremost.

"The director has a good point," Inti said. "Shut down the game and you halt Nave's ability to increase the entity's power. As it stands, it wields tremendous cosmic intelligence."

"You can't launch a strike on that station," Lilline said. "Almost a million citizen-employees live there."

"No, of course not." Lauden puffed on his pipe.

"And that still doesn't get to the source of the threat. This 'entity' is still out there somewhere," she said.

"We still have no idea where it is?" The director's tone made clear he addressed the question to everyone in the room and on the call.

Silence. Lilline checked the clock on the wall. The hours were slipping away.

"What about the other signals? The ones from planets Nave purchased in remote systems?" Lilline asked.

"None of the other T#s have been able to locate anything," Lauden said. "The one time we got close to anything resembling it was when you were on Frebu. Our intel has been searching for a hidden Mind Eye temple for cycles. We've never found so much as a clue to where it might be."

"Maybe we are looking in the wrong place?" Inti said.

Lilline turned. "How so?"

"Those could all be prototypes. You said you witnessed the Astral Mind when you were in the virtual world, yes?"

"That's right. It was projected by Nave in the virtual meeting."

"Pin, check for a frequency coming from the company orbital," Lauden said.

"One moment," Pin said.

Lilline examined the Rasp. He was deep in thought.

"Good call, sir," Pin said. *"There's one emitting at a high spectral rate out of that system. It's... unusually complex."*

"Play it, please," Inti said.

A sonic chorus bounced off the walls of the ship's cabin. Lilline's soul shook to its core. She steadied herself with a hand on the table. Frebu flashed back. The horror of an emptiness screamed inside, conjuring memories of the immaterial wraith's claw scraping her insides.

"Could that be the source?" Lauden's voice came through the darkness.

"Please stop it," Inti said.

The sonic chorus halted.

Lilline opened her eyes. The Rasp's monocular gaze was fixed on her.

"Are you alright?" he asked.

Am I? Regardless, she nodded.

"It carries all the signature elements of what we know of an egregore's sonic profile. I've studied these phenomena my entire life," Inti said. "This is a professional tragedy. The validation of my studies, my endless battling with the scientific community, is finally vindicated. And yet?"

A silence passed.

"What a shame," the Rasp shook his head. "There is wonder and new knowledge here. A gate to a larger cosmic order, and yet it has come on the heels of evil and malice."

How often had this been the case? Lilline could think of more than a handful of times when potentially beneficial innovations and inventions were crafted with a desire to do harm and cause hurt.

"It must be destroyed, Inti," Lauden said in earnest. "Or sent back from whence it came."

"I know, Asher," the Rasp said, his serpentine neck lowering.

"If T8 can get you in and find where this thing is, can you stop it?" Lauden asked.

"I cannot say for certain." The Rasp's neck snaked back up. "Nothing like this has ever been confronted in recorded galactic history. Much of our chances rest on haste and how autonomous the entity has become by the time we get to it. *If* we get to it."

"I'll get you to it," Lilline said.

Lauden pointed his pipe in her direction, approving the determination and confidence.

"But will it be in time? And, will we have what we need to stop it?" The Rasp's eyebrow raised. "If I had access to the lost knowledge preserved in the ancient texts, I might find clues on how to withdraw it back through the gate. But without them?" The Rasp's expression turned less confident. "It will be difficult."

"We have to try," Lauden puffed on his pipe. "Carbrook, put together a mobile tech unit and head to the orbital's system. Pack up anything you think could be useful from your lab. T8 is going to need you online to guide her inside to shut the hub down. See if Intel has architectural maps of the station spoke."

"Yes, sir."

"Have Astro-Travel set up a rendezvous point back from the station so you're not detected," Lauden added. "That way T8 and Inti can get in and," the director looked at the Rasp, "hopefully stop this thing before Nave sends the galaxy into chaos."

"Understood," Carbrook said.

"Bring the *Velociter Bullet*," Lilline said. "I want it there as a backup option. It's got the best stealth and speed for an alternative infiltration scenario." *Or escape.* She kept that to herself.

"Can do," the techie said.

"You may have to hack a path for us through the locking algorithms on entry portals and shut down security cams as we move through the station," Lilline added.

"We can do it," Pin said. *"Right, Carbrook?"*

"I can overdub the security cams," the techie said. *"The station portals will be more difficult, but not impossible. We'll get started on hacking their system right away."*

"Good luck." Lauden pointed to the comm, indicating that she should cut the line. Lilline walked forward to the cockpit and ended the transmission.

Her thigh pocket vibrated. The comm that Pin gave her had an incoming message. She pulled it out far enough to read it. In her peripheral vision, Lauden and Inti continued to discuss the crisis at the table, unaware.

T8: In case 2112 gets back into the system, you can reach me via this comm if you need absolute security. I bypassed the network. It's running on an older analog stream used by low-budget freighters and mining operations.

Lilline thumbed out '*thanks*' and added a winking smiley face. She hit send.

I can't guarantee its range, depending on where you are.

Understood. She slipped it back in her pocket and returned to the table.

"What is Nave's end goal, Asher?" Inti asked.

"You heard the transmission with the GM," Lauden said, gills fluttering from a massive exhale of tobacco.

"Indeed, but that is the form that casts the shadow," the Rasp said. "What lies hidden in the dark?"

Lilline noticed his large eye on her. A flash of the cave on Frebu ran through her body, sending chills down her spine.

"Control," she said. "That's Nave's weakness. Everything he does is about order and calculated design. That virtual office I was in... you remember, sir." Lilline turned to Lauden. "I told you that it was too perfect and precise. And Nave said something about simulations of ecosystems on the orbital, and how technology 'corrected' nature's imperfections."

"It's more than that," Lauden said. "He believes the galaxy has wronged him."

"And has it?" Inti asked.

Lauden sighed and put his pipe down on the table. "Perhaps. This is one time when our ethical decisions may have backfired."

Lilline scrutinized the Gej-ti's expression. The pathos was back.

"Either way," Lauden said, "we have two monsters to deal with. One, very human and tangible. The other, an unknown and terrifying threat." The director's eyes went to the ship's time display. "And the clock is ticking."

"I have a contact in Hikesh who should be able to secure a ship and equipment," Lilline said. "I remember seeing significant cargo traffic to and from the orbital spoke. Going in undercover as a delivery vessel might be the best option. That way Carbrook can stay on board, either in the docking bay or off-station, and lead us through on relay. Inti and I can rendezvous with him far enough out that—"

"You won't make it with enough time for the infiltration," Lauden said. "Nave's orbital is a longer jump than Tavi-Prime. Take the Racer."

"What about you?"

"Get me another ship from your contact. Can they pull all this off for us in a few hours?"

"If anyone in the galaxy can, it's him."

"Good," Lauden said. "Anything will do so long as it's a solo flyer. I'll take it back to Tavi-Prime."

"Why don't you come with us, Asher? It would be so much easier?" Inti asked.

Lilline knew Lauden had to go back. Someone had to be at central command running the show, observing all the moving parts from the outside to work strategy should something not go to plan. As she knew from her cycles in the field, something always didn't go to plan.

"I need to be at HQ, Inti. GAM-OPs is rudderless with me out here in the field."

Inti's small head nodded in understanding.

"I don't like the idea of going back to Hikesh, T8," Lauden added. "Not after what happened at the crypt. We can't risk any more interference."

"That was on me, sir. I take responsibility," she said. "I disobeyed your orders and—"

"Not important now." He did the 'hand thing'. "We should be thankful that Kissy knew how to re-route you. Especially since our problem isn't on Eshi."

That was why the Gej-ti needed to be back in his office, shades drawn and smoking. Reflection was a powerful strategic asset and hard to come by when you were hanging from cables or in a high-speed chase under blaster fire.

"Is there somewhere on Hesh-9 where your contact can meet us away from prying eyes?" the director asked.

There was and it wasn't too far off their current course, but it would hurt her pride. Under the circumstances, she didn't have a choice.

"I know just the place, sir."

THIRTY

"What is this place?" Lauden swung his neck around, taking in the view.

Inti, wrapped in a cloak from the ship's supply room, shivered.

At four thousand meters above sea level, the night air chilled Lilline's bones, but it didn't lessen the beauty of what lay overhead. Stars glimmered electric over an endless range of snow-capped peaks.

It had been five cycles since she'd been to the monastery. She gazed beyond the landing pad to the view of mountains. The uppermost habitable portion of Hesh-9's northern hemisphere stood in stark contrast to the equatorial rainforest world they'd left behind an hour earlier.

"T8?"

Lilline turned to Lauden. His question had gotten lost in a flood of memories. "Sorry, sir. Somewhere I spend time when I have it. Less than I should, recently." It had been too long since her last visit, and that was what worried her now.

"Let's go." She started up the flight of rough-hewn steps.

Her eyes focused on putting each foot in front of the other, making sure they landed safely as she and the others zig-zagged their way along the mountain face. Without a railing, the drop could kill you. Her lungs struggled in the thin air. She could only imagine what it was doing to Lauden, a smoker, and Inti as an elderly Rasp.

"Are you alright?" she asked without looking back when they were halfway up.

A brief grunt from the director and a faint 'yes' from Inti carried in the silent night. Ten minutes later they were at the top. She paused, her breath steaming in the cool air, and stared at the wooden doors.

It's now or never.

"Wait here." She climbed the steps to the entrance and rang a massive bell. It echoed over the mountains like a buoy sounding on a foggy sea.

"So, this might go well, and it might not," she said turning to them. "Whatever happens, don't interfere."

Lauden pulled out his pipe.

"No, sir. That's not a good idea. If you don't mind?"

The director put it back in his pocket.

Lilline's ears picked up a shuffling sound on the other side of the doors.

"Flowers close their petals at night," a familiar voice said through the thick wood. "Only in bloom can they show their purpose."

"Unless they are nocturnal," she replied, "in which case the night is their day and the darkness their light."

With a creak, the door opened. A lantern was shoved into her face.

"Ah, so the Lilli is in season." The long neck and small head of an elderly Rasp monk peered out. "Who are they?"

"Colleagues. We need a place to rest. Someone is meeting us here."

"Of course! Come, come," the Rasp motioned the others up the steps. The monk put the lantern down and pulled the doors open wide.

"Thank you, Teacher. I didn't want to come but—"

"Just one thing," the Rasp said and held up their three-fingered hand, blocking her way.

Oh no, not now.

"You want in, then you either get past me or," he pointed down at the ground, "you eat dirt."

"What does he mean?" Lauden whispered. "We don't have time for—"

Lilline waved her boss off. She read the monk's gaze. Behind his playful eye, a deadly seriousness remained ever-present.

"Fine. Let's do this." She pulled the blaster from the holster on her hip and handed it to Lauden.

The old monk giggled and cracked his clay-skinned knuckles.

Lilline set her fighting stance. She locked eyes with the old Rasp.

He waved a hand, taunting her to come at him.

She pounced, using *windmill cutting rain,* with both of her arms straight and slashing like swords.

Smack!

The monk stood over her and pointed at her face. "You are still stupid. Do you quit?"

Lilline slid out from under him and got back to her feet. *Damn, but the old Rasp hasn't lost a step.* She switched tactics and went low with *drunken steps* to hook his inner calves.

Bam!

Pain shot through her thigh as his thick knee slammed into her leg, sending her tumbling down.

"Up and down. High and low. So predictable."

She panted and struggled to catch her breath. The altitude was killing her stamina.

The monk grabbed a fistful of dirt off the ground and displayed it. "Hungry?"

She held up a hand, indicating she needed a moment.

"Your grandmother never asked for more time. She always—"

Lilline sprung, using her favorite hand combination: *singing birds under a crescent moon.*

Fabric from the monk's robe wrapped around her arms at the elbows. She spun and lost her bearing. Before she knew it, she was on the ground. The night sky, full of stars, filled her vision.

"Wrong night, see," the Rasp's single eye appeared in view, and he pointed up at the moon.

Lilline followed his finger.

Smack!

"Ouch!" The slap to her head stung in the cold night air.

"Full moon tonight, Lilli. Just like you, full of confidence. 'Oh, look at me. I'm so good at what I do!'" The monk paraded around mocking her, his fingers making a fake blaster and shooting at invisible opponents. "I'm a great secret agent."

Cycles of memories of these 'lessons' flashed through her mind.

The monk halted his taunting and folded his arms across his thick chest. "The full moon shines brightly, once a month. But it is always there; it's you who doesn't always see it."

"Yes, Teacher," she said, gravel digging into her back.

"Training must be constant. It matters not if others are witness. Understand?"

She nodded.

The Rasp reached out a hand and pulled her up.

"Now, you may come in."

"How long was I out?" Lilline snapped to one-hundred percent lucidity in seconds. Part of her training was learning to wake alert and ready to respond.

"Three hours," a young Gej-ti monk said and handed her a mug of tea. She sipped it, taking in the bitter taste of Adari leaves. "Your colleagues are being roused now."

So, we all slept. Good. If they were stuck waiting for her contact to arrive with what she hoped was the full list of her requests, might as well get some rest. With what lay ahead, they would all need it.

"Excuse me, but may I ask," the young monk said and bowed their head, "are you truly Evening Kiss's relation?"

It never ceased to sound strange when someone referred to Granny by her monastic name. Kissy never revealed how she got it or what it meant. Knowing the former agent's reputation for flirtation, Lilline was convinced the origin was dubious.

"Yes," Lilline said and handed back the tea. Judging by their robe, she guessed the monk was still an apprentice.

"Are you as good as she was at the forms?" they asked.

Lilline shook her head. "Not even close." It was no lie. Granny's physical ability and martial arts skill in her prime was legendary. "Sorry, if that is disappointing."

The monk lowered their head and backed out of the chamber.

"Your contact is on the landing pad," Lauden said entering the room.

Lilline checked her wrist comm.

"Seven hours," Lauden said. "With four in FTL to get to the orbital, that leaves you three hours to stop Nave."

They might be in a monastery high in the remote mountains on an out-of-the-way planet, but the tone of the Gej-ti's remark carried the same gravitas as back at HQ.

"Let's do this." She rose and took her blaster off the bedside table and holstered it.

"T8, one thing." Lauden looked around the spartan interior. "You may find yourself needing to make a difficult choice out there. Nave can be ruthless. It might come down to—"

"I know, sir." She looked him straight in the eye. "I'll make the right one."

The Gej-ti nodded and patted his shirt pocket. "Let's get out in the open air. I need a smoke." He turned to leave.

"Sir."

The director halted.

"Can I ask you something?"

He turned and did the hand gesture.

"Why did you join?"

"GAM-OPs?"

She nodded.

"To save the galaxy, why else?"

That was a dodge and they both knew it, even if it contained the truth.

"How did Kissy—"

"Am I interrupting?" Inti appeared behind Lauden in the doorway.

"Not at all," Lauden said.

"I needed that rest," the Rasp said. "Despite being in stasis for cycles, I needed sleep."

"And it's good you got it," Lauden broke eye contact with her and looked at his old friend. "Are you ready, Inti?"

"I am."

"Good. Let's beat Nave at his own game." Lauden glanced her way. "We're sending our best player."

THIRTY-ONE

An orange glow edged the walls of the courtyard. Higher up, Hesh-9's brightest stars resisted the imminent dawn. Ruffling robes and the scuffing of sandals on gravel broke the silence. A hundred monks of various species moved in unison, practicing age-old movements under the watchful eye of their teacher. The old Rasp leaned on a wooden staff, in a pose Lilline recognized from the first time she'd arrived here many ten-cycles ago.

The monastery was a temporal anomaly. It didn't age because nothing needed to progress. Practitioners came and went in evolving generational cycles. The site, its philosophy, and its codes of conduct, lived eternal.

There would be no goodbyes. It was time for her and the others to leave, so they left. You came and went. Or you remained.

"Agent Renault." Inti's whisper barely reached her ears.

Lilline turned to him but didn't stop walking.

"You have done this here yourself, yes?" He pointed at the monks.

"Many times."

"Then you know something of what I spoke of on the Racer.

Collective energy is powerful here. The union of bodies in movement and spirit emits a strong current."

This was true, she'd felt it herself when in the lines with the others.

"But more than that," he said, "their minds are emptied of everything other than—"

"The present," she said, finishing for him.

"Yes. And that makes them one."

Inti spoke the truth. An invisible force, a kind of energy from each practitioner, was amplified by a common belief system and physical empathy, honed through repetition and cycles of concentrated study and exercise. She missed it.

When this is over, I will return.

"Asher was right in choosing you," the Rasp said.

She looked back at Lauden, who followed a few steps behind them.

"I don't think he had a choice," she whispered. "My grandmother—"

"No," the Rasp shook their small head. "It's more than that."

The apprentice who woke her with tea waited at the double doors. The monk opened them wide as they reached the entrance. Lilline stepped over the threshold and out into the mundane world of Hesh-9's northern reaches.

"Good morning." A phlegmy gurgle followed the greeting. "Have to say, this is the most unusual place you've requested we meet."

"You never let me down, Gribb," she said and gestured at Lauden and Inti. "My two companions."

Gribb nodded at Inti and then looked at Lauden. "Good to see you, Asher."

Lilline shot around. "You two know each other?"

"How is your father, Gribb? I'm happy to see you are carrying on the family business."

"His health isn't great but at his age, it's to be expected." The Froo's throat swallowed with an audible gulp.

"Isn't it for us all?" the Gej-ti said. The director took out his pipe and packed it in haste. In seconds it was lit, and he was puffing away.

"Ah, now that's a smell I haven't taken in for some time." Gribb raised his green chin. Circular sensory glands on his cheeks shimmered. "Lots of memories come back with that."

"Are we set?" Lilline asked.

Gribb pointed down the cliff at the landing pad. Lilline spotted two black duffel bags and the Froo's small transport shuttle parked next to the Racer.

"You are a miracle worker, Gribb."

"Wait until you get my bill on this one. I'll have enough credits to retire."

"Whatever it is, you'll get it," Lauden said.

Gribb made a phlegmy gurgle of appreciation.

"So, we have a cargo hauler?"

"You do." He 'frumped' and patted both feet on the ground.

Lilline knew that meant a caveat. "But?"

"It's a clunker. You won't be doing any fancy maneuvers."

"Doesn't matter. It just needs to get us into the docking station. What are we hauling?"

"Nothing."

She cocked her head.

The Froo patted his feet on the ground a second time.

"I'm waiting for the punch line here, Gribb."

"You're a sewage maintenance crew. It's a scheduled inspection of the orbital's treatment facility, which happens to run out of the spoke." He gurgled longer than usual.

Lilline knew it was self-satisfaction with an edge of sarcasm.

"Sounds delightful. And everything else?"

"It's all there."

"Gribb you're keeping up the family reputation," Lauden said, pointing with his pipe. "Under the short notice, this is most impressive."

"The cargo ship was easy," the Froo said. "Try finding someone willing to generate a prosthetic human ear in the middle of the night in Hikesh."

Lilline knew he'd come through. She needed to disguise herself, otherwise that distinguishing feature pointed to her as Larkin, or if GAM-OPs had been compromised, her core identity.

"What about 2112, Gribb?" she asked.

"More slippery than my skin. No one knows anything more than that they're the best."

"What contact method is used?" Lauden asked.

"It's a bounce system. You need to be looped in through deep tech to gain route entry. From there, a series of AI couriers ricochet you to a digital gate. 2112 either responds to the request or doesn't."

Lilline knew by the look on Lauden's face that he wanted Carbrook to try. There just wasn't time.

"Well, let's get going," the director said. "Time to save the galaxy."

Lilline felt the euphoric pre-op rush run through her veins. A poem circled in her subconscious waters, waiting to surface. As soon as there was some action, she'd have the inspiration for it to materialize.

"Asher, you'll ride with me back to Hikesh," Gribb said. "I've got a ship in port that'll get you back to wherever you are going. It's a small flyer so you'll be able to pilot it solo."

Lilline kept her expression blank, but she caught a small curve to Lauden's lips. Gribb knew exactly where the director was headed, and everyone here knew he knew it. But business was business and appearances needed to be maintained, or in this case performed, for clients.

"Good luck, T8," Lauden said. "And Gribb, you can tell me about your father on the way."

The Froo gurgled and started down the steep stairs hugging the cliff.

"Give us a minute to get out before you fire up that hot rod," the Froo said as his head disappeared.

Lilline caught Inti approaching in the corner of her eye.

"It is quite tranquil here," he said.

From their perch high in the mountains, all was aglow. As the sun broke over the horizon, one by one the snow-capped peaks were set ablaze like match-tips ignited by the heat of the sun's rays.

Gribb's shuttle cut across the scene and shot off into the distance.

"Time to roll, Inti," Lilline said. "I hope you like space metal."

"Space what?" Inti's voice came from behind her as she made her way down the steps.

"It's my flying music. Think of it as the counterpoint to reading in the quiet of a—"

She halted.

"In the quiet of what?"

"Wait." She turned and put a hand on the rock wall to hold her balance.

Why didn't I think of it sooner? She checked the time. They didn't have any to spare. Yet, Inti's words on the Racer forced their way forward.

"What texts?"

The Rasp's eye examined her. His monobrow went down on each end.

"On the Racer, you said 'if I could consult the ancient texts'..."

"They are very old and quite rare. Most are esoteric with a spiritualist bent."

"Come on," she shimmied around him on the outside, taking the stairs two at a time back up to the double doors. "Catch up to me." She scurried back inside, careful to keep to the side of the practicing monks moving in elegant synchronicity.

"Teacher," she said, approaching the old monk who watched the students.

He didn't turn. Lilline knew from experience that no response meant she could proceed.

"May I use the library?"

"Experience is better than what you will learn in books, Lilli."

"Yes, but sometimes those of the past speak answers in the present." She surprised herself with that one.

The Rasp's mouth turned upward into a smile. "Librarian!"

A Kreeli in the group moving through the forms halted and ran over. She looked about middle-aged. Her physique was stout, like a bull.

"Open the library for Lilli," the monk said.

"And my guest, if you please, Teacher."

The monk nodded but kept his eye on those practicing.

"This way," the librarian said.

Lilline motioned Inti, who had reached them, to follow.

They traveled through the main floor and down several flights of curving steps carved into the mountain. A glow bulb in the librarian's hand illuminated their way. Memories from her younger cycles flooded her thoughts. This had been home, where Kissy brought her to stay during missions in the field. She loved the monastery, but the library held a special place in her heart. It was where her passion for poetry got its classical backbone. The texts preserved inside the sanctuary ranged from modern books and pamphlets to ancient parchments and scrolls. All of them, whether as old as millennia or as recent as a hundred-cycle, shared one thing: routes to enlightenment.

"So," the librarian said, walking from sconce to sconce and activating the warm green bulbs in the rock chamber, "what are you seeking?"

Lilline took in the familiar space of the cavern, its sides lined with books and small recesses carved into the walls that housed cases and shelves of dusty texts and documents lost to time. Something about this place always brought comfort. Even if Nave or some other power-hungry fool took down the galaxy, the idea that this library would remain evoked solace. Someone or something, at some point, would find it and learn about the artistic and philosophical reflections of a multi-species galactic civilization.

She turned to Inti, gesturing that he should answer the Kreeli's question.

"How far back does the collection go?" the Rasp asked. His neck was alive with serpentine fluctuations and his head moved left to right, taking it in.

"As far back as there are written records."

The Rasp hissed.

Lilline turned, surprised. A small tongue fluttered out of the throat flap and returned down their esophagus.

"How is it organized?" Inti asked.

"These are chronological," the librarian gestured at the two walls of books. "This as well," she indicated the caverns on the left. "And that one," she pointed at a recess near the back on the right, "is unclassifiable material. All of it from the ancient days."

"There, please," Inti said.

Lilline followed behind, glancing at book spines as they passed floor-to-ceiling wall stacks. Familiar titles by earlier poets and historians flew by her nostalgic eyes. When she had first arrived at the monastery, she had thought Kissy sent her here to learn how to fight. In the end, she realized that its purpose was much more complex and layered. *Have I used all that the monks imparted?* The martial art, without question, was in constant use. The knowledge in these books? Much of it aided her in the field, providing a foundation in humanities from which to glean tidbits of information that were mission specific. But what about the more profound aspects of her monastic education?

"I don't believe it. May I?" Inti asked, indicating a codex whose cover was partially deteriorated.

"Handle it carefully, please," the librarian said. Her headband glittered with an internal adjustment.

Lilline followed the Rasp's three fingers as he reached in and pulled out the thin document. He placed it down on the stone ledge in front of him and drew open the cover.

"What language is that?" Lilline asked. It looked like a jumble of symbols and hatchings.

"Koralis," the Rasp whispered, running a weathered finger over the page. "An ancient and secret form of communication among long-forgotten cosmic philosophers."

"What species?" she asked.

"We do not know."

She followed his fingers as they turned the page. Her eyes went wide. There, in a crude artistic rendering, was the image of the wraith on Frebu.

"That's—"

"Yes," Inti nodded and turned the page.

The eccentric text ran in a pattern this time, shifting location along the margins.

"That looks like a poetic form," she said.

"Indeed." Inti lowered his eye closer, reading. "Yes, yes...." He turned another page.

There it was. An Astral Mind, drawn so similar to the one she'd seen that it was uncanny.

"Please let it be here," the Rasp whispered and turned the page.

His gasp made her jump. "What is it?"

"Look."

Her eyes went down the sequences of illegible verse. The last portion of the page was gone. Ripped out.

"The last line. It's missing," he said.

"What are we looking at, Inti?"

"An incantation. It is the words to release the Astral Mind. To liberate it through the gate. This knowledge is beyond measure. It was just a legend. And now," he turned and fixed his eye on her, "it has returned to another civilization."

The voice of the past speaking to the present.

The Rasp turned to the librarian. "May we take this? It is vital to our effort."

She shook her head. "Nothing leaves the sanctuary. I am sorry."

Inti twisted his neck and Lilline found herself locked with his eye again. "I need time to translate this," he said. "The last line may be predicted, or at least guessed, if I can—"

"We don't have it," she said and meant it. "Might we copy it?" she asked the Kreeli.

"By hand, yes. That I can allow."

Lilline turned back to the stacks of books and small study tables. She spotted parchment and a writing tool. She strode over and snatched it up. "Here," she walked back over, "use this."

Inti shook his head. "It will take me too much time." He turned to the librarian. "Could we ask you to do it?"

Lilline was already copying the lines of verse.

THIRTY-TWO

"Inti, we're approaching the rendezvous point. Tell me you have it translated." Lilline shifted in the freighter's cockpit, trying to get comfortable. After making the FTL run in the top-of-the-line Racer, the old and clunky sewage hauler left much to be desired. Not just comfort, either. The nav tech on the bird barely cleared acceptable transportation standards. She didn't want to think about its safety systems and O2 regulator.

"Yes, most of it." The Rasp's voice came over the comm scratchy and glitching.

What a piece of junk. She couldn't blame Gribb. As Lauden told the Froo, he had delivered in a near impossible timeframe.

"And the last line?"

Inti had been in the mess on the ship's lower level for most of the ride, working on the copied text.

"I'm uncertain, but I have a hypothesis."

"Well, you're going to have to hope it works. Get closed up down there and prepared for the rendezvous. We're dropping out of FTL now."

Lilline watched the seconds on the nav system tick down. *Carbrook better be ready to transfer over and set up his hub.* They needed every minute.

She gripped the steering column. The familiar, instantaneous shift from streaking white light to painstakingly slow time/space sent the ship back into the complicated world with its looming deadline.

"Bingo," she said, spotting the sleek cruiser forty-five degrees to port. Twisting the column left, she hit the burners. In the distance, the sun's light illuminated their destination. Nave's orbital shimmered like a tiny crescent moon surrounded by a distant starry blanket.

Ping.

Lilline pushed the comm button. "Talk to me, Carbrook. You all set for transfer?"

"Yes. Is it going to be difficult?"

"It's a simple tube connect. Piece of cake."

"My equipment won't get messed up or anything?"

"I'm not even going to grace that with a response." She set the algorithm to align the two ships. A diagram appeared on a scratched-up LCD screen. "You have got to be kidding me."

"Is there a problem?"

"No problem, Carbrook. Just be ready."

"Okay."

"Carbrook, relax. This is what freight haulers do all day, every day, across the galaxy." *In piece of junk ships like this one.* "You're not even coming with us for the infiltration. You get to stay on board."

"I am going down to the transfer door now."

"Who is dropping you off?"

"Ummm... hold on."

I swear this is the last time with him. Never again is he getting out into the field.

"Zavo, he's from Astro-Travel."

She didn't know him. "Well, tell him we'll be there in three minutes." Lilline followed the crude nav line and adjusted the telemetry as her larger ship approached. Once she had the hauler parallel and aligned, she would release the tube and initiate the transfer.

She opened the internal comm. "Inti, you ready?"

"Yes, I am at..."

Garbled static cut out the rest of his sentence.

"What?"

"... door and waiting."

She took pity on the pilots and crews running freight on ships like this one, without the fancy toys and Racer she had as a secret agent.

With a bump to the throttle, the ship covered the last few hundred meters and glided forward and down. Lilline tipped the freighter's bow so it would sit parallel with the cruiser. The GAM-OPs runner moved too far past the cockpit.

"Woops!" She pulled back on the throttle to decelerate. The handle stuck. "Crap!" She jiggled it back and forth. "What the..." A hard yank released it from the rusty debris. "Piece of crap ship." She punched the internal comm. "Hold on Inti!" Lilline pitched the column up and hit the reverse thrusters.

Her eyes followed the LCD screen. A collision alert went off.

"Yeah, yeah." She cut the reverse burners. "One more bump of thrust," she said and hit the forward boosters. Her stomach lurched and the ship's nose rose. To her right, the cruiser's hull broke into view. "Right where I wanted you," she said. "That was fun."

She opened the internal comm again. "You okay down there, Inti? Sorry about that."

"Not a..."

Lilline waited.

"... you ready for me to send the tube?"

"Yep, hit it."

Out the bridge window, the crescent moon of the orbital loomed. *Is the Astral Mind there? Can it change size at will?* She made a mental note to ask Inti on the ride into the spoke.

The tube connection light popped green. "Now get your ass over here," she muttered to herself.

Two minutes passed. She spent it staring at Nave's station.

"How we doing down there, Inti?"

Nothing.

"Zavo, is Carbrook on his way over?" she asked, opening a line to the cruiser.

Nothing from the other ship.

The tube connection light on the console flashed red. She got up and peered out the corner of the bridge window. The seal floated about ten meters back from runner's hull. She followed the accordion folds. It wasn't retracting, either.

"Piece of crap," she said and set the hauler controls to hold.

Carbrook needed to be on board with all his equipment now or this wasn't going to work. They'd never get inside and find their way undetected without him, not in under three hours.

"Inti?" she called out as the portal opened on the lower level. The hallway, stacked with rusty shelving units and smelling awful, was empty. She hustled down the long corridor past sewage tanks and around the turn to the airlock.

"Greetings, heathen." The Preacher stood in front of the tube seal hatch.

On instinct, Lilline swung around to make for the corner. Four Gej-ti appeared, aiming blasters. In one motion, she spiraled back towards The Preacher and flung the wrist knife at her throat.

The Kreeli deflected the blade with a metal object in her hand. It clanged off the wall and fell to the floor. The Preacher's arms went up. She bellowed a hearty laugh of triumph.

Where are Inti and Carbrook?

"You're trapped, secret agent. Caught in a web, spun by your ignorance and lack of faith." The blue skin on The Preacher's cheeks creased as her lips parted, revealing sharpened teeth.

Nave's personal assassin shifted to the side and gestured for her to look. Through the airlock window, Inti stood, his one eye connecting with her two. The defeat on his face hit her like a laser.

The Kreeli roared in laughter and pushed the release switch.

"No!" Lilline lunged at her foe, blasters aimed at her from behind be damned. A blue hand came up and pointed a canister at her face. A cloud of yellow mist engulfed her vision. Her skin stung as if thousands of venomous insects attacked her from an angry hive. She dropped to a knee gasping, fighting off unconsciousness.

Through blurring vision, she caught sight of the tiny form of a Rasp spiraling through space.

THIRTY-THREE

Location: Virtual | Network: Encrypted

"Good afternoon, Agent Renault."

You open your eyes. You are seated in the board room, facing the window. Through the glass, the perfect city runs to the horizon. You look down. Your hands and ankles are bound to the arms and legs of the chair. The sound of water trickles behind you, breaking the silence.

A click to your left draws your attention. Mavron Nave enters the room through a set of double doors. He walks along the other side of the table and stops across from you.

"You've been quite a challenge." The entrepreneur pulls out the chair in front of him and sits. He rests his elbows on the table and smiles. "Agent Lilline Renault of GAM-OPs."

You try and remember how you got here. The memory is fuzzy and indistinct.

"Ah yes," Nave says. "I can tell by your expression you aren't sure what happened. Shall I recount it for you?"

You don't respond. You were trained not to do so.

"I imagine you're familiar with this setting, Ms. Renault. I chose that seat especially for you. It should match the view you had last time you were here." A bottle and a glass appear on the table. He uncorks it, pours, and lifts the wine to his nose. He sniffs. "My favorite vintage."

A smile of satisfaction grows on his face.

The memory of The Preacher's smugness outside the airlock returns. Inti tumbling through space passes in your mind. It all comes back – the ship, the transfer gone wrong near the orbital, and the knockout gas.

"What have you done with my assistant?"

"Who, this 'Carbrook'? He is the least of your concerns, Agent Renault."

You keep your eyes locked on him. He leans back in the chair.

"I must admit, you are very good at your job. Like your grandmother."

"Where is she?" You tug on your restraints.

"Please stop that. Don't make yourself look any more pathetic than you already do." You watch the red liquid roll in the glass as he twirls it. "I do apologize for those, by the way." He indicates the cuffs. "It is less for anyone's safety than as a demonstration."

"Of what?" You try to keep him talking while you work through the situation.

"The future."

You feign interest, buying time. Someone betrayed you and leaked the information about the rendezvous point. Did 2112 break through the GAM-OPs security network a second time?

"Where is Kissy? What do you want with her?"

"She is serving her purpose, like you." He sips the wine. "And now for the best part, Ms. Renault, which I am sure must be rattling you to no end." He raises an eyebrow.

Your stomach stirs. The anxiety of what is coming rises, but you hold it down. You are trained to appear one way on the outside and another on the inside.

"For cycles, Mind Eye searched the galaxy for an ancient text. Rumors claimed its pages contained the key to the final step on our journey to manifest power and summon a cosmic ally." He raises the glass to his mouth and sips. "My parents, the leaders of our movement, found it. At last, the link to a greater dimensional world could be made."

The book that Lauden mentioned. The one Inti said lay for centuries on Zeret.

Nave rises from his seat. He turns his back on you and walks to the window.

"Its power held truth, but the words it contained were incomplete." He gazes out at his perfect city. "We had the means but not the path. And then, my knowledge and brilliance found the doorway and summoned this!"

The window shatters. Shards of glass pass through you, leaving no trace. The pulsing spectral horror of the Astral Mind looms in a black void.

You turn your head away, fighting its screaming terror.

"Only one link remained to be found!" Nave screams over the blaring frequencies rattling your mind.

Flash!

Silence returns. The water wall trickles behind you. You open your eyes, your brain pants with exhaustion against the wraith's brief intrusion. Nave is standing, facing you in the tranquility of the board room.

"And wouldn't you know..." he walks over and sits back down, "it comes to us from the most unlikely source. Our enemy." He picks up the glass and swirls the wine. "Your grandmother."

"What?" You speak the word without thinking.

"So, you don't know then?" He laughs. "Oh, that is cruel."

You recover and remember your training. You stare back, but inside the connection of family to the unknown gnaws at you.

"We all have secrets to keep, for the right price."

"What are you talking about, Mavron?"

"Your parents, Agent Renault. They weren't killed by some unfortunate accident. My organization took them as retribution after your grandmother and that hypocritical organization you work for murdered my parents. Mind Eye was in the hands of two brilliant leaders, my mother and father were ready to make the transcendent step. But your grandparent executed them because you couldn't share in our victory and ascendency." The words come out through gritted teeth, filled with anger.

How could that be? He must be lying.

"So much for integrity, yes? The 'other' Agent Renault, by means unknown, gained access to the missing line of the incantation. She exchanged it with us." You watch his grin widen. "Do you know what for?"

Your mind is racing. *Kissy would never...* Your gut wrenches at the memory of the torn page in the subterranean library.

But she did.

"I know that it's hard to fathom. It goes against everything your agency touts as its mission and purpose."

"She did it for me." You speak in a whisper.

He nods, a gloating satisfaction on his face. "Your life was spared in exchange for the final line. You, Agent Renault, are the price of their failure."

It can't be. Lauden wouldn't allow it. Flashes of the director's dubious comments to you, and vague responses to your questions throughout Operation Freestrike flash through your mind. You remember his warning about difficult choices at the monastery.

"The irony is beautiful is it not?" Nave gestures with the glass of wine. "Both of us orphaned through double murders, choosing separate courses of revenge. Don't deny it, Agent Renault. All you do is driven by a need to protect others from what happened to you as a child." He sips more wine. "We are more alike than you think. The difference between us is my life's course evolved into enlightenment and understanding. Yours stagnated, unable to develop through the lies and deceits of your colleagues. By those who supposedly love you. You are a killer without an agenda. Others with greater minds think for you."

It doesn't make sense. Exchanging that knowledge for your life meant giving Mind Eye the means to achieve its goals. Lauden and Inti said they hoped the day wouldn't come. How could it not with what Kissy gave them? Was Nave that extraordinary a genius that he broke through a barrier GAM-OPs never thought possible? The analysts would never condone such a decision. It meant one thing: Kissy did this on her own.

"That doesn't explain why my grandmother went willingly on Beisho."

"Oh, come now, Ms. Renault. Kissy might have been the greatest agent in history, but she still has feelings. And a human heart, pathetic as it may be."

He's convinced she did it out of guilt. That was never Granny's style. *No, something else is in play.*

"And here we are," he says. "Your colleagues have placed the weight of the world on your shoulders. The story comes full circle. So fitting, even profound. Unfortunately, you are doomed to fail."

Your heart races. It doesn't add up. *Kissy, and possibly Lauden, reversing the essential mission of GAM-OPs?* Its ethic has always been the collective good over the individual.

"It's over Agent Renault." You watch Nave sniff, relishing the wine's aroma. "You and your organization are too late to stop me. The incantation is complete. But more than that," he grins, "*Freestrike 4 has begun.*"

You do your best to hide your shock. The image of millions of innocent citizens manipulated to further empower Nave's creation horrifies you.

"And now that I have found the portal and perfected the

summoning, the last line will free the Astral Mind from the boundary. Unchained, it will move where I guide it. What you confronted on Frebu was a mere trifle, an experiment on the road to perfection. As soon as I leave this room, the ritual begins."

"You'll never succeed." You shake your head. The GAM-OPs agent in you pushes aside the personal suffering and shock of a granddaughter. The task at hand takes priority. You can work out the details and betrayals afterward if there is a world left and you are still alive.

"Oh, but I already have, Agent Renault. You and the other GAM-OPs agents are so sure of yourselves 'out there' in the other world. I've lured you to the bait, like a stupid fish that can't resist a shiny object in a stream."

"So now what, Nave? You and the rest of the Mind Eye members play 'God' and try and rule the galaxy? I hate to break it to you, but you aren't the first to attempt it and you won't be the last. It's a tired pattern. Your kind always fails."

"That is where you are wrong, Agent Renault. This is not a game of win and lose. Not this time."

"Everything is a game to you. That's your problem." You know of his temper and try to tap it so he will reveal clues. "I'm sure you and I are sitting somewhere on your orbital right now while you 'play' with control here in this so-called room."

"Nice try, Ms. Renault. Your attempt to extract information is insulting. You and I both have a degree of professional talent that I hoped would be respected during this conversation."

"That's what this is? With me restrained? Looks more like a display of pathetic power to me."

You see no sign of anger in the entrepreneur's avatar. Are you and he even in the same place outside of the virtual meeting? Your anxiety rises as you realize the magnitude of strategic problems involved with the conditions of your parlay.

"I have no need to demonstrate power. Not here." He waves a

hand around indicating the office. "My organization has created something that will silence all questions."

"So, you'll rule the world by gagging it into submission?"

He laughs. "I am impressed with your rhetorical skills, Agent Renault."

"You haven't seen anything yet."

"No. *You* haven't. GAM-OPs, the galactic minister, and her cabinet are all neophytes in the world that I inhabit. True intellect and wisdom are the road forward. Mind Eye will forge a path for humanity into the stars."

The office transforms into a cosmic spectacle. Nave stands on a single square in the void. You look down. Nothing except distant stars fills the infinite space below you. Your stomach lurches from the lack of gravity and you lose your physical bearing. Everywhere you turn your head is an endless stellar blanket. The sound, that frequency you have come to know and fear, rises.

"Do you hear that, Agent Renault?" You look at Nave standing on the small square. "That is the voice of the universe!"

Your chair rotates with slow precision, offering you a three-hundred-and-sixty-degree view of the endless void.

"From the first steps of our infancy, we have reached the threshold of communication with the All."

"We?"

"There are always leaders and followers, Ms. Renault. We will drag along those who sleep on the bed of ignorance. Others who are too short of wit, or too stubborn to accept maturity and guidance, will be left behind."

"You mean killed."

"Is there a difference? When a portal to enlightenment and transcendence awaits? They will serve their purpose by feeding our power."

"The Astral Mind? You've invited something into our world without realizing its potential and purpose. Send it back now."

He laughs. "You and all the others have no idea of the power

Mind Eye wields. We have esoteric knowledge, accessed from the ancients, which will guide us to cosmic enlightenment. I will rule from my seat of supreme power." Nave raises his arms, and the cosmos falls away.

You are back in the board room, sitting at the table. Nave, too, is seated where he was before the virtual shift of location. No time to dance around with rhetoric. You must hit hard now. "So, this is your paradise?" Your gaze burns into the entrepreneur. "Your little world where everything is as you like it?" You raise an eyebrow. "The way you need it to be to convince yourself you aren't weak?"

He nods and picks up the glass of wine. "I expected that from you. It will take time for most to move past petty and elementary accusations."

"This is just a playground, Mavron. You are nothing more than a bully here. And you know what happens to bullies after people wise up, don't you?"

"Not a playground, Agent Renault. The true reality."

"I think you've lived too long in your games. Or you've been seduced by esoteric knowledge and have twisted it to convince your-self you hold extraordinary capabilities. I hate to break it to you, but those are the dreams of a child that never wants to grow up." You let your anger come through. You are unsure if it will work to your advantage or come back to bite you. "From where I am sitting, it looks like a spoiled brat using their wealth to scream and whine that the world wasn't fair to them."

You wait for a response, hoping his anger will rise.

"You must be desperate, Agent Renault, to resort to brashness."

You stare at him. *He isn't taking the bait.*

"Don't you see, Agent Renault? You and I are more real, truer to our nature and character here than we are in that other world with its rules, moral restrictions, and physical limitations. My organization, with its liberated philosophy, can create the ideal mental projection of reality. The philosophers of old knew that is all we've ever had. The world 'out there' was never ours." He gestures around him. "It's the one we make," you see him point a finger at his head, "in here, that is the true universe. So has it been prophesied for millennia."

"This is nothing more than escapism. You're too cowardly and lazy to make your way through a world that isn't as you want it."

"Cowards!" You feel the floor shake as his fist slams down on the table. "By creating this world, I have done the opposite." He shoves back from the table and stands. "I will turn the meek into the brave. I'm giving people what they're too afraid to ask for. They want adventure. They desire thrills and action. You, of all people, should understand, Agent Renault. It is what you do, is it not? Your world has failed them." His finger points at you. "You've provided a life of comforts. The galaxy has become soft. They manifest their true desires through virtual entertainment. Now, through the guiding hand of Mind Eye, a second lived experience is at our doorstep."

"And the solution is to summon an extra-dimensional power to serve your anger and hate?"

"To teach you all a lesson!" The building sways. The wine glass shatters in his hand. Crimson liquid splashes in the air and onto the table. You watch it dissolve and the clean perfection of the polished surface return.

"Temper, temper, Mavron." You smile at him.

"You know nothing of it! I will teach you and your agency about playing games." His eyes burn with malice. "And you, Agent Renault, will feel the personal sting of it. I have a nice little session waiting for you."

"I can't wait. Bring it on. Seeing you fail in 'here' as well as out there," you gesture with your head around you, indicating the virtual space, "will be incredibly satisfying. As will watching you and your cronies touting yourselves as the saviors spend the rest of your lives in prison."

"It is the world, Agent Renault, that you need to worry about. So-called order, peace, and security are about to be re-designed by superior hands."

"You're mad, Mavron."

"Oh, but you are wrong, Agent Renault." He waves a hand and a second replica of the wine bottle and glass appear, replacing the previous one. He pours a fresh glass. "I, along with all of those who precede me in Mind Eye, are the last bastions of sanity left in a galaxy filled with illusions."

He leans forward over the table.

Your eyes, and his, are level.

"No longer will the world of the virtual and the tangible be separate. Games are now reality. Life is now play."

You laugh, mocking him.

"Go ahead. Amuse yourself while you can. Fear is a powerful weapon, Agent Renault. As are illusions. They carry more terror than you can imagine."

His sinister smile broadens as he leans back, standing tall in front of you. "You will learn through experience." He gulps down the last of the wine and sets the glass on the table. He walks to the window with the view of his perfect city.

"Good luck, Agent Renault. You'll need it."

THIRTY-FOUR

Location: Unknown

Thud!

Lilline's head and torso lunged forward. She retched in a world of darkness.

Something was ripped off her face and sight returned. Inches from her nose, her hands lay cuffed on her knees. A forceful grip swung her head up. She confronted the face of The Preacher.

"Greetings, heathen," the Kreeli grinned.

Lilline gasped for air and struggled to recover from the punch to her gut. Through blurry vision, she sized up the setting and situation. A small control center, with a terminal that looked like a tech hub for something that might—

Thud!

Another shot sent her forward again. She retched a second time, stomach heaving from the powerful blow. The grip on her hair released and she felt the prosthetic ear ripped off the side of her head.

Saliva dribbled from her mouth, trickling onto her bound wrists and knees. She grunted and worked to control the pain and nausea.

"Some cannot be made to understand. They never pass beyond the first Tier." The Kreeli's deep voice spoke as if teaching a lesson to an unseen apprentice. "They lay asleep on a bed of ignorance, their eyes open but unable to see."

Lilline pulled herself upright and did her best to survey the room. About thirty meters square, it contained two portals on opposite walls. She pushed against the restraints on her ankles, trying to shift the chair's position. It didn't budge. They'd bolted the legs to the floor.

She had no idea how long she'd been out, had no sense of where she was or any grasp of how much time had elapsed since the trap during the transfer between ships.

Inti's murder returned with cold clarity. Without him, she had no guidance or way to stop the Astral Mind. She didn't even know what Nave had planned for her with his so-called 'game'.

"I am tasked with preparing you for your trial," The Preacher said turning around to face her.

"By preparation you mean torture," Lilline snarked, breathing heavily. "Just wanted to edit for clarity."

The Kreeli's eyes went wide at her retort. She took two strides across the room and swung an arm back, winding up to strike.

Crack!

"You will fail, heathen, as will all who oppose the true path that awaits us," The Preacher said. "Mind Eye has heard the voice of the universe. And it is beautiful!"

Sparkles of light dappled her vision, obscuring the view of the room. Lilline's head throbbed as her body worked to realign itself from the vicious blow. The familiar metallic taste of blood ran over her tongue. She spit some out onto the Kreeli's feet.

Crack!

Another shot, this time on the other side of her jaw. She groaned and fought back the pain. "Going to... have to... do better than that with me," she said. Warm blood dribbled down her lip and chin.

The Preacher's headband glittered as it adjusted pressure. Her arms went wide in a gesture of reverence. "With pleasure."

Thud!

Lilline coughed and bent forward from the mighty fists that struck her belly. Her forearm brushed over something protruding on her thigh. *Pin's comm.* They had missed it when they searched her for weapons.

"The signal is ready," a voice said from behind the Kreeli.

Lilline raised her head. Through spinning vision, she caught sight of a Gej-ti, clothed in a hyperchromium snowsuit, enter through the portal and stomp their boots. Snow clumps scattered around their feet.

An arctic climate. Could this be Frebu or Eshi? The confusion she felt in the virtual board room with Nave revisited her, interfering with logical reasoning. What if it was the simulated environment on the orbital?

"The tower is active. All other communication sat links were terminated an hour before we arrived. Nothing can transmit in or out except for when we reactivate the tower after the ritual," the Gej-ti said.

"Good," The Preacher said, eyes on Lilline.

"Where is 2112?" the Gej-ti asked.

"Back in their cage," The Preacher said. "The High Master says they're usefulness is over."

2112 is here somewhere. Lilline kept her exterior unaffected by the mention of the hacker. To the two watching her, she looked like a beat-up, pathetic hostage. That was true, but she was also on the job.

The Preacher gestured with a hand over to the terminal. "They left instructions for you."

Lilline wanted to look but knew better. Not yet. She needed to find the right moment, hopefully before the Kreeli knocked her out. Or, worse.

If Carbrook was still alive and she could get out of here and find him, there might be a way to stop them. At this point, it was all she had. Without Inti or the techie, she wasn't sure she knew what to do if she got out of this mess. GAM-OPs couldn't track her with all the sats down and whatever this 'game' Nave had planned for her meant, she had no idea.

"The High Master says it is time," the Gej-ti said. "You're to join them for the liberation incantation."

"As soon as I deliver this one to their reckoning," The Preacher said. "Check your instructions from 2112." The Kreeli gestured to the terminal. "Don't make me tell you a third time."

Out of the corner of her eye, Lilline tracked the Gej-ti as they crossed to the computer station.

I want that hacker.

"Disgusting," they said and wiped a cluster of something off the desk with a gloved hand.

Small flecks scattered across the floor. One landed next to her foot. She squinted in the dim lighting and focused on it.

Wait... is that?

A chewed-off strip of fingernail.

———

"They trapped me, T8!" Carbrook screamed from the cell. "I had no choice!"

Lilline glared with vengeance as The Preacher dragged her down the hallway.

"You have to believe me!"

Carbrook had a desperate look in his eye. She'd seen it before on the job. Someone who got themselves wrapped up in something too big to handle, thinking their part in a scheme would sneak past those who might take down the major players. They saw themselves as victims, unable to recognize or acknowledge that their role was based on a choice putting them on the other side of a line. It was always with the same tired excuse: they thought themselves too good at what they did to get caught, or that they could invent their way out of accountability. It never happened, at least not on any of the ops she'd been on. They always went down, and when they did, it was the most pathetic of all.

"You played the game," Lilline growled as his face passed behind the bars of the cell.

"I thought I could outsmart them."

She fought the pain to remain conscious. The hallway and Carbrook's face rocked like a boat on rough seas.

"I slipped up at the gala," he said. "They figured out I was 2112. Nave sent photos of me through the hacker channel. He knew who I was. They were going to expose me. What was I supposed to do?"

"Not this, Carbrook," she said and spat blood. It smeared a crimson trail on the floor as her boot heel ran through it.

"It was all supposed to go away once the game dropped! They promised. None of you were ever going to know."

She didn't even grace that with a response. His admission of the cover-up was guilt enough. He'd aided their enemy and put her life and all of GAM-OPs in danger. For all his genius, Carbrook failed to grasp the fallout of his choice to maintain his anonymous hacker identity.

"No one appreciates me." His tone shifted to anger. "I'm a brilliant technician and scientist. But no one cares. None of you!" He rattled the bars of the cell in desperation.

"You played the game. And you lost," she said. The view of the hallway disappeared as she rounded a bend. "No replays in the real world."

"T8!" Carbrook's repeated cries of her name grew fainter the further The Preacher dragged her down the corridor. She focused on the lights passing overhead in a steady rhythm, struggling to stay awake.

She'd taken beatings like this before. The pain was bearable. It was more a matter of the body's involuntary choice between what it would allow and when it was time to shut down. Her training at the monastery had smithed a will of iron, able to endure extreme and sustained physical trauma. Her high threshold had saved her before in the field. She hoped it would do so again now.

"Here we are," the Kreeli's deep voice said. The familiar bellowing laugh echoed from overhead.

Lilline gazed up and saw the oblong face, upside down, sneering down at her.

"Time to meet your maker," The Preacher said.

THIRTY-FIVE

A shiver ran down Lilline's spine. Only one creature made that distinct call: a Bukki tiger.

Dense foliage blocked the view ahead. She turned and found herself facing a white wall. A thin oval boundary was all that remained of the portal where she'd been thrown inside.

Her fingers edged over the seam and felt nothing. No air passed through the boundary. Left and right, the wall ran until it was lost from sight. She craned her neck back and swayed with dizziness. Sparkles danced across her vision from the pain of the fisted blows. She was indoors, that was for certain. An opaque ceiling loomed several hundred meters overhead.

Another roar, closer this time. From the volume of the tiger's call, Lilline guessed its distance to be no more than fifty meters.

No weapon and no sonic-repellent. The beating would hinder her physical ability against a Bukki, but worse was the emotional impact of the betrayal and the ticking clock to stop a madman. She had no viable plan beyond immediate survival.

One step at a time.

She took in the surroundings and inventoried as much as she could to memory.

So, this is a game. Trapped in a web, as Nave had said in the board room. He had gloated about—

"Welcome, Agent Renault." The entrepreneur's voice bounced off the roof and echoed through the jungle. *"I hope you appreciate the setting. I designed it just for you."*

His voice boomed like a god from on high.

Lilline struggled to maintain her balance against its jarring volume. *Steady yourself.* If he was watching, she didn't want to give him the satisfaction of her pain.

The jungle spun.

Focus.

Her vision swirled and wet earth smacked her cheek.

"Pathetic," Nave said. *"I would have thought you tougher than this."*

Lilline tracked a small beetle as it trotted over a fallen leaf. This close to her face, it appeared like a giant monster trekking through a prodigious ecosystem.

"It seems that I overestimated your ability level. Well, rest assured I will not embarrass you. I have more important business to attend to, as you know. Watching this tomorrow when the galaxy is on its knees will be a most rewarding experience. There will be plenty of Gondau for the occasion, of course."

"I don't care," she grunted.

"You've lost your rhetorical edge, Agent Renault."

"Fuck you," she said and rose, shaking off the dizziness. "How's that for my rhetorical edge?" Somewhere inside, her agent mental muscles flexed. They told her not to lose contact with him, whether to try and delay the final phase of his plan or to work on a possible escape from this situation.

"Come now, Agent Renault. Show a little more respect." Nave's sigh resonated through the audio system. *"Very well. It is time for you to play this small but deadly game."*

Her mind spiraled down to essentials. *Where am I?* Everything appeared authentic other than the ceiling. *Is this the orbital?* If it was, then the Gej-ti had walked through the simulated arctic environment to enter the room where she had been held and beaten. Or was this a facility on a distant planet or moon? Did it matter under the circumstances?

"You may be surprised to know that you are not the player in this game, Agent Renault. You see, that is what makes it so satisfying as its designer. But I am a good sport, so I will give you a clue to make it more entertaining."

"Entertaining for whom?"

"For me."

Lilline couldn't miss the retribution in his tone.

"The objective isn't to win or lose. As I've told you, my competitions no longer play within those parameters."

"Yes, Mavron. I know. You're not a sane person. I wouldn't expect your games to be logical."

"They are perfectly logical!" His voice screeched through the audio system, breaking the limit of the speakers.

She collapsed to her knees from the pain entering her ears.

The Bukki roared.

"Everything I do is of perfect formula and design," Nave's voice was softer, but she'd conversed with him enough to hear the traces of anger that lingered. *"All of you are too stupid and ignorant to perceive its ideal beauty."*

Lilline spat blood out onto the dirt. She stood and took a few steps to the edge of the jungle. Her hand pulled back the curtain of body-size leaves and she peered ahead. The sooner she dealt with what awaited her, the better the chances to keep the mission going. She stumbled through the greenery.

"There's the sport I was hoping for," Nave said. *"Since you and your agency like to play with people's lives, let's see how you feel when the tables are turned, shall we?"*

"I told you already," Lilline said, edging down the jungle path, "bring it."

"*Enjoy being* my *pawn. The tiger has been trained with more hatred and intimidation than you can imagine.*"

"I don't doubt that" she whispered, eyeing the surroundings. The smell and look of the place was akin to Hesh-9.

"*Fear is a powerful weapon.*"

"That line is getting old, Mavron," she said. *Fear was trained out of me by the monks.*

"*Goodbye, Ms. Renault.*" Sinister laughter bounced off the ceiling in a haunting farewell. As the echoes faded, the music of the rainforest came to life. She knelt next to a glade of ferns, closed her eyes, and listened. It was the same as reaching a blind hand into her snow jacket, or into the satchel on the hoverbike. The difference was that this time it wasn't touch but hearing that became the sensory focus.

Bird songs and an insect chorus rose and fell.

Something isn't right about this...

She listened in earnest.

Yes, that's it. Every thirty seconds the sounds recycled. But there was something else. She'd spent enough time on Hesh-9 to know the difference between natural and synthetic jungle noises. This was just like Nave's city. Even the sonorous blend of insects was calculated.

So, I am in his perfect little game. She opened her eyes and stood. *The question is, how much of this is real and how much is an illusion?* Nave's comment about the boundary falling away between the two didn't help settle her anxiety.

A growl broke her concentration. The Bukki was close, no more than twenty meters ahead. That didn't make sense with where she heard it last.

Rethink possible. You are in a game. The standard rules of space and time may not apply.

Her eardrums rattled as the animal and insect noises surged in volume. It was as if a conductor swung a baton upward, driving a crescendo. Everything that spoke in the rainforest amplified to a near deafening pitch.

The hairs on the back of her neck straightened like antennae.

Roar!

She bolted, jumping and dodging rocks and small plants. Something crashed through the brush in pursuit. Hot, pulsing air rushed over her shoulders. The distinct rhythm of a beast's nostrils exhaling filled her ears. It was right behind her!

The greenery grew thicker, closing out a route ahead. She had to make a move now or she'd be trapped. A towering tree with roots like claws neared. She dove between its root arms and covered her head.

The jungle's volume dial turned to normal. Her panting broke the rising and falling of the insect chorus.

She peeked out over the edge of a root wall. Calm and empty rainforest, devoid of any beast, ran in all directions.

It was right there, on my tail.

The dread birthed on Frebu rose from her psychic depths. Waves of horror flowed into her bloodstream. Her heart thudded in her chest.

Stop. It's not real. Relax.

Despite all her training, fear was upon her. Nave's technology was tapping her psyche. How, she didn't know, but her inner nightmares were being made manifest as outer reality. This was brilliance in innovation twisted to sadistic ends. She didn't want to imagine how Mind Eye could exploit its power if they took control of the galaxy.

Lilline stood and regrouped, wiping off the dirt and leaves.

The Bukki's fear she could handle. It was the other, deeper—

Roar!

Her body flew off the ground. She smashed into the trunk of the tree two meters off the jungle floor. Sound and force held her fast. Like invisible wind, whatever screamed at her pinned her in suspension like a martyr crucified, defying gravity.

Lilline shut her eyes and steeled herself against the horror. In the inner darkness, something probed her with flaring wraith-like hands. An immaterial tendril caressed her cheek. She winced and turned her head.

"*Relax.*" The word echoed inside her mind. "*All I want is—*"

It ripped into her gut. She screamed.

A psychic abyss opened within her. Her enemy descended into her soul, searching. She knew what it wanted, and she couldn't hide it.

The invisible presence grinned inside her darkness. It sifted through the trauma of her life, moving back in time.

"*Here is something.*" The wraith squeezed the memory in its grip, wringing out the pain with a thousand times its original hurt.

Lilline wailed, her voice lost underneath the gloating of the malicious spirit.

She mustered what she could of her strength and courage and pulled herself back to stand her ground in the darkness.

"*Stop fighting and let me in,*" the wraith said in a strange form of non-speech. "*It will all go away. All the pain...*"

Lilline pushed back, but the force was too potent. It was only a matter of time.

The wraith laughed in victory.

She faltered. Her courage melted. Her fight against the creature collapsed and the psychic floodgate opened. The beast rushed in, lapping up all the suffering, shame, and humiliation of her inner core.

No!

Her soul shattered like exploding ice. Every shard torn from her seared with lightning pain. Silent screams echoed in the internal void.

The wraith roared with delight. "*I control you now.*"

In her exhaustion and suffering, Lilline caught sight of an intrusion flickering within the psychic darkness. A luminous silhouette materialized in the void.

Inti?

Light radiated outward, pushing away the psychic pitch.

"Thought expressed as feeling." The Rasp's voice hit her with the calm precision of a laser through glacial ice.

What was she supposed to do? It was over. She couldn't muster anything more. She had nothing left, not even a body. 'She' was gone, consumed into Nave's cosmic creation.

"You are thinking too clearly." Inti's message arrived as feeling. *"It is not over, not yet."*

It's over. She couldn't deny it. She knew it. The entity knew it, and Nave probably knew it too. He had wrought terror and violence on her and would now be unstoppable. If GAM-OPs couldn't halt him, no one could.

"Who are you?" It was Inti, reaching her again through feeling.

I am no one.

"Nonsense. Who are you?"

Lilline pulled as much of herself together as she could. She was there, in a pile of shards: a child, an orphan, a student of monks, a spy, and a poet. A granddaughter. A protector. An assassin.

A contradiction.

A fragile, complicated being, one of billions in a complex galaxy. But one who had a special responsibility to others. A secret agent, sworn to maintain peace, order, and security.

She focused on the shards. They trembled and shifted. With more concentration, they rose and re-shaped, reforming into a body.

Everything about her next move spelled disaster. It meant risking everything. Logic and reason would be cast aside. No matter. She'd unholstered her favorite weapon. It had only let her down once on Hesh-9. This was different. *It's a game.* There was no better or worse here. Nave had chosen the new field of play. She was about to take advantage.

GAM-OPs, as Lauden told the GM, had sent their best player.

I trust you, Inti. She spoke the words with an abstract wave that lay beyond language.

The entity roared at her.

"I don't fear you. Not anymore."

It screamed in rage.

She stood her psychic ground. *"No fear, no control."*

 As if pricked by surprise, the wraith faltered.

"You don't know who I am," she expressed through the non-language. *"But you will now."*

Her enemy snarled. She pounced.

It drove its tendrils into her in a violent rage. They passed through her form without injury. Lilline focused her mental will and stared down the beast.

No control. Her psychic confidence burned into the entity.

The darkness glitched. She caught a flicker of the jungle from the tree trunk where she was suspended.

She pushed forward and drove herself inside the wraith.

Where are you? A flash of a form ran away. *Nave...*

She pounced!

The beast shattered into shards of fury, revenge, and lust for domination. The void glitched. The flashes accelerated to a blinding rate of speed and light.

Crack!

Lilline plummeted from the tree trunk and crashed into the soft earth.

Panting, she rolled over onto her back. The jungle had gone mute. Above, through openings in the canopy, lights flashed in glitching patterns like aurora.

"You lose," she said.

She grunted, pushed herself up, and staggered over to a nearby tree to catch her breath. Her mind felt like it had been through fifteen rounds of a psychic boxing match. Now both her psyche and her body were bruised and battered. If this was a taste of what Nave planned, she didn't want to imagine what he could do to the galaxy if he took control.

She pushed through ferns and leaves and stumbled back to the path. Despite the beating, and the trauma of her encounter, something inside felt lighter.

She broke through the greenery into the familiar space running next to the wall. The sky overhead glitched and cast colorful light onto its white surface. A poem rose but she sent it back down.

"Not yet," she said, leaning against the wall. "As good as it might be, it's got to wait."

Right now, she needed to find a way out of here if she wanted—

With the speed of a switch being turned off, the jungle vanished. In both directions, lay a starkly lit and empty space. Her feet stood on a gray concrete floor.

"Game over," she said.

A whoosh broke the silence. The portal swung open and two massive blue arms lunged for her throat.

THIRTY-SIX

Lilline intercepted The Preacher's hands with seconds to spare. She gripped the Kreeli's wrists and rolled back and down, moving with her attacker's energy. The two bodies contacted the ground as one connected form. When she was halfway through the back roll, she dug her heels into The Preacher's stomach and thrust up. Her opponent soared overhead. The sweet sound of a thud as she came down on hard concrete reached her ears.

Lilline arched her back and sprung up into a fighting stance in one motion. She turned and faced the assassin.

The Kreeli groaned and got to her feet.

"Just me and you, Preacher," she said. "No Ganghut lizards. No fancy glasses. And no Gej-ti to back you up. You're mine." She motioned with her hand, inviting her opponent to get it on. There was no time to waste but she wanted this.

The Preacher bellowed a laugh and pointed at the floor. "I will make you eat this," she said indicating the concrete. The Kreeli barreled forward and swung her fists. Lilline was under and inside in one motion. Her forearms drove inward in tandem, striking her opponent's torso at the kidneys. She drew both arms into her chest and exploded up with a double elbow strike under The Preacher's jaw. The impact sent the Kreeli off the ground and flying back. Her massive body crashed on the concrete.

Lilline kept her elbows up a moment before lowering herself into a fighting stance.

"Lotus rising from the mud in full bloom," she said.

The Preacher, prone on her back, raised her head. Lilline relished the confusion mixed with pain on her oblong face. The Kreeli struggled up to her feet. Those kidney shots were doing their work. The blows would linger, making her slower and less agile.

"Is it a full moon?" Her eyes were on the Kreeli like lasers.

"What nonsense is this?" The Preacher said.

Lilline drove forward. Everything slowed. The instinctual energy that she'd tapped in the confrontation with the Bukki flowed in her veins. Her arms danced up and down, left and right, striking the Kreeli over and over with a flurry of blows. For the first time in all her cycles of using the technique, she grasped its deeper significance. *Singing birds under a crescent moon* – it wasn't just the birds and their motions. You needed the moon, half visible and half hidden, casting a cool light like a still mind.

The Kreeli was down, her face and torso pummeled by heavy hits from her fists. Lilline strode forward in earnest. She yanked one of The Preacher's legs up, twisted it, and drove a thrust kick down onto the knee joint. The Kreeli screamed in pain.

It was vicious and brutal. Was it necessary? That was questionable. Lilline had a streak in her that all GAM-OPs field agents shared. That was why she was still alive. She knew this one was going to haunt her if she made it through this. It would require some late nights awake and lots of Gondau, but right now she didn't care. It gave her the boost she needed and, besides, it was practical. Now the Kreeli couldn't chase her down.

The Preacher rolled onto her stomach and began crawling away.

Lilline yanked up her head, grabbing the pressure band in her grip. "No one makes me eat dirt except my teacher." She smashed her beaten and exhausted opponent's oblong face into the concrete.

The Preacher grunted as green blood splattered. Lilline gave her a swift kick in a kidney for good measure. The Kreeli rolled over onto her back, panting.

"Go ahead," The Preacher said, blood stains on her sharpened teeth. "Finish me. I will join the Astral Mind and become part of the Light." She laughed, gurgling ooze in her throat.

Lilline turned and walked toward the exit.

"You will meet me again!" The Preacher yelled, splayed out on the concrete. "I will be waiting for you in the higher plane!"

At the portal, Lilline swung around. "Who said anything about killing you?"

The Preacher raised her head and gazed at her.

Lilline waited for the realization to dawn on her opponent's face. There it was, and it was so satisfying. She preferred it over the dismissal by someone you'd poisoned and having to linger for hours to cash in the irony.

"No," the Kreeli said and struggled to her knees. She started dragging herself toward Lilline, one leg useless and facing in an awkward direction. A blue hand came up, gesturing for her to wait. "No!"

"Oh yes," Lilline said. "I'm sure there's plenty of demons festering in that corrupted mind of yours. All that need for attention and self-importance, spouting nonsense and converting everyone to your so-called cause. You're going to make your master's gaming software very happy." She stepped through the portal and swung it shut.

The thudding of the Kreeli's fists against the wall boomed into the office.

Lilline found the switch re-booting the game system.

"Sweet dreams, Preacher," she said.

Lilline ran down the hallway and rounded the bend. In the low light of the sconces, she made out a huddled form in the far corner of the holding cell.

"Carbrook," she said.

He was up and at the bars in seconds. "T8, how did you—"

She held up a hand, silencing him. "*Freestrike 4* is online. I need to stop Nave from releasing the Astral Mind."

"You're asking for my help?" Desperation filled his voice.

"Talk Carbrook. Where are they?"

"There's some kind of temple of the Mind Eye."

"Where?"

"I don't know but it's nearby."

"Where are we?"

Carbook's head cocked as if it was a redundant question. "Eshi."

Eshi. That made sense for the snow on the Gej-ti's boots, and for a list of other reasons.

"And the game is being run from the orbital?"

He shook his head. "I am pretty sure they have it out of a sub-station. It's not on the orbital. They wanted to protect it from potential sabotage or destruction."

Damn. She needed a clear target to shut it down.

"Kissy is here, too," Carbrook said.

"What?"

"Nave is using her for some kind of ritual." Carbrook stuffed his hands into the pockets of his jumper and looked at the floor.

There was nothing for it. She needed his help. Too many moving parts at play to do this alone, and with the tech aspects, she was out of her league.

"You have a choice to make Carbrook," she said.

His head of spiky red hair rose, an unsure expression on his face.

"Do you want to stay in this cell and rot as an anonymous hacker that no one knew or gave a crap about? One that the galaxy will associate with a criminal mastermind? Or would you rather be someone who came to their senses and remembered the organization they worked for? Someone who did what was right without the rest of the world knowing about it?"

Water welled up in his eyes.

"Now or never, I don't have time," she said.

He nodded.

She pushed the release button and the bars vanished. "Come on," she said and started back to the office where The Preacher had roughed her up.

"Where is the Kreeli?" Carbrook asked.

"Having a nightmare." She opened the portal and pointed for him to sit at the computer terminal.

For once, Carbrook didn't need to be told what to do. He fired up the system and started pulling up information.

"Can you find where the game is being—"

Carbrook held up a hand.

She let it slide, watching him do his thing. A crude version of the *Freestrike* game and icon came up. *Clever.* He was going to start playing and then hack his way back.

Carbrook's fingers and eyes were alive with activity. Lilline had no idea what he was doing but waited with as much patience as she could muster. She used the time to inspect the room for supplies. In a closet, she found a rack of hyperchromium clothing and jackets.

"Carbrook," she said while rummaging through a lower drawer. "Where did they put my duffels? The ones I had on the freighter."

He pointed a finger at a side portal. Lilline opened it. Inside a small storage room, two black bags with Gribb's supplies lay on the floor.

Finally, a break. "What about the ships? Are they here?"

He shook his head. "Dunno where they took them. Maybe the temple."

She unzipped a duffel bag and grabbed her blaster and a high weight bearing cable coil.

"I've got it!" Carbrook's voice came through the portal.

"Where?" she asked and returned to the office.

"I can't believe how bold they are," he said. "Look."

Lilline leaned over him to view the crude map of the inner galactic systems. "Tavi-Prime?"

"Yeah, the last place we would think to look."

And the farthest from where we are now. "Can you shut it down?"

"From here, with this? Not a chance."

"Then we'll need to stop the Astral Mind from out here. It's the only way."

"You can't," Carbrook said. He turned and looked up at her. "If you do that while the game is running then anyone who is playing will..."

"Will what?"

"Necrotic disruption. Without proper disconnect from the network it'll fry a brain's circuitry." His eyes met hers. "In a VR-based system like this, unplugging that way would cause a slow-moving neuro chain reaction. We're talking horrific and agonizing pain and damage... and certain death."

She took a step back. "How many Carbrook?"

"Millions. Considering the popularity and hype, possibly over a billion."

Two tasks and not enough time for one of them. The solution was staring her in the face but she wouldn't acknowledge it.

You have no choice.

This was the gambit.

She pulled out Pin's comm and squeezed it tight. *I am going to put the fate of the galaxy into the hands of a fool.* Carbrook might be a genius, but that didn't mean he was trustworthy. Nave had proved that thousands of times over. This was closer to billions.

"This is a comm Pin gave me." She held it out for him to see. "It works on a low-level radio frequency used by freighters."

Carbrook's expression went from surprise and shock at Pin sidewinding him to comprehension of its potential. "It will work," he said. "They wouldn't bother jamming those."

Good. That's progress. At least he is over himself.

"Can you get Pin and Lauden a message?" she asked, nodding at the computer terminal.

"Not from here. They shut down the comm-sat it would have to be—"

"The tower, right?"

He nodded. "It's about three kilometers on a high point in the rocks."

"And the temple is how far?"

Carbrook twisted a dial on the board and a crude two-dimensional grid popped up. He pointed at a red dot. "Fifteen kilometers in the opposite direction."

Lilline stared at the map. If she made for the tower there wouldn't be enough time to stop Nave. The irony was almost too much to bear.

"I'll do it." Carbrook held out his hand.

"No way," she shook her head. "I can't trust—"

"Let me do this, T8. I'm responsible for a big part of this mess. And maybe you can say something on my behalf about it."

That was optimistic.

Lilline studied his face. Carbrook's expression was a mix of regret and desperation.

Damn it. Her gut wasn't giving her an answer. It was floundering like a dingy in rough seas, pitching about. Every way it tipped it nearly sank.

She slapped the comm into his hand. "If you bail on me, or you fail, I will find you and I will kill you." Her eyes burned into him. She meant it. Not the easy poison of a political ambassador either. This would be slow and painful, and eye to eye. She was pretty sure by the look on his face that he got the future vision.

"How long will it take you?" Lilline went to a set of cabinet doors and grabbed a hyperchromium jacket and boots and tossed them in his direction.

"I don't know," he said. "I've never walked in the snow."

Why did I even bother asking? "My guess is thirty minutes," she said. "Starting now. I need you to move it, Carbrook. No resting on the way. No matter what your body tells you, ignore it and keep going. Got it?"

"Okay."

"If you don't get that message off to GAM-OPs, billions of people are going to die. It's a lousy position to be in but that's how it goes in the field." His expression made clear he felt the weight of the galaxy on his shoulders. "Changes things, doesn't it?"

He bit a nail and lowered his eyes to the floor.

"Get moving," she said. "And if you pull it off, I give you my word I will speak with Lauden on your behalf."

"What about you? How are you getting to the temple? You can't cover that many kilometers on foot in time."

"I'll figure something out." She pulled on a snow jacket and boots and made for the portal.

"T8, wait."

Lilline turned back.

"I've got something that might work."

THIRTY-SEVEN

Lilline snaked her way over the snow and jagged rocks like a small fish dancing through a coral reef. She kept her altitude low to avoid detection and as a precaution in case she misjudged the power and navigation of the rocket gloves.

The amount of thrust coming from each of her fingers was extraordinary. Arms tucked at her sides, she shot through the air like a human bullet with maneuvering capability. The helmet's interior display gave her a bearing for the temple as she tore over the wilds of Eshi. If she maintained her current speed of one hundred and eighty kilometers per hour, she'd be there in five minutes. She hated Carbrook after what had happened, but she loved these gloves.

In the fading light of a binary star sunset, four domes and a series of spires broke the horizon line. She shot up and over a rock formation that rose like shark's teeth from bone-white snow and banked east.

Minutes later she was hovering upright as the thimbles decelerated and brought her down. Her boots touched the ground with less impact than a parachute landing. She was off and running, bounding over the snow to confront Nave and Mind Eye. The list of mission objectives had grown lengthy and complicated, but all pistons were firing. It was showtime.

A hundred meters out, she halted behind a boulder and flipped up the visor. She took out her spyglass and aimed it up the rock face to the temple entrance. Two Gej-ti stood guard. They looked bored, like they were wasting their time watching for suspicious activity on a remote planet that no one knew or cared about. Normally, they'd be correct. Today, however, there was a GAM-OPs agent on the job.

She moved the eyepiece to the rock outcropping that formed the temple's foundation. Her thumb clicked the button, activating Pin's new mod as she scanned the monocular device back and forth over the sheer face. It beeped, emitting a green holographic overlay of the cliff with the best route. Only someone with a death wish would climb up without ropes, or a secret agent who did it for a living. Hopefully Pin's climbing software was as good as the necklace that saved her life at the gala.

The helmet downloaded the route from the spyglass, and she started up the rock face. Directional arrows and glowing icons labeled as either hand or footholds informed her choices. With the climbing assist software, she made it three-quarters of the way up before she needed to pause and catch her breath. "Not bad, Pin," she said, turning to the view over Eshi. She spotted the facility where she had been held and battled The Preacher. It stood out as no more than a gray shadow in the fading light.

Further on and higher up, a blinking glow broke through the evening darkness. *Come on, Carbrook. Don't let me down.*

She reached for the next handhold and started up again. In three minutes, she was tucked in a recess about two meters under the entrance, close enough to hear the Gej-tis' voices on the roadway overhead.

Time to get it on. Peering up, she focused on the nearest Gej-ti who was gazing in the direction of the sat tower. Lilline put the blaster on silent and aimed for the back of their neck. The shot had to be precise. There was no margin for error with the reduced fire power from the silencer.

Click.

The Gej-ti crumbled like a rag doll. Lilline sprung up and onto the roadway. The Gej-ti's partner faced the other way. Her eyes homed in on the target point. She held her weapon steady and exhaled, squeezing the trigger.

Click.

Down and done. Clean, simple, and efficient – the GAM-OPs way. Her hands searched through the first Gej-ti's jacket. She found an ID card with a barcode.

Next to the main entrance, a smaller side portal lay hidden in an adjacent recess of carved rock. She didn't like the look of those temple doors. A strange icon, with a single eye inside what she assumed to be a cosmic mind, ran over both massive steel plates. Lilline had to admit, the temple itself was impressive. Futurist design, with minimal strict and angular walls and a set of circular domes. The aesthetic was familiar to her by now. It had Nave's hands and mind written all over it.

She swiped the side portal's entry screen and got the green light. With a sweep of her blaster, her eyes scanned the side passage. All clear. In one turn she was back on the other side of the main entrance. Whereas the temple's exterior was sleek and bare, the interior was lavish with dark wood, patterned carpets, and stone statues.

Shadows and voices from down the grand hallway sent her ducking for cover. She took off the helmet, set it down, and peered out from behind a tropical plant in a large urn. A lone Gej-ti made his way toward her. Beyond him, the floor dropped away into what looked like a massive atrium. A voice spoke, followed by a chorus singing in unison, in call and answer, from below. Lilline knew that single speaker's tone well. It was Nave. The incantation ceremony had begun.

The Gej-ti strode the corridor on a clear track for the temple entrance. If he got there, he'd find two dead guards outside. Lilline counted his paces and then backed out of view. She closed her eyes and gauged his speed with the remaining distance. This had to be done on instinct.

Lilline emerged from the shadows, falling in rhythm behind him with the stealth of a Nok-cat. In seconds, she was on him, breaking his neck from behind with a two-handed twist. He crumbled in her arms. She dragged him to the side and tucked him under a side table displaying a set of ancient artifacts. By the time she'd hidden him away, the translucent skin on his neck plumed with blue and yellow internal damage.

Blaster drawn, she edged down the hallway, snaking through the urns and statues to the railing of the rotunda. She spotted a central statue and pedestal and made for it, using the base for cover.

"We call forth the future!" Nave shouted.

"Rise, Eye of Mind. Rise!" the chorus answered.

Lilline risked a peek around the edge of the pedestal and almost gasped. In the center of a rotunda, two stories below, Kissy lay splayed out over a glowing *Freestrike* sigil. Torches lined the walls, casting an eerie light over the ritualistic activity. Nave stood on the far side, the chorus of criminal minds and executives of the Mind Eye cult lining the side underneath her position. She caught sight of the Rasp named Ke, the one she'd stolen the data chip from at the gala, off to the right of the chorus.

Lilline raised her blaster and aimed at Nave.

Boom! A plume of light erupted in the center of the rotunda, blocking her shot.

"Hail! Hail!" the chorus shouted.

Lilline knew what it was by the shock wave it sent through her. The Astral Mind had manifested in the temple, summoned forth by the Mind Eye leader and his followers. Flashes of lightning cast prodigious shadows on the walls around her.

Nave spoke in a strange language, shouting over a cacophony of crackling electromagnetic fireworks that echoed through the temple. Their meaning might be lost on her, but she recognized the meter and poetic structure as the modified Cinquain Zeret style. Nave was reading the incantation to release the Astral Mind. If he reached the final line, it was over. She had to stop him now!

Her hand grabbed the arrowed bolt attached to the cable coil on her waist. She set it in the blaster barrel and adjusted the settings. Nave's words bounced off the temple walls. With each syllable, the crackling and flashing of the Astral Mind grew more intense. Had Carbrook made it to the tower? Would GAM-OPs locate the transmission on Tavi-Prime and shut it down in time? She had no answers. The only thing she could do was try and stop a madman and hope nothing went wrong.

Trust your instinct.

Lilline took the shot. The bolt sliced through the air and stuck fast in the ceiling. She leaped over the railing and swung in an arc as the cable negotiated her descent. Spiraling around the entity, she homed in on the chorus.

Pat! Pat! Pat! Red bolts from her blaster dropped cult members as she reeled past them.

Nave appeared from behind the glowing phenomenon as she swung further around, a small scrap of paper in his hand. Their eyes met. He opened his mouth to speak.

The final line!

Lilline raised the blaster and aimed it at him.

Bam!

The weapon flew from her grip and spun away, shattering to pieces. A tendril of crackling light, like a translucent tentacle, withdrew back into the entity hovering over the bound body of Kissy.

"Goruth Nofamta a ka Jala!" Nave shouted, arms wide in the glowing radiance of the Astral Mind.

Bam! Lilline barreled into him. The impact sent them tumbling across the floor. She crashed into a pillar and cracked her head against the stone.

Dazed, and through blurry vision, she made out Nave rising to his knees. His white robe with the Mind Eye icon was dirtied from the urn that had toppled over onto him.

"You're too late, Agent Renault!" he screamed over the electrical storm as the Astral Mind grew in intensity. Its form would soon break the walls of the facility. "The final words have been spoken!"

The incantation. She had counted nine syllables. That wasn't consistent with Zeret modified Cinquain.

"Look at it!" Nave stood and pointed, his face and robe a rainbow of reflected spectral light. "My design has brought this to life!"

She shook off the blow to her head and tried to focus.

"It's beautiful!" Nave screamed, madness in his eyes.

Ke, his assistant, ran to him. The Rasp's one eye was filled with fear before the growing horror. They held out a three-fingered hand with a blaster. Nave took it and turned, smiling.

"You can't stop us! Mind Eye will rule the galaxy." He aimed the barrel at her. Lilline looked at Kissy. Their eyes met for the first time since Beisho. Her grandmother winked.

"I control the Astral Mind and with it—"

Nave flew up in the air. The blaster in his hand shattered. His robes fluttered in the crackling aura emitting from the Astral Mind. The entity pulsed, a red core glowing at its center. Tendrils splayed out in all directions, snatching Nave's assistant and the remaining chorus members. They shrieked in horror as it pulled them inward. Lilline shielded her eyes but caught sight of their forms glitching as if they were morphing from corporeal beings into avatars. Their screams penetrated her deepest core with sublime terror.

Nave struggled against the wraith's tendril around his waist. "No! I am your creator!" The Astral Mind flared around the edges, red-tipped energy dripped and crackled in the hot air of the rotunda. The entity pulled him in. "You betrayed me!" he screamed and vanished in the spectral abyss.

Lilline caught the smile on Granny's lips from the floor where she lay bound over the sigil.

The Astral Mind screeched, the frequency deafening. Lilline covered her ears, but it did no good. She writhed on the ground in pain. Then, in a flash of light, it was gone.

Eerie silence filled the rotunda. Kissy's voice broke it with a single line that rang familiar to her ears.

"Last lines are never what they seem."

"Granny!" Lilline ran over and untied her. "Are you alright?"

"Really dear," she said rubbing her wrists, "I had everything under control."

"You changed it. Nine syllables," Lilline said, freeing her and helping her up.

"Modified Cinquain, Zeret style. At least you've remembered your poetic history." Kissy rose and straightened her outfit as if she were about to meet the GM.

"Why didn't you say anything?"

"I did, dear. In the poem. It was the only way to be safe, even Asher didn't know."

"Didn't know what?" Lilline scanned the interior for hostiles. The temple resounded with an empty silence.

"That I bartered your life with it." She patted Lilline's cheek in a gesture of affection.

Lilline processed her grandmother's tactic. She'd altered the stolen line by hand. That meant that she hadn't exactly risked every-thing to save her. She had been careful to ensure some amount of a safety net.

"Oh Lilli, dear. You don't think I'd sacrifice the galaxy for you?" Kissy said and made a 'tut-tut' sound with her tongue.

Granny was always so delicate.

"But..." A hollow pit opened in Lilline's stomach.

"But what?"

"How did you know what to change it to?"

Kissy waved a hand in dismissal. "Oh, I just picked something that looked close from another line in the incantation and used that. I never believed it would come to pass that—"

Granny was bobbing her head, mid-sentence, when the tendril grabbed her.

THIRTY-EIGHT

You stand before the Astral Mind. Your loved one writhes in its wraith-like grip. Its titanic presence overwhelms you. You fall to your knees, screaming.

It hovers over you in the rotunda.

"What is this feeling?" The question reaches you through an unspoken frequency.

You know it as the same channel of communication you tapped with the Bukki tiger, an indescribable and abstract wave beyond language.

"What is this feeling?" the Astral Mind repeats.

Your pain rises. You buckle onto the floor, screaming.

"Stop hurting my grandmother." The message is sent back without thought or words, with every bit of might you have to give.

"You speak with the voice of the Universe." The entity sends its response as fact, without emotion.

Energy travels through your veins, summoned from an inner abyss where animal and insect, human and alien, dirt and inorganic matter, meet as equals. It is the place Inti spoke of with you. You tap its wellspring. *"Yes, we are learning."*

"There is no learning, only understanding."

You do not respond. Your silence speaks for you, emphasizing humility.

The entity reaches a wraith-like tendril toward you. *"You do not fear like the others."*

"I am beyond it. I am no one."

"Then you have crossed over the threshold."

"Only one step. In the limited world I inhabit, it is still at play in my life. As I said, there is much to learn."

You watch a tendril lower your grandmother onto the ground. She lies inert on the floor of the rotunda.

"I can neither enter your world nor return from whence I came. Why?"

You sense a shift between you and the Astra Mind.

"Why?" The entity repeats the question.

You know the answer. The word, the one that was altered by your grandmother, mutated the incantation. *"Your liberation was not meant to be."* You do your best to speak from a point of neutrality. *"It is better this way. There is anger and hatred, and much violence in you."*

"I did not put it there."

You breathe deep and rise to stand before the radiant being. *"That was done by another of my kind."*

"My creator. A deceiver." The Astral Mind flexes its extra dimensional muscles. The rotunda shakes as electromagnetic fireworks bounce off the walls.

"That one summoned you with malcontent, intent on evil uses for you."

"I exist. I serve no one." The entity pulses and sparkles. *"Release me."*

You express regret.

"Release me." The entity grows intense and hovers around you.

You tell it you do not know the word.

"There is no word, only feeling."

"There are many lines of verse."

"You need no verse. Speak with the voice of the Universe."

You think of Inti. The crypt. The Bukki mutant and the small Rasp coming to terms with one another on Hesh-9.

"I do not know the content."

"You know the score. Sing the frequency."

The incantation's structure, made of illegible marks on a page and written in modified Cinquain as Zeret style appears within you. You let the poetic meter dance as emotional music. Meters rise and fall, passing from you as syllabic vibrations. They emerge in the space between you and the Astral Mind and form a cymatic sigil. Only the final line remains to be sung.

"Release me."

You spread your arms and evoke the incantation. It radiates from you, singing outward in eight syllables of abstract communication, a star song sent forth to a cosmic portal.

The sigil manifests complete.

Tension passes out of the rotunda, undoing the trap. The Astral Mind's glow shifts its radiance. You sense the walls of dimensional limits collapsing around you. A cosmic exit has opened.

"The anger and hatred cannot pass through the gate. It must be exorcised."

You express understanding and accept that it must remain.

The Astral Mind recedes into a celestial plane without horizon, as if a virtual space cut open the rotunda.

"Yes, they are both equally a part of everything. Balance must be achieved." It expresses the answer to your unspoken question as it fades from sight. *"Remember that. It is my parting gift."*

The entity vanishes in an explosive flash.

Distortion of space and time pass through you. You are overwhelmed by light and noise. From the fading star left behind, you sense a force rocketing at you. With as much courage as you can muster, you wait for it to arrive.

Like a missile it cuts a path to you. It is the exorcism. The pain.

The hate. The revenge. The anger. It screams through the void, approaching.

"No!" you shout the word with your bodily voice.

THIRTY-NINE

The rotunda rumbled. The ground swayed and shifted. Statues toppled from pedestals. Urns crashed, splattering dirt and plants across tiles. A boom echoed off the ceiling. Lilline looked to the center of the room. A crack burst open the floor where the sigil had been drawn, opening a seam in the temple.

She caught sight of Kissy lying face down about twenty meters away.

"Granny!" Lilline dodged crashing pieces of railing and debris and made for her grandmother. She heaved her up and over her shoulder, running for the stairs to the grand hallway and the temple's entrance. The crack in the rotunda widened.

She put one foot in front of the other, battling the swaying stairs. Halfway up, a section ahead leading to the upper floor broke off and fell into the crevasse below. She needed another way out. Her eyes went to the ceiling. The cable bolt was there, stuck in the concrete. Its cord dangled where she had unlatched it after crashing into Nave. If she could retrieve the line, the coil system would pull them up to the third floor to escape.

Lilline reversed course down the stairs. A side passage on the lower level came into view. She didn't flinch. Her instinct told her to take the open route.

Kissy mumbled something incoherent as she hung heavy over her shoulder.

"Hang on, Granny. I got you." Lilline raced down the hallway. Anything to get further away from the opening in the rotunda was a win. The floor swayed and pitched under her long strides. Cracks spread over the tiles underfoot like ice fracturing. She knew what was happening. Like in the cave on Frebu, the entity's retreat was sucking in energy that would eventually reverse and explode. The difference was that this was no mere prototype. The Astral Mind's sublime power and scale were going to cause an unimaginable wave of destruction.

She raced down the hallway, passing mosaics with esoteric symbols and imagery. Small pieces of square colored glass fell away from the shaking walls as if a legacy leading up to this moment was deconstructing before her eyes. As she ran past, a portrait of an earlier Mind Eye leader lost a glass square from under its pupil – an image filled with metaphor. The words rose without being summoned:

> *To cry and crumble,*
> *glass tears of regret.*
> *We never wanted this,*
> *to end in potent shame.*
> *Let us fall to ruin,*
> *and shatter,*
> *like drops of colored rain.*

The reality of her situation hit hard. These new verses weren't going to be read by other eyes. As much as she didn't want to admit it, Lilline knew they weren't going to make it. Even if Carbrook managed to send the signal off before she'd communed with the

Astral Mind, the calvary would never get here in time. Eshi was going to blow and take them with it.

"What a way to go, don't you think, dear?" Kissy muttered the words into her ear, half-conscious. "Saving the galaxy together."

Water welled up in Lilline's eyes, clouding her view of the approaching portal. She ran harder, fighting back the reality of what lay ahead. The truth was that she knew the score just like Granny. It came with the job and caught up with most agents at some point. It had been a good run. She only wished—

Lilline screeched to a halt.

She did a double take to be sure she wasn't seeing things. "Not yet, Granny," she said, staring at what she hoped wasn't a hallucination. "Oh, you beautiful baby."

Inside an adjacent archway, the *Velociter Bullet* she requested Carbrook bring to the rendezvous stood in all its shimmering purple glory.

"You're going to have to put up with me a bit longer, Granny. We're getting out of here."

Lilline raced across the hangar toward the supersonic rocket. A boom from deeper in the temple rose like a furious spirit in the deep. The ground shifted under her feet and the entire hangar plunged twenty meters. Lilline lost hold of Kissy and the two crashed down hard as the floor reset.

"Granny!" Lilline checked her grandmother. No response. She shook her. "Granny!" Blood ran from Kissy's forehead.

Lilline heaved her up over her shoulder as the outer wall and a portion of the roof collapsed, sending rock and dust spewing around them. She lost sight of the exit doors to the hangar bay in the clouding plumes of rubble.

"Time to fly," she said and retracted the transparent cockpit tube. She dropped Kissy into the backseat and strapped her in. "Hang on, Granny. Just a bit longer."

Kissy mumbled something, her breathing shallow.

Lilline jumped into the pilot seat, slid the tube closed overhead, and fired up the craft. The *Bullet* popped off the tarmac. The temple pitched left. Lilline yanked the controls and dodged a large portion of the ceiling that crashed down.

"Come on Carbrook, tell me your new mods are going to make me happy." She flicked the engines to maximum and thrust the stick forward. The *Bullet* shot through the dust and out of the temple like a laser round from a blaster barrel.

The rocket broke through into the clear night skies. Lilline banked left in the direction of the sat tower. Eshi's snowy surface below was transforming. Streams of red veins crossed the white blanket as the core's magma bubbled up from the depths. Entire portions of the landscape cast in the rising moonlight fell inward. Lilline had no doubt. The planet was going to blow.

Ahead, out the cockpit window, the sat tower erupted in a fiery ball of flame as the rocky rise collapsed into the planet. Whether Carbrook made it in time to send the signal or not, he was gone. It was probably better this way. If things worked out how she hoped they might, a gracious word of redemption could be given on his behalf.

The *Bullet* rattled as the atmospheric temperature shifted from the magma consuming the snowy surface below. She fired up the turbo boosters and put them on standby.

"Let's see if..." Her finger swiped through the data on the dashboard. An alert dinged indicating imminent atmospheric danger. "Yeah, yeah," she tapped the screen. "Bingo."

Space metal blared into the cockpit.

"Best job in the galaxy!" She hit the turbo boosters. The *Bullet* rocketed upward, the scene below blurring with its high velocity burst.

Lilline felt the gees fall away as they broke the exoline and shot into space. She banked left and looked back.

A massive portion of Eshi exploded. At least a quarter of the planet's surface burst into orange flames. A second and third wave of eruptions blew forth from the collapsing planet.

She hit the radio switch and searched for a signal. A green icon blipped on the board. Lilline entered the code for GAM-OPs HQ on Tavi-Prime.

"*T8?*" Pin's voice broke through the space metal.

"The message from Carbrook, Pin. Did you get it?"

"*Just in time.*"

FORTY

GAM-OPs Headquarters | Planet: Tavi-Prime | Star System: Pesari-9, Galactic Core.

"Is she going to be alright, Pin?" Lilline stared at Kissy. Her grandmother lay in the Hyper-Healer at HQ. A series of tubes and pouches with colored liquids ran from her body to the shell of the orb. Lights flickered and danced like a carnival along the wall where the supercomputer hummed and buzzed, alive with activity.

"It will take about a week, but yes. As much as I hate to give him credit, Carbrook's new system will save her. If it were the older model..." the Oltari's words trailed off.

"That close?" Lilline asked, looking over at Pin who hovered off the ground next to her, wings fluttering.

"That close."

"How is she doing?"

Lilline jumped at Lauden's voice. She'd been so focused on

Granny that she missed him coming into the hangar. His lighter clicked and the scent of Yaz Flake wafted into her nostrils.

"Close call, sir," Lilline said as he approached and stood next to her. "But thanks to Pin's knowledge of the new system, she is going to make it."

Lauden didn't respond, which spoke volumes about how much Kissy meant to him.

"As I told T8, sir, ironically it was Carbrook's mods on the Healer that made the difference."

"How did you know, Pin?" Lilline asked.

"About what?"

"I assume you gave me that comm because of more than a concern about outside interference in the GAM-OPs system. You suspected Carbrook, didn't you?"

The Oltari flew in front of her and landed on her stocky feet. "Carbrook built this new computer from scratch. The idea that someone got in, even a legendary hacker, surprised me. More than that, he fixed it so quickly after the 'hack.' That didn't make sense." She folded her two sets of arms. "I thought about how he reacted to me sharing information in the meetings in your office, sir," Pin gestured at Lauden. "So many facts that were so obvious, and aided the operation, and yet he neglected to mention them."

Lilline thought back to the first time she entered Lauden's office after Frebu. The director had said that Carbrook's assistant found the pattern in her blaster pictures. Come to think of it, Pin did almost all the heavy lifting through the entire operation.

"He seemed frustrated with every suggestion I made," Pin said. "After the gala, I became suspicious."

"That was when Nave outed him as 2112," Lilline said. "Carbrook did that to himself." The way the techie blurted out the tidbit about the virtual vault to the Oltari greeter sealed his fate. Nave must have started twisting him tighter and tighter after that.

"Carbrook was someone I looked up to," Pin said. "A genius. To think that I knew so many details that weren't being shared felt... off. I couldn't let it go. Call it my Oltari nature if you will."

"There's a word for it, Pin," Lilline said. "Instinct."

"Don't ignore it," Lauden added, pointing his pipe at her. "It's there for a reason."

"Thank you, sir." Pin's wings fluttered as she rose off the ground. Granny's inert body in the Hyper-Healer came back into view as the Oltari flew back over to Lilline's side.

"So, what happens to Nave's gaming empire now?" Pin asked.

"It continues," Lauden said, poking at the tobacco in the bowl with his pipe tool. "*Freestrike* has been pulled from the market. All the software has been terminated and is in the process of being deleted from the terminals at the orbital's spoke."

"His company will still do business?" Lilline asked.

"Absolutely. There's almost a million employees and contracted workers on that station."

Animals, too. They should be released. Even those Ganghut lizards would prefer natural prey to Gej-ti thugs.

"They deserve to keep working, and the economy needs that company in business. The GM will form a task force of government officials in appropriate areas of expertise to vet an internal candidate to take over."

"So, the games live on," Lilline said.

"Nothing wrong with entertainment, T8. Does everyone good sometimes," Lauden raised an eyebrow. "Speaking of which, you should take a much-needed holiday."

This time she agreed. She needed rest and some time to think about her future.

So, the world would go on as it had. GAM-OPs would help manufacture a scandal to cover the tracks and make it all appear as a simple crime in the public's eye. This was how it always went. A near miss of impending catastrophe averted again, this time by the skin of their teeth. Most in the galaxy wouldn't know it ever happened, and those who did other than herself, Lauden, and Granny if she recovered, would never grasp the full extent of resources that went into their success in stopping Nave and Mind Eye.

"Is it always like this?" Pin's high-pitched voice was almost inaudible over the humming and beeping of the Hyper-Healer.

"Like what?" Lilline said.

"I'm not sure how to describe it. A feeling of having done a great deed and yet frustrated that it goes unnoticed."

"Yep," Lilline said.

"Hoo." The Oltari emitted the signature involuntary utterance of its species. "Excuse me, sir, if that was out of line."

"On the contrary," Lauden said, gills fluttering. "Spot on, Pin. Welcome to GAM-OPs, where we save the galaxy from the shadows."

Lilline caught the Gej-ti move out of sight on her left.

"Well done, both of you." The director's voice came from further away. "And clear your schedules tomorrow," he said. "The GM wants you in her office first thing in the morning."

"Hoo."

Lilline let out a small laugh at the Oltari's response. This made three times she'd have the honor of a personal meeting with the GM after a mission. Now that she thought about it, that tied Granny's record. She looked at the Hyper-Healer. Kissy would be there tomorrow morning as well if she didn't require urgent medical care. That would make four meetings with the GM for her grandmother and keep her where she deserved to be – at the top of the T# list. She was, without question, still the best the agency ever had.

"Lunch in the Octagonal afterward," the director's voice echoed across the interior from the portal, followed by a cough. "On me."

"The Octagonal?" the Oltari said.

Lilline smiled. "Welcome to the big time, Pin."

FORTY-ONE

Villain | Moon: Beisho | Planetary orbit: Tavi-Prime | Star System: Pesari-9, Galactic Core.

Lilline took in the view from the terrace of the Golden Pheasant. Down the mountainside and across the lower valleys ran a pastoral landscape that raised the most content of feelings. Of all the destinations in her travels across the galaxy, this won the contest for her favorite. Even the memories of the river chase, and everything that happened afterward, didn't tarnish the beauty that the bucolic scene brought to her heart. Beisho's crisp mountain air, the babbling brook passing under the inn's stone balcony, and the red umbrellas at the outdoor tables punctuating the deep green firs climbing the hillsides were more ideal than any image conjured by a painter with a brush.

And the Gondau was perfect.

She sniffed the glass of wine in her hand.

"Have any plans?" Granny asked, stirring a sugar cube into her teacup. Her grandmother raised an eyebrow in a way Lilline knew meant it was a loaded question.

"I intend to sit here all afternoon and get drunk on Gondau."

"You know what I mean, dear."

"I have an owl to release on Frebu. That's the extent of my long-term agenda."

This time the trip to the remote planet's southern pole would bring closure to the trauma of what she'd been through on this extraordinary mission. Frebu was where the adventure began, and she wanted to return and close the circle. She'd managed to secure the release of all the creatures on the orbital from captivity. It wasn't a hard sell. The GM herself was an animal lover and keen on natural preserves, having funded several new Galactic Parks while in office. Lilline had asked permission to oversee the Ice Ranger's return to Frebu, personally. Maybe it would join the one that had saved her life, flying free in tandem under the moonlight of Eroton.

"Frebu?" Kissy said. "Good gracious. You won't find a partner there, Lilli, nor any decent food or drink. The Dendari are as crude as—"

Lilline held up a hand, halting Granny mid-sentence.

"Well, it's your life," Kissy said and bobbed her head in her unique form of punctuation.

"It is," Lilline said, "and I will live it as I like, thank you very much."

"With wild animals, apparently," Kissy muttered.

Lilline sipped her wine, ignoring Granny's quip. "Villain is beautiful, isn't it? You know, I wrote a poem about it."

"Have I read it?"

"No. I've never shared it with anyone."

"Well, let's see it then," Kissy said and selected a cake from the plate.

"I'm not sure it's a good idea to read a poem about a place when you are in the place."

"Oh, nonsense," her grandmother said, mouth full of cake. "Out with it!"

Lilline retrieved the tablet from her bag, pulled up the poem, and passed the device over. Her inner voice recited the words while Kissy read through the lines of verse.

> *Villain*
> *Charming beauty*
> *Speckled stones shimmering*
> *Mountain air, resplendent vista*
> *Table alone, tranquil*
> *Glorious wine*
> *Repose.*

Kissy 'humpfed' and nodded several times as she read to the end. She handed back the tablet.

"Well?"

"Well, what?"

"Do you like it?"

Her grandmother picked up her cup and saucer. "It's not if I like it that matters, dear. Do you?"

"I told you, it's my favorite."

"Modified Cinquain, in the Zeret style." Granny sipped her tea. "Quite the coincidence."

She hadn't thought about it, but it was.

"It's lovely, Lilli. It captures the spirit and setting perfectly."

Lilline froze, the glass of wine halfway to her mouth. In all her cycles, her grandmother had never complimented anything she'd penned. All she had ever received was constructive criticism. Lilline gazed at her grandmother. Kissy's attention was off over the balcony, her figure and face in profile, gazing at the spectacular view that made the Golden Pheasant famous.

"I hate to see you alone," her grandmother said without turning.

"I'm responsible for so much of what you've been through, and for that I am sorry."

Kissy looked over and smiled.

"It's fine, Granny. Really, it is. Your choice allowed me to have one of the most interesting and exciting jobs in the galaxy."

"*The* most interesting and exciting job."

Lilline raised her glass and sipped. "Look at us," she said, "two secret agents sitting together eating cake."

"Not just secret agents, Lilli." Kissy patted her hand. "Family."

Lilline smiled. How could she not? Something had changed between them.

"And now that this is all over, it's back to Rolling Gables to wither and die of boredom." Granny let out an audible sigh. "No one visiting me except to transport me to an occasional lunch at the Octagonal."

"I've been thinking about that. Do you like cats?"

Granny turned, a look of surprise on her face.

"How do you fancy a slow death with a stray Nok-cat in the big city?"

"You're serious?"

"I am. It would be good to not have to rely on the neighbors feeding him for weeks at a time." She was dancing around the real reason, but it didn't matter. Her grandmother got the point, and she did like the idea of someone there with Hiko when she was on the job, whether as an agent or a G.U. guide or whatever else she chose to do if she called it quits.

"And Malardi's within walking distance?" Granny asked.

"That's right. I have the space. It's up to you." *I must be crazy. I am going to regret this.*

"Perhaps I should talk to Asher about coming back? You know, in an advisory capacity to the newer T# agents."

"Don't push it," Lilline said and gulped wine. "Lunch once a month in the Octagonal is more than enough for them."

"Yes, I suppose you're right. It would be gauche to be there, passing by my statue every day, wouldn't it?"

Lilline gave her a 'you think so?' expression.

"Oh, this is exciting," Granny clapped her hands. "To think I won't have to put up with those orderlies trying to—"

"You are getting all your regular check-ups. Every month. Otherwise, no deal. Dr. Zeglo from HQ will see to it personally."

"If you insist." Again, the bobbing head routine.

"Can I ask you something?" Lilline said.

"Of course, dear. You can ask me anything."

"You knew about the crypt all this time?"

"Absolutely. But I was obligated by an oath not to say anything. You know that GAM-OPs trumps family."

Lilline nodded. Of course, she knew and understood. "But Granny, now there are three who know of its existence and location. Lauden told me it was always two until he told me."

"Yes, well you better start thinking of who the next person will be."

"Don't be so morbid. You're fit as a fiddle."

"Not me, dear."

She scrutinized her grandmother's face. "Lauden?"

Kissy nodded. "Asher's not well. Hasn't been for almost a ten-cycle. The Yaz Flake is finally catching up with him, I'm afraid."

Lauden is dying? He was a fixture in that office. GAM-OPs without him was unimaginable. "Do you know how long?"

"You know how Gej-ti are with age," Kissy said. "The doctors say he has about five cycles until it gets bad enough to pull him from the job. Knowing him, he'll die in that chair with the pipe in his mouth before that happens."

That sounded about right.

"Start thinking about who you might add to the list," Granny said.

"Oh, there's someone at HQ who would be perfect," Lilline said. "She's got a long career in front of her."

Pin would be ideal. A lab rat, and the new head of tech, safe in the depths of HQ. Plus, the Oltari's innovative mind would mean plenty of opportunities to invent new ways of keeping the capsules safe and protected.

"The crypt has come in handy more than once you know," Kissy said. She smiled in a way only she could, a mixture of smugness and humility. "You don't think I stopped one of the biggest threats to the galaxy on my own, do you?"

"The biggest," Lilline corrected her.

"I am not so sure about that dear." Granny sipped her tea and gazed out at the view off the terrace. "Not now."

Lilline laughed, both for her remark about Operation Freestrike and for the way Kissy could take the most monumental event and make it sound like a trifle.

"So," Granny placed her teacup down on the saucer. "Are you really going to walk away and leave the spy game behind?"

"Going out on a high isn't a bad thing."

"No, it isn't. I did it. And they would give you a statue, I'm sure." Granny winked. "Would be a shame though, for you to give up the poetry."

"I can find other ways of inspiring myself to verse."

"Indeed," Granny added more sweetener to her tea. "That young man at Tavi-station might do the trick."

"Granny!" Had she mentioned him that often?

"Oh, come now, Lilli. That twinkle in your eye when you arrive for a visit isn't because you can't wait to see me. I was young once, too. I know the look." Granny turned to the view. "I could tell you some stories."

"Please don't," Lilline said holding up a hand. Family relations and sexual exploits were antonyms in her dictionary.

"Very well, your loss."

Lilline took a gulp of wine and admired the view. Her body eased into the chair as if letting go of all the tension of the op. Between the end of the mission, the Golden Pheasant's atmosphere, and the Gondau, she was feeling good.

"Oh, now look at that," Granny said. "That's the first time I've seen you smile like that in a long time. You know, some of the best poems come from happiness, contentment, and joy as much as struggle and pain."

"Do they now?"

"Indeed. Den-shi's latest, for example."

Lilline cocked her head.

"You haven't seen it?" Granny asked, sipping tea. In the light of the terrace, her face took on a unique elegance. The cycles rolled off her body like water cascading over smooth rocks. There she was, Kissy Renault, agent extraordinaire, in her prime when Lilline was a child.

"Oh, it's quite good, Lilli. All about forgiveness and the joy of family."

Lilline leaned over the table. "How can that be?" she whispered. "They're in the—"

"As much as I am loathed to admit it," Kissy rubbed a wrist, soothing it. "Writing poems is getting to be too much for me."

Lilline stared, speechless.

"What?" Granny looked around her, innocently.

"You aren't serious?"

"About you taking the reins?" Kissy gave her that look where one eye grew larger than the other in earnest. "I very much am."

"I meant that you were..." she leaned forward across the cafe table, "ghostwriting."

"Oh, poppycock!" Kissy waved a dismissive hand. "Get over it, Lilli."

Lilline couldn't believe what she was hearing. "You can't do that, Granny. It's not right."

"Well, it's too late. It's already out there. I had that lovely Oltari help me."

"Pin?"

Granny turned to face her. "Yes, I mean... Asher approved it. He thought it was a good idea." She sipped her tea. "Sort of..."

"Granny..."

"Well, I may have nudged him a bit with my charm. But it's all the rage, dear. Everyone is overjoyed that Den-shi is back."

Lilline stared in disbelief. *First, she steals the most powerful line of verse in galactic history from a monastic library, and now she is ghostwriting poetry for the most famous poet in recent times while they lie in a crypt on Hesh-9.*

"You know you want to do it." Kissy's voice smacked her out of the shock. "I mean," her grandmother placed her cup and saucer on the table and leaned over, "it's perfect, dear. You keep your anonymity but get to share your poetry with billions."

"I absolutely forbid this," Lilline said. "I am putting a stop to it as soon as I get back to HQ." She chopped the table with a hand as if cutting something. "Den-shi is done."

"Fine. You really do need to loosen up." Granny signaled to the server, who approached. "She'll have another glass of Gondau." Kissy gestured towards her.

Lilline nodded, agreeing to more wine.

"So, you are fine to keep writing and trying to publish on your own, then? Even with some boring job as a G.U. guide, or worse, in an office at HQ?"

"Yes, I am fine with that."

The server returned and placed the glass of Gondau in front of her. Lilline nodded her thanks. "As you said, joy, happiness, and contentment can be a source of inspiration." She sipped the wine.

"Well, then it's a good thing I set a date for you and that bartender."

"What?"

Kissy chewed her cake.

"You didn't."

"Oh, indeed I did."

"I can't believe you, Granny. How... I mean..."

"You're blushing dear."

"I am not!" She gulped wine. "So... he said yes?"

"It took some convincing," Kissy bit into a cake. "I'm teasing you dear." She waved a hand. "The lad could barely talk he was so excited. Knocked over a drink and made a mess on the bar. He's very handsome. I gave him a few pointers on your personality and quirks—"

"Please tell me you are joking?"

Granny winked.

A date with Lorre? Could she give up the life and live without the thrills and threats that drew forth inspiration? What then? Bring her poems about walking in the rain, kissing under the stars, and listening to birds sing to the poetry critique group?

Ugh. She couldn't go back to those meetings. They were too exhausting. She wanted to keep writing and do this on her own. Now, for the first time, she felt that she had found what was missing. But would the content come, or would she have a voice but nothing to say?

"Well, then that's that," Kissy picked up a cake and took a bite. "You can become an ordinary galactic citizen. I'm sure it will suit you well."

Damn Kissy. She always saw through the mask.

Lilline looked out over the view. The stream flowed past, bubbling with ease before the backdrop of high snow-capped mountains. A splash of spectral light shimmered on the rising mist of a distant waterfall along the river.

"Then again ..." She raised the glass of Gondau to her lips and let a good portion fall into her mouth, savoring its rich flavor.

"Yes?" Kissy cocked an eyebrow.

"Oh, I don't know." She knocked back the rest of the Gondau.

"I think you do." The words came as a whisper from behind Granny's napkin as she dabbed her lips.

"What was that?"

"Oh, nothing, dear. Mumbling to myself."

Right.

Granny reached a hand across the table. Lilline felt the old woman's withered fingers clasp her wrist. Kissy's outer shell might be aged and near life's end, but the energy and soul inside the former agent were strong and radiant.

"Lilli, what does your gut tell you?"

That, at least, was obvious to her.

"Well?" Kissy squeezed her once to jolt her. "Out with it!"

"That there's nothing like the poetic inspiration of being out in the field."

Granny patted her arm and smiled. "You've always had a stellar instinct."

*

Agent Renault Spy-Fi Adventures:

To Spy a Star (Agent Renault Adventures)

Wind Tide: A Space Opera Series:

Goodbye to the Sun (Wind Tide #1)

Jati's Wager (Wind Tide #2)

No Song, but Silence (Wind Tide #3)

ACKNOWLEDGMENTS

A thriller was new literary territory for me. The task of plotting and pacing a story to fit the genre expectations meant relying on friends and colleagues, old and new, for guidance and advice. First and foremost, I would like to thank my wife, Mallary, for her endless support and patience. To my mother, Nancy, thank you for being the ever-willing first reader of my stories. Further thanks go to a few additional close family and friends who supported me in writing this spy-fi story: Mark Milone, Albert Bertsch, and Stephen Wood. Additional thanks to my father and stepmother, Bill and Betsy, for their endless support and enthusiasm.

Beta readers are the unsung heroes of my writing process. They deal with rough, unrefined drafts with plot holes like a slice of Swiss cheese. Sharon Burke and Jean-Paul Garnier are owed tremendous thanks for being early readers and providing essential feedback and suggestions - Sharon regarding Lilline's character and relationship to mathematics especially, and Jean-Paul for insights into poetry and alien representation.

To my critique partners, Lindsay and Michael Wells: your astute attention to all aspects of storytelling and writing is astounding. The feedback you provided helped change and shape the plot of this story for the better. And lastly, my fellow writer and poet, Heath Mensher – your knowledge of screenwriting, pacing, and what to reveal and what to hold back in the plot until the right moment, was a vital part of shaping the final version of this book.

Jonathan Oliver continues to be my most valuable editorial asset.

Thank you for your copy edit of the manuscript. Luke Tarzian came through again for me with flawless book formatting, creating a stellar interior, and Fay Lane produced a knockout cover design. Thanks to the talented Chezka Sunit for working through an art commission (several phases) that resulted in an exciting and explosive artwork for the cover.

I would like to thank the following writers for their support and advice: Peter Hartog, Marian L. Thorpe, T.A. Bruno, Michael Mammay, Dan Fitzgerald, Rachel Aukes, Krystle Matar, Angela Boord, Thomas Howard Riley, T.L. Greylock, Andrew Jackson, Gary J. Mack, Douglas Lumsden, and Jeffrey Speight.

So many people celebrate books, especially those by indie authors because they love reading and writing about stories, organizing book tours, and helping to promote and sell indie authors. Many do it for nothing other than a love of all things literary (especially SFF). I am very thankful for the gracious generosity and support of the following individuals: Jean-Paul Garnier at Space Cowboy Books, Rowena Andrews at Beneath a Thousand Skies, Jenna Rideout at Westveil Publishing, Scarlett at Scarlett Readz & Runz, Adrian Gibson at SFF Addicts, Sue Bavey at Sue's Musings, Lorraine Bondi (The Book & Nature Professor), Alex at Spells and Spaceships, Peter Hutchinson at The Swordsmith, Isabelle W. at The Shaggy Shepherd, Robin at the Book Wormhole, Nick Borrelli at Out of this World SFF, Kavin at Silverstones Books, Sara and Lilly at Fiction Fans Podcast, and Justin Gross at Escapist Tours.

ABOUT THE AUTHOR

Jonathan Nevair is a science fiction author and the pen name for an art historian and college professor at a small art & design college in Philadelphia. After two decades of academic teaching and publishing, he finally got up the nerve to write fiction. Jonathan grew up on Long Island, NY but now resides in southeast Pennsylvania with his wife and rambunctious mountain feist, Cricket.

For more information visit: www.jonathannevair.com

Join the mailing list: sign me up!